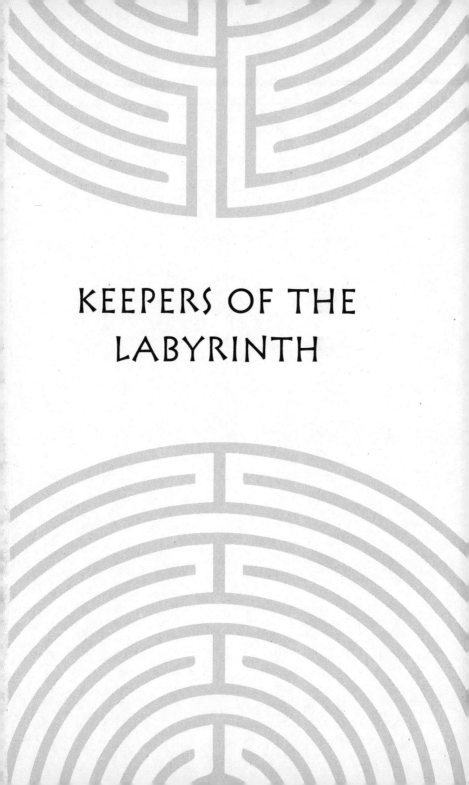

KEEPERS OF THE
LABYRINTH

KEEPERS
OF THE
LABYRINTH

ERIN E. MOULTON

Lola,
LIVE BOLDLY!

ERIN

PHILOMEL BOOKS
An Imprint of Penguin Group (USA)

PHILOMEL BOOKS
Published by the Penguin Group
Penguin Group (USA) LLC
375 Hudson Street, New York, NY 10014

USA | Canada | UK | Ireland | Australia | New Zealand | India | South Africa | China
penguin.com
A Penguin Random House Company

Library of Congress Cataloging-in-Publication Data is available upon request.

Printed in the United States of America.
ISBN 978-0-399-16459-0
1 3 5 7 9 10 8 6 4 2

Edited by Jill Santopolo.   Design by Semadar Megged.
Text set in 11/16-point Horley Old Style MT Std.
The publisher does not have any control over and does not assume any responsibility
for third-party websites or their content.

For Pa,

who checked on the body count and messages
from beyond the grave

*The urge to discover secrets is deeply ingrained in human nature;
even the least curious mind is roused by the promise of sharing
knowledge withheld from others.*

—John Chadwick, *The Decipherment of Linear B*

PROLOGUE

The wind blew in from the Aegean and swept toward the Libyan Sea. It tumbled rocks from mountaintops, sending them echoing into the bellies of gorges. It whipped toward houses, filling hanging clothes with its hot breath, stretching them to wick away the last of their water. It danced through the olive groves, pulled the fruit from boughs, and sent it careening to the ground. It disrupted a goat grazing under the cypress trees before it sailed down the dirt road that led to Melios Manor. It knew the place well and took a moment to admire it. The building stood austere and looming. It was the best of the old and new, leaning into the mountain like a child into its mother's embrace.

When the wind had had its fill, it dove toward the garden and lifted a few bees from their work. It stoked the outside fire pit and licked the olive oil off a hanging pot of lentil soup before it sailed past the open kitchen. Then it bulleted upward and into Athenia Pelia's study, toppling a stack of manila envelopes on her desk. Athenia rushed to clasp the window and snatched at the envelopes as they landed at her stockinged feet. She was a small woman with black ringlets that would tumble down her back if she let them. Instead, they were pinned into a rough twist at the nape of her neck.

"Mitera Gaia, Mitera Gaia," she said under her breath as she pushed the envelopes back into a pile. Athenia's quarters were striped with every color—like a candy-monger's den, only instead of candy, the colors were ribbons and yarns that hung out of stacked baskets. A wooden rack heavy with decorative buttons leaned into a corner. And from the top of that rack tumbled a stack of stained olive-wood boxes filled with metallic charms.

A knock came at the door, but before Athenia could answer, it swung open.

"Ah, Bente, kalimera," Athenia said, pulling a pair of glasses from her face as she surveyed the older woman. "You look worried."

The tall Norwegian swallowed, entering the room. "It's nothing. At least not yet."

She clasped her hands together, stretching veins taut from her knuckles to her wrists. Despite her age, Bente was strong, agile and nearly as sinewy as she had been in her youth.

"Shall we?" Athenia said, reaching up to a cast-iron sconce that stuck out of the stone wall and yanking it downward. The stained-glass window at the top of her door swung in its spot and came to rest upside down in its frame. On the other side of the room, pendants shimmered as the wall behind them swung open. The women slipped inside and sealed the door.

Athenia pulled a lighter from her pocket, gave it a flick and set it to the nearest wick, which peeked out of a cast-iron arm on the wall. The flame caught, and moments later, as if by magic, another one lit in the opposite corner. But that wasn't all. Flames rose in a spiral, climbing the stone of the antechamber. Higher and higher they streamed, until they met the rafters. Then they bloomed along the beams, sitting like clusters of birds. Finally, upon reaching the center, the flame stopped at the chains of an ancient candelabra.

Athenia waited, wondering if she needed to have Trudy repair it again, but a moment later, with a snap, the candles sparked to life like a wave of fire. Then all went quiet.

On the opposite side of the antechamber, another door swung open, and in walked Trudy and Colleen. Trudy brushed a curl away from her face as she removed her lab coat from her shoulders and took a seat. Colleen pulled a clipboard from underneath her arm and a pen from her pocket.

"Shall we begin?" Athenia asked, stationing herself at the head of the table. She pulled a small wooden peg toward her. It was decorated with ten buttons showing old pictographs, and her thumb made quick work of punching in the code.

A square of the far-left wall swiveled, revealing a pedestal holding a large tome. It sat open on the wooden stand. She moved swiftly to it. It was heavy in Athenia's arms, and as she returned to her seat, she set it carefully on the table.

She plucked a cracked leather strap from the center and flipped the book open to the selected page. It was split into four columns. She took a moment to let her eyes fall on the familiar letters in the third column. The letters of her ancestors. Greek. She had studied the ancient alphabet and knew it well.

She cleared her throat and began. "As you know, we have completed our recruitment selections. In just a few weeks, we will begin our leadership conference and assess each pupil to see who best displays the four virtues. To see who will follow in our footsteps." Athenia gestured to the pile of manila envelopes next to her. "We have a promising group of young women from around the world."

"And we have a promising set of challenges for them to face," Bente added, sitting up straight and clasping her hands in front of her.

"Yes, throughout the week, I suspect all will have a fair chance to display their skills." Athenia gestured to Colleen. "Do you have the assessment sheets for us, Col?"

Colleen nodded curtly, her short black hair swinging in a bob around her face. "Yes," she said, taking a sheet from the top of her clipboard and passing the pile to her right.

"Very well," Athenia said, accepting the papers as they reached her. "We must be sure to evaluate thoroughly in every workshop." She looked at the ancient Greek, examining the parameters of the first virtue. She read the old phrases, her mind working them into English. "First, we seek the Historian, whose virtue is knowledge—mainly, the ability to cull and access information through the written word." She looked across the table at Colleen. "Col, as current Historian, what is your plan to assess these attributes?"

Colleen clipped the extra assessment sheets onto her clipboard. "I'll be discussing knowledge foundations worldwide, information storage and knowledge sharing. I'll also be looking for someone particularly interested in history, its interpretation and how to access and assess archives."

Athenia nodded, scribbling in the margins of her paper. She placed a finger back on the page. "Next, the Inventor, whose virtue is creation. We will be watching for the ability to think outside the box, innovative spirit and a scientific mind. Trudy, as current Inventor, have you settled on a plan to assess these attributes?"

Trudy set her glasses on the table in front of her. Her Irish brogue filled the room as she spoke. "I have several challenges set up for them, but we'll be exploring genetic experiments, natural energy storage and climate-control solutions within our workshop modules."

"Very nice," Athenia said. She looked down at her sheet. "Next is the Artist, whose virtue is empathy. I will be looking for the ability to connect and sympathize with even the darkest and most brutish of spirits. My classes will cover cross-cultural art and universal relation to expression."

The others around the table nodded as Athenia's eyes fell to the Greek once more. The final virtue.

"Finally, we seek the Protector, whose virtue is boldness.

Attributes are strength of body, mind and spirit." She looked up from the book. "Bente, as current Protector, do you have a plan for assessing these attributes?"

"I've made some adjustments to the course on the back hill," Bente said, "where I will be watching for their endurance, strength of will and team-leading abilities. The ropes course on the first day should help us weed out those who lack a call to adventure."

Athenia surveyed the book and gave a satisfied smile. "I think we're in line with the tenets." She closed the book and returned it to the pedestal on the antechamber wall, and pushed a small button on the stand. It swiveled away from her and out of sight. She stopped to look at the picture that now took its place. **HELENE BENNETTE, ARIADNE 400** was inscribed on the bottom of the frame.

"Do you think her daughter will be anything like her?" Athenia asked as she ran her fingertips across the inscription.

"I have a feeling she will be very much like her," Bente said.

Athenia turned and looked across the antechamber at the others. Trudy and Colleen both stood with bowed heads.

"She won't be exactly like her," Trudy muttered. "Not with that sort of baggage."

"Let the process take its course and we will judge her skills fairly," Bente snapped.

Athenia nodded, and folded her hands into the sleeves of her sweater. "If she does not pass, she does not pass. And she'll be none the wiser. Regardless, we will have four new initiates. The best of the best."

Athenia made her way back to the end of the table. "The meeting is adjourned. Zeis tolmira. Live boldly."

"Zeis tolmira," they said as they departed.

1

Lilith Bennette ran at midnight. She ran at midnight because her mind was moored upon the hour. Unable to slip past it, her eyes blinked open. She got up, placed her shoes on her feet, waved to Dad, who was sitting at the dining room table plucking his guitar, and disappeared into the dark night. Up Caulder's Lane, down the dirt road that led out to Braggs Hill. Past Mr. Garsh's farm stand and through the small town center. She beat the pavement around the bend to the quiet post office and up the stairs of the general store, the sound of her tread turning hollow as she ran over the porch, then down the stairs on the other side. She passed the town's silent sleepers, nestled in their dark-windowed bedrooms. She wound her way along the river's edge, following the trail along Snake's Vein Road. She ran harder up the steep hill before she paused for a moment to take in the view of the village below. Her eyes darted from post office to Olsen's Grain and Supply to St. Patrick's steeple. The moon shuttled out from behind a cloud and illuminated the face of the town clock. 12:30.

Her mind had worked the hour relentlessly for years—three to be exact—trying to solve the impossible riddle. To put the pieces together. The smell of lentil soup in the night. The shuffling. The smoke sounding the alarm. The rope, tied so effectively over the ceiling beam. The word *suicide* that everyone seemed to believe. The funeral, with its religious tones that no one seemed to believe. The smoke of the twenty-one-gun salute. The flag, folded in surrender. The bruised hearts hanging from pins, kissed and given back.

The tears of her father, unable to believe that his Helene would quit on him.

Lil jumped three times, pushing back the tears that sprang into her eyes, and kicked out toward the woods, the ropes course. As she met the tree line, she reached over and set a timer on her wristwatch, told her body to move and her mind to silence. She raced across the balance beam, leaping onto the zip line, and sailed between the trees. Planting her feet at the end, she darted toward the rock wall and jumped to the highest handholds she could reach, climbing, unharnessed and breathing quickly. She crawled over the top of the wall and stood for a moment, gazing between the trees.

From here she could see the airfield and the hangar sheds in the distance. The airplanes sat like awkward birds, wings bathed in moonlight and blanketed in patchworked fog. She glanced at her watch. Already a few seconds behind her normal time. Lil looked to the rope hanging from a high tree branch just seven feet away. Her fingers itched, and she tried to disregard the image of the rope on that night. She hesitated, clearing her thoughts with a long exhale.

The leaves rustled as if carrying the whisper of her mother's voice. "*Min zeis aplos. Zeis tolmira.* Do not just live. Live boldly."

Lil swallowed hard, stepped back a few feet, aimed for the rope, ran and jumped. Her hands closed like knots around the fibers, but she didn't linger. She clung with her right fist and reached with her left, grasping another rope and then another until she'd swung to a webbed ladder. Bouncing toward the forest floor, she took off toward the airfield.

She stretched her arms as she soared beyond the shelter of the trees, her reach slicing through pockets of fog as she made her way between planes to the Longhorn. Her mom's plane. They still paid the storage fee, and old Mickey didn't mind not having to find someone else to fill its spot—now a monument more than anything else.

Lil jumped, peering into the cockpit, then reached up, grasped the latch and opened the door. She felt under the seat and pulled the leather-bound journal from the shadows, flipping to the very back and slipping a picture from between the pages. She glanced at it in the moonlight. Her mother when she was younger. Lil's age, she thought, about sixteen. Strong and muscular, with her arm around the waist of a tall woman with silvery hair. They both wore T-shirts and leggings. Their calves and shoes were caked with mud as if they'd just finished a long spring run. They stood on a mountaintop, a rocky vista behind them. And in the shade of a tree, Lil could see an etching of a double-headed ax inscribed on the face of a large, smooth stone. It matched the necklace her mom wore. Her mother had called the ax a labrys. Lil flipped the picture over and looked at the back.

Helene and Bente
Future Leaders International
1990

She folded the picture, reached down and tucked it into her sock, then placed the journal back in its spot, closed the cockpit and circled the airfield. Her watch indicated that it was 12:50. She turned right out of the fenced-in field and headed toward home.

Lil rounded the corner on the east end of Caulder's Lane and slowed her step as she reached her backyard. Her watch beeped 1:00.

"To a new day," Lil said as she crossed the yard and strode into the dining room.

Her father was standing at the counter, pouring hot water into a ceramic mug. He slid the mug of tea and a glass of cold water across the countertop. "Late night for an early plane ride."

Lil yawned and took a sip from the glass.

Picking up another mug, her father rubbed at the circles under his eyes as he sat back at the table. "You'll need your rest if you're going to get on a plane in six hours."

"I'll sleep in the air," Lil said, downing the rest of the water and taking the chamomile toward the stairs.

The scrapbook was out on the table, and Lil noticed the laptop as her dad flipped it shut.

"Checking e-mails," he said, sliding the computer away. "Updating your aunt on the farm. She might come visit this fall."

Lil nodded, though she knew he was lying. Just like her, he was up looking for Mom. In their own ways, they were always trying to find her. To unearth the truth.

Peeling her shoes off, Lil eyed the rifle that had come to sit by the door these past few nights. It had taken the place of her dad's guitar. As if he were waiting for something.

"Fox's getting into the coop again," he said, nodding toward the gun.

"Ah," she answered, though she found it suspicious that he hadn't mentioned it previously. He usually mourned any chickens that got plucked from the coop, and stormed around the house, wondering aloud how the fox had made its way in under the radar. How the fox had made its way in despite the extra boards he had put up to keep them out. No, the gun was not there for a fox. Lil would have known about it by now.

Her dad rubbed his hands together. "I'll wake you in three

hours"—he spread his arms apart in a grand gesture—"and you shall be off to see the land of your mother."

Lil appreciated his efforts to keep things upbeat, and she smiled toward the wall as she pushed her shoes against it. She rounded the banister. "Love you. See you in the morning."

"Lil."

She looked sideways as her father lowered his hands to the table once more.

"I'm serious. Your mom would be glad you're able to see her homeland. It had a special place in her heart."

Lil trained her eyes on the stairs. "I know." She nodded, winding the string of the tea bag around the handle of her mug.

"All right. Get some sleep. I love you, but I'm still waking you in three hours."

"'Kay." She headed upstairs and into her room.

Lil set the mug down on her desk and finished filling the duffel bag that was already sitting open on her chair. She'd meant to finish packing earlier, but as always, she'd had things on her mind. She rolled several clean shirts and a few pairs of shorts, and tucked them neatly beside her pants, sweaters and active-wear. She checked her travel kit for shampoo and hair ties and soap. Nothing to exceed three ounces, Lil thought, turning the travel bottles so that the side displaying the size was visible.

She yawned and put down her checklist. The manila envelope that she had received weeks ago peered out at her from beneath the edge of her duffel. She retrieved it, staring at the flowing red ink on the front. *Ms. Lilith Bennette.* The brochure landed on top of the pile as she opened the folder and upturned the contents onto her desk. She stared at the images of the bright, whitewashed walls, the blue water, the flowers that, according to this brochure, stretched down lanes, unsuppressed.

Discover Crete, it said. Discover Mom, Lil thought as she pulled out the official welcome letter.

Lilith Bennette,

Welcome to Future Leaders International. We are so pleased to have you join us at beautiful Melios Manor in Crete, Greece. We believe your unique leadership skills will shine here on Crete. Get ready for a conference full of sun, fun, team building, invigorating discussions and enlightening workshops.

The manor itself looked amazing, with its cobbled walls and sunny flowers lining the walkways, bright blue sky above. *Eco-friendly, agrotourism, nature's haven,* the trifold brochure proclaimed. The pictures that pocked the inside pages showed gardens, sheep, winding roads and beautiful natural vistas. Lil wondered if she would see the same sights as her mother. If she would smell the same smells.

She reached into her sock and pulled out the picture of her mom and Bente, then shuffled the papers until she found the one labeled *Teacher Biographies.* There it was. *Bente Formo.* The exact same spelling as the inscription on the back of the picture. It couldn't be a coincidence, could it? How many people were even named Bente? How many Bentes could possibly be counselors at a Future Leaders International conference in Greece, no less? And why had Mom kept the picture in the back of her journal? Surely they were close.

Lil pressed the picture flat and ran her finger along the necklace her mother was wearing. Even though the charm was too small for Lil to see clearly, she had captured it in her mind's eye.

It was circular, double sided and metallic. Lil had wondered what it was made of. One side was etched with a spiral and little symbols. Lil remembered sitting on Mom's lap, tracing the spiral with her finger. The other side, dark like soot, was much simpler—a double-headed ax centered in a circle.

Sometime during the week of the tragedy, Mom's necklace had gone missing. The coroner hadn't seen it. Or so he said. It wasn't in her room, or in the cockpit of her plane, or anywhere around the house. It had simply disappeared. But it was here in this picture. Preserved. Lil wondered if maybe it was a friendship necklace. Or maybe it was something much more important, like the wing insignia Mom had worn on the lapel of her uniform. Something to do with honor.

She would ask Bente. Bente would know.

Lil tucked the flattened picture underneath the paper clip in her registration packet.

She looked down at her watch. The number flipped from 1:44 to 1:45. She closed the folder and dropped it into her duffel bag, then jumped into bed and counted herself into dreams.

2

Ares Slynn heard the phone in his Fifth Avenue apartment ring before he reached his door. He groaned as he pushed his grocery bag into the crook of his right arm and fumbled to get his keys out of his pocket. He jingled the other keys free of the first, opened the door and wandered into the kitchen without giving the incoming call the benefit of a glance. He just couldn't. Not after the day he'd had. It was constant interactions. Constant meetings at the university. Everyone seemed to need him: the students, the faculty, the incompetent lab assistants. Of course, this was a curse of being a teacher who inspired people the way Ares did. He didn't expect others to reach his level of aptitude.

Who could possibly require his time now? As if understanding his train of thought, the ringing stopped. He peered through the doorway at the screen, a momentary green glow in the shadowy living room, then breathed a sigh of relief as it went dark without indicating a voice mail. He dropped the grocery bag onto the table and placed the teakettle on the front burner.

The papery deli bag crinkled as he pulled out the baguette and laid it on the cutting board. He selected a wheel of Brie from the refrigerator and inhaled the aroma as he unwrapped it. His stomach growled and his mouth begged for a slice, but Ares restrained himself. It was better at room temperature, anyway. He took the time to wipe off every corner of the kitchen sink while the water in the teakettle came to a rolling boil. Then he made a cup of weak tea, submerging the tea bag only three times before discarding it in the trash. He placed a lemon wedge in the cup, then sipped the detoxifying mixture.

He made his way to his favorite chair in the living room, setting the tea on a side table and pulling a chenille blanket over his shoulders. He took his noise-canceling headphones from the chair arm and selected Beethoven's "Moonlight Sonata" on his iPad. The notes soared into his ears, and Ares felt the tension leave his body. He leaned his head back against his chair and listened, slowly scanning for any knots that might be hiding inside his muscles. City life, he thought as he stretched his fingers, curled his wrists and then dropped his hands into his lap. After ten minutes of relaxation, he reached between the cushion and armrest and retrieved his journal, feeling the familiar weight in his hands.

Ares had had this type of journal since childhood. It was one that his mother had required him to begin. His journal of truths. Each day he would write down and reflect on a famous quote or philosophy that had appealed to him in some way. He flipped the pages, spotting names as he went: Socrates, Carnegie, Sartre, Plato. His fingers paused on the page, and he read his favorite quote: "It is a rough road that leads to the heights of greatness." Seneca. He felt fireworks fly up his spine as the words rang with the music. He knew this quote to be true. He'd paved his own road. Never had he been given chances. Never had his greatness been acknowledged in his youth. He had fought tooth and nail for it. All Zephylites were required to build themselves into true men and women. To become more than their forebears. And just like these people, Ares would have his name in the history books.

Only he would reach farther, be greater, leave a legacy like no one had before.

His thumb flicked the page, and he wondered if he should call a meeting tonight. He heard the dull sound of the phone ringing once more, barely audible over the sonata. He looked at the wireless receiver next to his chair. *Number unavailable,* it said. Perhaps it wasn't the college? But it couldn't be one of the Zephylites, for he knew all their numbers, and none were unlisted. As he lifted his hand from the page and reached for the phone, the noise ceased and the screen went dark. He lowered his hand, waiting for the beep of the voice mail to tell him there was a message, but once again silence followed.

Ares picked up his pen and flipped to an empty page. He had long ago decided that he might add his own quotes to the anthology of greatness, so he had recently abandoned the old philosophers and scientists and looked within. He twirled a pen between his thumb and index finger and thought. Then, with great purpose, he bit the tip of his pen, unclipped the cap and began to write.

> *May one self-made man lead the world to glory. May his teachings be great. His pen mighty. His ledger bright. His mind clear. His body and will strong. Then, and only then, will his name go down in history, and those who are wise enough to follow find their feet in footprints of gold.*

He pressed the pen between the pages, slid his book back between the cushion and the armrest and let the music envelop him.

As the sonata wore down, his stomach begged for nourishment. He went into the kitchen and sliced into the room-temperature

Brie, placing a gooey triangle onto his plate. He neatly sawed off a few pieces of bread and wiped the crumbs from the counter into his hand. He sat down at the table and flipped on the kitchenette light.

As he lifted his first slice of bread and Brie to his lips, the phone rang again, making his hand jerk so violently, the Brie dove from his grasp and landed upside down on his plate.

He groaned, hurried into the living room, lifted the receiver and slammed the Call button as he brought the phone to his ear. "What is it then?" he shouted.

"Ares?" a hushed voice said.

Ares cocked his head to the side. The voice was thick, low and had obviously been mechanically enhanced. But the stranger had used his Zephylite name. He had only received one call like this before.

"Perhaps," he said, careful not to sound too eager, though he did begin to salivate as he flipped the bread and Brie over. "And who is this?"

"That is not of importance. What is of importance is the information I am about to give you."

"Do you always make such presumptions?" Ares said, but he did not hang up the phone. Instead, he walked back to the table and sat once more.

"A new recruitment session will be taking place at Melios Manor this week. The teachers will be distracted with the leadership conference"—the voice faded for a moment and Ares squinted, trying to grasp every word—"the nebulous chamber."

Ares' eyes shot open. "Who is this?"

"It means . . . the Icar—"

"I know what it means," he said, his lips sliding into a smile like a snake, stretching the width of his face. He placed his hand on the End button, silencing the phone before the speaker could continue. He felt his hair rise around the back of his neck as though electricity had suddenly filled the air.

He strode into the darkening living room and retrieved a box from beneath the coffee table. He set it down in front of him and lifted the cover. Pulling a round emblem with a jagged line from within the shadows of the box, he placed the chain around his neck so that the pendant dropped just over his heart. A leather scroll had been tucked in the corner of the box, and he gently lifted it, unwinding it. He picked up the phone, noting the dial tone before he punched the numbers.

The line rang twice.

"Come on, come on," Ares said, taking a breath, willing Horatio or Felice to pick up.

Rrrrrrrrring. Rrrrrrrrring.

"Hello?" a voice said.

"Felice?"

"Yes?"

"It's Ares. Meet me at the ward. It concerns the Icarus Folio." He heard a gasp at the other end.

Yes, it would be easy to persuade them to go on a sacred quest. He had guided them, prepared them for this from youth and he knew their faith was deep. He knew they had nearly memorized the writings of Hexalodorous. He knew their childlike zeal. Especially the eldest. "Bring Horatio and Byron. Call the others."

He hung up the phone and reached for his jacket. He did not need food now. This. This could sustain him forever.

3

After nineteen hours of travel, Lil found herself foggy-headed, tired and boarding a shuttle bus with the initials **FLI** on the side. She went to the back and jammed her duffel underneath the seat in front of her before sitting down.

"We're going to be full, everyone, so please make room in the seat beside you," the man in the front said. "My name is Aestos, and I am your guide to Melios Manor today. You will be seeing me around the manor all weekend, and you should not hesitate to ask me for something if you need it. It is our duty to make your stay here in Crete one you will never forget."

He clasped his hands together and repeated what he had said in French, German, what sounded like Spanish, then choppy Chinese and finally Greek.

She recognized a little bit of Greek, her mother's accent ringing in her ears. But she was unable to understand anything but a few words. It wasn't like she hadn't asked to know more, but her mother had been somewhat reserved about it. "You are an American," she would say to Lil. But Lil had not ever been so sure of her identity. The kids at school had families who had been in Vermont for generations and seemed to think she was foreign even though she had been born there. And yet, Lil thought she certainly couldn't be Greek. She had never even been here before. It was like wearing a pair of mismatched shoes. Neither fit exactly right. One unwelcoming and uncomfortable. The other like no shoe she had ever seen. Greek, her heritage and her mother, were a mystery to Lil. One she desperately wanted to unravel.

Lil looked out the window, wondering if anyone else had come from the United States. Moments later, one last girl got on the bus. She was short, and her hair was loose and long but sprung out around her head in uncontained twists and curls. A pair of purple glasses framed her brown face, and she had a crease between her eyes. The kind one might get from considering the world for too long. She stopped near the front and struggled to put her suitcase in the luggage hold, then continued to the back.

"May I sit here?" she asked as she approached the vacant seat next to Lil.

"Please do," Lil said, happy to hear words she could understand.

"I'm Sydney," the girl said as she sat down and swung a backpack from her left shoulder into her lap.

"I'm Lil," Lil said.

"Nice to meet you," Sydney said, unzipping her backpack and pulling out a handheld device that looked like an inside-out walkie-talkie. Lil could see wires running across a computer chip at the front. Sydney flipped it, revealing a gray, pixelated screen. Then she hit a little button on the side, and the screen glowed green.

"Commence trilateration," Sydney said into the side of the device.

"What's that?" Lil asked.

The device beeped and then displayed a little winding line across the screen. "Essentially it's a homemade GPS," Sydney said, holding it out to Lil. "It just pinpointed where we are in the world." She pointed at a little X that began to move as they pulled out of Chania Airport.

"Did you make it?" Lil asked, staring at the tiny flecks of solder, meticulously round, holding down the ends of the wires. She had once made a noisemaker at a library program, but this seemed far more advanced than anything Lil would ever attempt, even with guidance.

"Well, yeah," Sydney said, setting it on top of her backpack, screen up. "I wouldn't exactly buy this."

"Why do you need a GPS if you were planning on taking the bus?" Lil wondered.

Sydney looked at her, scowling. "I was bored. Besides, did you see the road we're going up? It's insanely dangerous looking. Steep. Lots of turns. Very narrow."

Lil had noticed that the manor was in the middle of nowhere. But she was fairly used to that, being from the middle of Vermont. She wondered if that was why Mom liked Vermont.

"It *is* off the beaten path," she said.

Sydney leveled her with a stare. "That is the understatement of the century."

Just then, Lil became aware of the girls on their left giggling and eyeing them from across the aisle. The girl doing most of the laughing had sleek black hair that she wore in a ponytail, and eyebrows that had been plucked into sharp points.

"*Regardez la pauvre nerd qui peut même pas acheter un poratble approprié,*" she said. The dowdy girl next to her started laughing again.

Lil glared. "I don't know what she's saying, but I can tell it isn't good."

Sydney's eyes landed on the device. "I know what she's saying," she said, indicating a maple leaf pin she wore on her sleeve.

"You're from Canada?" Lil asked.

"Yeah, Winnipeg," Sydney replied. "Just ignore her."

"Well, what did she say?" Lil said. "It depends on what she said. She can't just sit there and say—"

"She seems to think this is the only cell phone I can afford." Sydney tapped the side of her temple. "Not too bright."

Lil smiled, but a moment later, the girl in the seat across from them looked at her again. This time she spoke in English. "They must not have hair salons in Canada."

"They must not have manners in France," Lil said, standing up.

The bus pitched around a corner, and she clung to the seat back in front of her to keep her feet.

"That's Vivi Lancaster."

Lil looked down. The girl in the seat she was clinging to turned toward her. She had short brownish hair that twisted in the front like a ski slope sliding to her forehead. Her skin was pale and her eyes were bright blue, and she wore a pair of plain suspenders over a white collared shirt. She was retro and stylish, like a mix between a black-and-white movie and the front of a modern magazine cover. And she had a slight French accent— perhaps a touch of a British one, too. Lil couldn't quite tell.

"She's been trying to lose me since the layover in Frankfurt. I'm Charlie." The girl extended a hand over the seat. Lil took it and shook.

Sydney looked up from her device and peered over the seat.

"I'm Lil; this is Sydney," Lil said.

"Ah, *oui*," Charlie said. "It's a pleasure."

The van twisted around another bend, and Lil sat down. Charlie leaned up, lacing her arms over the back of the seat.

Sydney glanced back at her device. "Here goes."

"What's that—" Charlie started, but before she could finish what she was saying, the bus took a sharp turn, upending several bigger bags and suitcases from the luggage hold. Once the girls had righted themselves, Sydney leaned over Lil to look out the bus window, then pushed the device between them. Charlie appeared just above the seat again.

"It's a handmade GPS," Lil said.

Sydney pointed at the screen. "We're coming up on another turn, heading up the mountain now. This is going to be sharp turns all the way up."

Lil watched the X as it embarked on a series of S-turns.

"You were right about the road," Lil said, looking out her window, trying to get a glimpse of where they were going. The bus tilted, carrying them higher and higher. As they continued, the shuttle got quieter and quieter. Lil pulled the window open, searching for some air. The Cretan wind blew in, and she sucked in a breath as she watched the world below become smaller with each turn. The road was narrow, and without guardrails. The only thing stopping the van, if it started over the hill, would be a few rocks, some shrubbery, maybe a roaming goat. Otherwise, they would tumble, perhaps for miles.

A tiny church on a pedestal marked the next corner, and Lil could see the stems of some flowers poking out of it.

"Do you think that's for religious offerings?" Lil asked.

Sydney looked up and shook her head, staring back down at the GPS. "No, that's where people've died. Crete has an extremely high percentage of automobile deaths. One every couple of days or so."

"Every couple of days?" Charlie's knuckles grew white as she clutched the seat back.

"Give or take," Sydney said, nodding. "Another turn."

They climbed onward, and Lil watched the bees spin between wildflowers that marked the side of the road in big colorful splashes. She wondered if Mom had climbed this road. Had seen these wildflowers, had felt this breeze on her face. Lil closed her eyes and breathed in the aroma.

Opening her eyes once more, she watched as houses disappeared in the distance. They climbed to a rocky mountaintop where the road leveled off, and drove along a straightaway for a moment. The passengers on the bus seemed to take a collective sigh of relief as the sheer drop-off became guarded by trees on both sides. A mile or so later, a long stone wall cropped up on their right and hugged the bank as it wound its way toward a large sunny spot in the distance. Finally, they rounded a corner and the trees peeled back, revealing a large stonework building.

4

WELCOME, FUTURE LEADERS OF THE WORLD! The banner on the front of the manor waved like a flag in the wind. Lil made her way down the shuttle steps behind Sydney and Charlie. She slowed to a stop and stared at the manor. This was going to be their home for the next twelve days? Lil had never seen anything like it. Windows were splayed open-eyed by wooden shutters. The late-afternoon sun reflected in the glass. Below, old urns and modern plastic buckets sat side by side, holding flowers of every color. Some careened forward in floral waterfalls, and others climbed up the wall toward the balconies above them. There were two stone stairwells that wound from the ground floor up each side and plateaued into simple but decorative gardens before melding into the mountainside. Lil craned her neck, taking in the scene before her.

The natural beauty of the place seemed endless. Back on the ground, over to her left stood a large vegetable garden, and Lil took a deep breath as a warm, salty aroma sailed toward her on the breeze. She spotted a large fire pit with several roast chickens spinning above it. The grease spattered into the flames, as if asking them to rise higher. The garden reminded her of her mother's herb garden. And the herb on the chicken had to be rosemary.

That was Mom's favorite, and the smell seemed to surround Lil, fill her senses. She stepped toward it without thinking.

"Is that—"

"Dinner," Aestos said as he handed the last bag to the last girl, closed the bus door and headed toward the garden. "And that's not all, so do not be late."

"We'd better check in," Sydney said, dropping her device into her backpack and retrieving her welcome packet. Charlie led the way to the back of the line as Lil picked up her duffel bag from the dirt driveway and followed.

After about fifteen minutes, they had wound their way to an arched wooden door. The top half of it was open, and an oval sign swung in the breeze next to it. **PEΣEΨION (RECEPTION)** was carved into the raw wood.

Lil looked into the office. A short, flustered-looking woman stood in front of them. She had curly hair that had erupted into flyaways all around her head. A set of round spectacles, held together on one side by several pieces of duct tape, were propped on her nose. She wore a lanyard that held her name: Trudy. She flipped to the final page of a logbook and placed a large folded piece of paper in it.

"All right," she said, looking up at Lil. Lil cocked her head to the side. Was she imagining it or had Trudy's lips turned up in a smile? The way her eyes twinkled, it almost seemed as though she recognized her.

Lil cleared her throat. "Lili—"

But before she could finish, the woman had retrieved a registration packet from the box in front of her and held it out. Lil saw her name on a sticky label in the upper right-hand corner.

"Welcome, Lilith," Trudy said in a lilting Irish accent.

She hadn't imagined the look, then. "How—"

"And this must be Sydney Bennington," Trudy said, pulling the next one out and handing it to Sydney, "hailing from 'O Canada.' I have family on the East Coast."

Sydney nodded a thank-you and accepted the folder as Lil stepped aside, feeling foolish for thinking that there had been a connection.

"And last, but not least, we have Charlotte Babineaux."

"Charlie, *s'il vous plaît,*" Charlie said, accepting the folder.

"Very well," Trudy said. She pulled her glasses from her face and waved her hand as she looked out over their shoulders. "It's a hot one. Let's get ye in out of the sun." She swung the door open, and the girls spilled inside, hauling their luggage with them.

"Now, your room number is on your registration packet. Please fetch your keys from the rail," she said, pointing toward a set of hooks that sat next to an interior door. Lil peered at her folder. She was Room 4D. She went to the wall and picked up a wooden lanyard attached to a large cast-iron key.

Trudy rattled on while Sydney and Charlie retrieved their keys.

"You're all in Hall D, which is the one just above us. You'll take a left toward the kitchen and head up the back stairwell to get there. I'll see ye at dinner, I'm sure." Trudy herded them toward the interior door.

Lil grabbed the knob and pushed it open into a cool stone hallway.

"Second floor, all right?" Trudy called after them.

"Yes, ma'am," the three replied as they passed into the hallway.

"Wait!" Trudy said.

Lil turned back.

"Ye can't forget your candles. Remember, we're an eco-friendly, self-sustaining facility, which means that the whole building is solar powered." She held up three candles by their wicks with one hand.

"I have a flashlight," Sydney said.

Trudy stared at her, still holding out the candles. "That's fine if that is what ye require, but we're in favor of sustainable living here, and while your flashlight's batteries fill landfills, these candles were made here at Melios Manor using our very own beeswax."

Sydney looked skeptical. "A little dangerous, everyone running around with candles."

Trudy's eyebrows rose. "The building is stone. We've never had a problem before." She turned to the others. "Bring these to dinner—you'll want them on the way back. There will be extras in the lobby if ye need them."

Lil took all three candles, passing one to Charlie and another to Sydney. Sydney hesitated and then took the candle.

"Fine, I'll use it as a backup."

"Preserve the water," Trudy shouted after them. "Kindling is set in the fireplace should you need it. Become acquainted with the materials in your folder!"

They hurried to the end of the hall, where another cluster of girls stood in front of a sign that said **KOYZINA**. Lil didn't need the translation that was spelled out: **KITCHEN**. The smell of the chicken had spilled into the hallway.

The girls turned. It was Vivi again, and two others.

"Oh, are you in Hall D?" Charlie said, not masking the disappointment in her voice.

Vivi bristled, and then a smile snuck into the corner of her mouth. "No." She reached out a hand and patted Charlie on the shoulder. "Hall D is like servants' quarters." She jutted her chin toward the kitchen. "We just came over to see what the smell was."

"Servants' quarters?" Lil said as they passed her and scurried down the hallway. Lil watched as they went to a large spiral staircase that circled up from the foyer. "Do you think we're really in the servants' quarters?"

"I have no idea, but I like the smell," Charlie said.

The delicate acidic smell of tomatoes, sliced garlic and onion poured out of the kitchen. And herbs. The aromas mixed together and made Lil's stomach dip and churn. "What time is dinner?" she asked.

"We'll have to check the schedule," Sydney said.

Charlie peered through a window on the side of the door, and Lil looked over her head. The interior of the kitchen boasted a large counter and a wood-fired oven where three large loaves of bread grew brown in front of the open flames. Lil had seen flatbreads made in something similar. Beside the oven, copper pots and pans of every width and height leaned against one wall next to equally large wheels of cheese. And there was Aestos in the middle of it. He moved quickly, working a mortar and pestle in front of him. Without removing his eyes from his concoction, he lifted his right arm and freed a few thyme leaves above his head, where bundles of herbs were swinging in the breeze.

"Is that the bus driver?" Charlie asked.

"Yeah," Lil said.

"Of course it is," Sydney said. "Didn't you guys read the brochure? It said right in it that Aestos Trika was in charge of the food." She stared at them. "It talked about how all the food was made on the grounds. Everything is organic. Remember? Eco-friendly."

"Hippies," Charlie said, lifting her eyebrows. Lil grinned.

Her mom and dad had been called hippies simply for owning a family farm. Nowadays it seemed that any place that was self-sufficient, or even anyone who had a garden and canned their own food, was somehow associated with the free-love era.

"Not exactly," Lil said, smelling the rosemary roast chicken. Lil suspected the chickens had been freshly killed and plucked that morning.

Sydney turned and attempted to hoist her rolling bag onto the first step. Lil grasped the bottom of it with her free hand, and they climbed toward the landing. A stained-glass window spilled colorful sunlight down the stairs as they rounded the corner and continued up to the secind floor. There was a little wooden plaque right next to a stone archway: **ΑΙΘΟΥΣΑ Δ (HALL D)**. The girls pushed a wooden door open.

"This is me," Charlie said, stopping at the first room on the right. Lil looked up at the top of the door. It was crowned by a rectangular stained-glass window. The corners of the window were blue and wavy, and in the center was a white bull with a woman sitting on its back.

"Oh, that's interesting," Charlie said as she pushed the key into the lock.

"What's interesting?" Sydney said, setting her side of the bag down for a moment. Lil did the same.

"It's Europa."

Lil tried to remember where she had heard the name.

"You know," Charlie continued, "the myth about Europa and Zeus?"

Sydney shrugged. "Never heard of her."

Charlie tilted her head and looked down the hall.

"Ah *oui*, and that is Daedalus and Icarus." Her eyes lit up with a smile. "They're all Cretan myths."

"3D. That's me," Sydney said, going to the door and sliding the key into the lock. Lil grabbed the handle of her bag and followed her. How she had ended up being the bellhop, Lil wasn't exactly sure.

"Remember Daedalus and Icarus?" Charlie said, coming with them. "They build wings and fly too close to the sun?"

Lil looked up at the stained-glass window and nodded. She did remember it from when they had studied mythology in elementary school. Everyone knew the story of Daedalus and Icarus.

"Oh yeah," Sydney said. "I read about them in the brochure, too. They were in the 'mystery and lore of Crete' section."

"You've not read the *Metamorphoses*?" Charlie asked.

Sydney raised an eyebrow and pushed her door open. "Have you read *A Brief History of Time*?"

"No," Charlie said, "but—I thought you would have read—"

"I mostly stick to applicable reading," Sydney said matter-of-factly.

Lil gave Charlie a glance as she set the suitcase down next to Sydney. Charlie didn't seem to be very offended by Sydney's abrupt way of talking. Instead she smiled and fired back, "One might argue that they are both applicable, in separate disciplines."

Sydney shrugged. "Anyway, thanks," she said to Lil, accepting the suitcase and turning back to her door.

"No problem," Lil said as she grasped her key. Sydney was in 3D, so that would mean that 4D was directly opposite. Lil turned to place her key in the lock and froze.

A chill reached from the stone floor, up her legs, and curled around her shoulders. The stained-glass window above her door was different. She shook her head and looked again.

"Ah, you have the story of Ariadne and Theseus," Charlie piped up next to her.

"What?" Lil said, trying to steady her hand.

"Ariadne. She gives the ball of thread to Theseus so he can make it to the center of the labyrinth." Lil stared at the woman holding out the ball of thread. That wasn't what had bothered her. It was what was on either side of the woman. The shapes were barely visible in the patterned glass. One might not even detect them if they weren't familiar with them already. On one side was a spiral decorated with pictographs. On the other was a double-headed ax. A labrys. She'd traced the designs a thousand times. They were the images on her mother's missing necklace.

5

il opened her door, and her gaze darted around the room as if she might find her mother there. But only sun spilled in and lit the beautiful interior with a warm glow. A bed was tucked into a nook, framed by bright red curtains, and Lil made her way to it, dropping her duffel bag on the mattress. The azure pillows popped against the blanket, and Lil lifted one of them, squeezing it to her chest. It was soft and smelled like flowers. She unzipped her backpack, and pulled out the registration packet and the picture of her mother and Bente she had clipped to the front of it. Then she passed the window seat, which was a stone slab propped on two large urns, kicked her shoes off at the balcony door and stepped out into the sun.

She stared around at the scenery, looking once to the picture and then to the terrain to see if she could identify where the picture had been taken. The land was a mash-up of soft and hard. Tree lines folded into jagged rocks, and shrubs sprang up from what looked like parched dirt. Lil could see an olive orchard sloping downhill from the garden, twisted trunks climbing up to lush, fruit-bearing branches. The sound of bells sent a flurry of birds skyward. She thought she saw a few rushing sheep and a turbaned head ducking in and out of the trees. The clouds above rowed their way across the sky, their dark bellies lit by the fire of the dying day. The wind picked up, drumming across the rooftop, and Lil could hear her mother's voice in it, as if this was where it had always lived: *Min zeis aplos. Zeis tolmira.* Do not just live. Live boldly.

A knock came at the door and Lil jumped, shoving the picture into her pocket.

"Lil? Lil?"

She rushed inside, pulling the balcony doors shut behind her, and opened the dormitory door. Sydney and Charlie looked in at her.

"It's six fifty now," Sydney said, holding her watch out for Lil to see. "Dinner?"

"Sorry!" Lil said, grabbing her folder.

"Don't forget your candle," Charlie said, holding hers up.

"Or you can both leave your candles and I'll bring the flashlight," Sydney said. "I actually have rechargeable batteries in it." She waved it in front of Lil. "Who's sustainable now?"

"Yeah, but if we don't come back at the same time," Lil said, wondering if she might see . . . might talk to Bente.

Sydney shrugged.

Lil picked the candle up from the dresser and pushed it into a waiting candleholder, then joined the others in the hall.

They made their way downstairs, past the kitchen and office into the foyer. Girls began to trickle down the spiral staircase. A large wooden door hinged to its frame with strapped iron stood open, welcoming them into the dining hall.

Lil scanned the room, savoring the simple beauty of it. If this was Greek, maybe she was Greek after all. The idea was definitely growing on her.

One long wooden table cut the room in half. Beeswax candles warmed the bellies of large and small glass jars. The dark stone that made up the walls seemed to absorb the twinkle, but a fading beam of sunset silhouetted the hollyhocks that had reached the windows and craned their cheerful faces inside. Kindling had been set in a squat fireplace on one end of the room, and a large fresco of a woman holding a ball of thread ornamented the wall just above it. More Ariadne. But without the other symbols this time. Lil wondered how long the fresco had been there. It looked faded, salmon colored, barely detectable. The chairs that hugged the table were short-backed and wicker. Each seat was set with a copper-rimmed plate and a matching porcelain bowl. And the mugs looked to be handcrafted and ranged from deep blue, to sea green, to blood red.

"Want to sit over here?" Charlie asked, heading across the room to a few seats in the middle.

Sydney nodded, and Lil could see no reason to disagree. It was a small group, much smaller than she had realized it would be. It didn't really matter where they sat. They would be able to see the counselors' table and the podium that stood next to the fireplace. Lil just wanted to spot Bente. She hoped the woman might notice her in the crowd.

Lil pulled out a chair and took a seat. The roasted chickens had been placed evenly down the center of the table. Little cast-iron pots sat between them, the ends of ladles poking out like flags. And big bowls of salad were filled with smile-shaped tomato wedges drowning in oil. Lil was tempted to snatch one out of its bowl.

The intercom crackled, and a voice emanated throughout the manor.

"Hello, future leaders. This is your grand counselor, Athenia Pelia. Opening remarks will commence in five minutes, followed by dinner. Please make your way to the dining hall." She repeated herself in Greek, German, French, Spanish and Chinese.

By the time the announcement came to a close, most of the seats at the table were occupied. Sydney pulled her packet onto the table, and Lil noticed that she had several notes sticking out of each end. Charlie, also, had a journal and a pen out.

Lil reached for her pocket. She hadn't even thought to bring a pen to dinner. Or a notebook. Had the packet said they should? She had gotten so wrapped up in the picture and the stained-glass window . . .

"Do either of you have a pen I could borrow? I forgot mine upstairs."

Charlie's face lit up as she produced a cloth roll. She unwound it to reveal many pens held against the cloth by leather loops.

"Take your pick," Charlie said as Lil examined the variety. One was silver and gold, another was bright blue with a silver seal across the cap and another was slick black with copper bands. Charlie pulled the cap from one and displayed a fountain pen tip that curved into a fine point.

"They're all filled with series three because they took my black serpent class away at customs."

Lil reached for the black one. "What's black serpent class?"

"It's an ink." Charlie looked at her as though this were obvious. "Series three is not as good as the black serpent class. It just doesn't move as well on the paper."

Sydney nodded, and then flipped her notebook open to the first tab and busied herself reading.

Charlie continued. "Margo goes to book expos all over the world, and she gets me a fountain pen and a journal from each country." She rolled the case back up and put it into her pocket.

"Who's Margo?" Lil asked.

"She's my foster mom," Charlie said, her eyes falling back to the pen. She twirled it along the top of her paper and then smeared her pointer finger across it.

"We run an antique-book store. We have a branch at home and a branch in London," she said. "I-I don't see her much these days, but the pens . . ." She held her pen up again, hesitated. "I love the pens."

Lil smiled, even though she didn't buy the idea that fountain pens could replace a parent, but maybe it was one of those things a person hangs on to. Something to believe in.

The bell rang behind them, and a small door near the counselors' table opened. The counselors walked in. There were four of them, and Lil's breath caught as she saw the one on the very end. It was Bente. At least she thought it was. She pulled the picture out of her pocket and looked down at it and then back up at the woman who now took her seat in the last chair at the table. Same sinewy build. Same straight hair. It was all silver now, but the way it hung around her face was exactly the same. It had to be her.

"What's that?" Charlie whispered, jutting her chin toward the picture in Lil's hand. "Is that you?" She glanced back toward the counselors, to Bente. "Do you know her?"

"I'll explain later," Lil answered. What could she say about it, anyway? she wondered. That she had found her mother hanging from a ceiling beam, and that she and her dad couldn't sleep at night and that she had come to find some answers about a random missing necklace that for all she knew could have been something dumb like a charm bracelet? Lil pushed the picture into her pocket. She would have to think of a better way of putting all of it. Or maybe not say anything at all.

"It's strange, isn't it?" Sydney mused, not looking up from her paper.

"What is?" Lil said.

"They all seem much older than I expected," Sydney said. "For camp counselors."

Lil nodded. It *did* seem like all the counselors were older women. At least forty-five or older, but, Lil thought, the packet had said they were at the top of their fields. It took time to climb, didn't it? The one who now made her way to the podium seemed like she was close to Lil's dad's age.

"Welcome, future leaders," she said, tapping the microphone twice. "I am your grand counselor, Athenia Pelia. It is an honor to have met many of you already today. I am the director of your conference this week. I hope that this is going to be a memorable learning experience for all of you and something you can look back on fondly in years to come. There is no doubt in my mind that connections will be made, knowledge will be gained and challenges will be conquered. Before we eat, I would like to introduce you to the mentors you will be studying with this week." She gestured toward the counselors' table, and the woman closest to the podium stood up.

"Colleen Umeo Hashiro, hailing from Kauai, USA, is our resident historian with more than twenty-five years of experience in the fields of archaeology, world history and information services. You will see her for workshops on knowledge foundations, archives, history and mythology, information science and the future of information technologies."

Charlie nodded and scribbled. "That one's on my itinerary."

The next woman stood up, and Lil recognized her from registration earlier in the day. Her hair had been only slightly tamed since then, and she had a new shirt on for the dinner.

Athenia smiled and continued. "Trudy Finnegan. Known

across continents for her groundbreaking work in particle acceleration. You'll be seeing her this week in the lab. You will not want to miss her series of workshops called Women in Science and Technology: The Next Generation."

Sydney's eyes seemed to light up and she jotted a few notes in her folder.

"Just past Trudy, you will see Bente Formo," Athenia continued.

Lil's heart shot into her throat at the sound of her name.

"Coming to you from Krigsskolen Academy in Norway, she is here to lead the workshop on women in military service, leadership roles and the future of women in combat."

Lil watched Bente stand. Shoulders back. Chin up. Jaw tight. A serious face, but not unkind, like Mom, someone you wanted to make proud. She looked a little older than the rest of the women, but stronger, too.

"Oh jeez." Sydney capped her pen. "I am not going within fifty feet of her. Do you see the size of her biceps?"

"I'm pretty sure the schedule is nonnegotiable. Rotating through each workshop every day," Charlie whispered.

"No way. I'm getting a headache during that one. Do they have a nurse here?"

"I'm excited about it," Lil said.

"Do you really want to go into the military?" Sydney hissed, leaning across the table toward her. "Do you realize how dangerous that is?"

"I'm going to fly," Lil said, involuntarily looking out the window.

"Are you speaking metaphorically?" Charlie whispered, looking up from her journal. "I do love metaphors."

"No," Lil said. "I mean, I'm going to fly . . . a plane . . ."

It took a moment for Lil to realize that the room had gone quiet and several pairs of eyes were looking at her. Athenia paused with hands in the air, and when her gaze finally landed on Lil, she looked almost as if she had seen a ghost. Lil felt her face flush.

Athenia cleared her throat. "If we are quite ready, we will continue."

Lil's eyes found her hands. She heard a giggle and didn't have to look to know it was Vivi Lancaster.

Luckily, Lil felt the focus return to the front of the room as Athenia continued. "And lastly, I will be teaching Women in Arts and Culture: Present, Past and Future." A few claps resounded around the table as the artists made themselves known. "I will also be holding open studio hours all week long, so you will have plenty of opportunity to explore the wonderful world of art."

Athenia paused and checked a notepad in front of her.

"Should you need anything throughout your stay, there will always be someone on duty in the office in which you registered." She indicated the small office through the door and on the other side of the foyer. "Furthermore, as noted in your acceptance packets, this week is meant to be entirely unplugged, giving you time to meet, connect and make bonds as well as the chance to enjoy the beautiful grounds of Melios Manor. Should you need to reach home, the office is also equipped with a computer and phone, which will be available to you twenty-four hours a day."

She gave a look around the room, nodded and smiled.

"Once again, we would all like to welcome you to this wonderful meeting of minds and hearts. We look forward to getting to know you. And we expect a great conference"—she nodded to the table—"beginning with this delectable homegrown meal from Aestos' unsurpassable Cretan kitchen."

Lil looked up to catch Athenia's gaze fall on her once more as she left the podium. Lil stared back, locking eyes with the older woman as the dining hall erupted into applause and a clatter of dishes and utensils took over.

6

The clock on the dining room wall wound its way toward nine as the plates began to empty and the stomachs began to fill. A large dog strode between the tables, sniffing, consuming crumbs and leaving large gobs of drool wherever a savory morsel had been found.

Lil lifted the tag on the dog's collar.

"Her name's Crumbsy," a girl with long dark hair that was gathered at the left side of her neck said. "The grand counselor has a weak spot for street dogs. Do you mind if I join you?"

"Not at all," Lil said, lifting a scrap of chicken off her plate. She gave it to Crumbsy, who accepted it with drooling jowls.

"That's disgusting," Sydney said from across the table as she placed her empty bowl in the center of her empty plate.

"What's your name?" Lil asked the newcomer.

"I'm Katrina Andrande. I heard you three are in Hall D, too."

"Oh." Charlie pulled her napkin out of her lap and set it beside her plate. "Are you across the hall from me?"

"1D," Kat said, nodding. "Oooohhh, who's that?" she said, looking over Charlie's shoulder. Lil followed her gaze. A boy about their age was making his way toward the table with a tray of copper cups with shiny, long stems. The boy had dark hair that had been lightened by the sun. His face was tan except for around his eyes, as though he was used to wearing sunglasses all the time.

"Hello, my name is Atticus. I will be serving tea and dessert," he said, coming to their table.

He plucked a bowl of strawberries from the center of his tray and lowered it between the four girls. "Freshly picked this morning."

Kat nabbed one of the berries before the bowl hit the table and popped it into her mouth.

"Can I interest you in any tea before you return to your dormitories?" he asked, gesturing to the copper cups on his tray. Up close now, Lil could see that they were bigger than regular cups, more like small, long-handled saucepans. They were each filled to the brim with liquid that varied in hue.

"We have mountain tea for clarity, sage for digestion, mint to cleanse the palette and celery leaf to calm jittery nerves."

They each chose one, except for Sydney, who placed her hand over the top of her mug definitively. Atticus began pouring the steaming liquid.

"Are you just working here for the summer?" Kat asked as Charlie lifted her mug and Atticus poured more tea.

"No, I live here. My father—" He stopped and placed the cup back down. "My father and I run the kitchen. I also tend to the sheep."

"You're a shepherd?" Lil asked, picturing the turbaned person she saw slipping through the trees earlier in the day. It must have been Atticus.

He nodded, lifting the mint infusion and pouring it into her mug.

"Thank you. *Eefcharisto.*"

He looked up and smiled at her. *"Parakaló,"* he said, then moved down the table.

Aestos appeared on the other side of them with another tray of tea and fruit. "No *raki* for the youths. Would you like mountain herbs instead? Freshly harvested this morning and steeped to perfection." He questioned the other conference attendees as he walked down the opposite side of the table, filling Atticus' silence with his jovial chatter.

Lil sipped the tea and put the mug up to her cheek, comforted by the warm cup.

"He's cute, isn't he?" Kat said, looking at the opposite end of the table, where Atticus was lowering another bowl of berries.

"Easy, Juliet," Charlie said.

"Yeah," Sydney said, grimacing. "Is *that* what you're here for?"

"No." Kat looked serious as she placed her mug back down on the table. "I am here for the seminars on arts and culture. Athenia is one of my father's mentors. He works at the Museu de Arte de São Paulo."

"São Paulo?" Lil asked. "In Spain?"

Charlie laughed as she sipped from her mug. "Try Brazil."

"Yes, Brazil. Where I'm from," Kat said.

"Sorry," Lil said, feeling her face flush. Everyone here seemed so well traveled, or had parents who traveled. They each were able to speak at least two languages and seemed so cultured. Her few Greek phrases felt even more inadequate now.

"You okay?" Kat said.

"Oh yes," Lil said. "Sorry. I'm just embarrassed."

"Not to worry. I don't know much about America. That's where you're from, right?"

"Yes," Lil said. "Vermont." She paused, realizing it would be a real task for anyone who was not an American to know all the states in the United States. Just like she didn't know the provinces of Canada or the counties of the United Kingdom. "New England."

Kat stared at her blankly.

"Northeast," Lil said.

Charlie shook her head.

"Near Boston," Lil added.

"Ohhhhh." The girls nodded.

"That's a very important American city," Charlie said. "I got a quill pen from there in 2005."

"What are you all here to study?" Kat asked. Pulling a piece of string from her pocket, she began to knit with her fingers. Pink and blue bands spun around her knuckles and seemed to grow longer within seconds.

"Attention, ladies!" Athenia said, interrupting their conversation. She made her way to the podium and tapped the microphone. "Before we disband, we have one more matter of business. As was noted in your registration folder, each morning will begin with a unique challenge. The team that wins the majority of these challenges by the end of your two-week stay will win the manor team scholarship."

Clapping and cheers erupted from around the table, and Sydney dropped her folder and sat up attentively.

Athenia continued. "The first challenge will commence tomorrow morning on our very own ropes course." A ropes course? Lil sat up, too, suddenly alert. Maybe it was the same one that Mom had done. Maybe she would find herself on the same bluff shown in the picture of Mom and Bente.

"Oh, great," Sydney muttered.

"And each team will have a mentor."

A girl with a sweeping blond braid that wrapped elegantly around the back of her head started speaking. "Is this mandatory?"

"No interruptions, please," Athenia said. "We will split up into our teams now so that you will have time to meet your mentor before your challenge."

Lil's stomach flipped. Please be Bente, she thought. Please be Bente.

Athenia placed a pair of glasses on her nose and lifted her notepad. "Hall A. Team A. Your mentor is Colleen. Please meet briefly at the left wall." Cheers erupted, and the four girls from Team A, including Vivi, separated from the table, making their way to Colleen. Each one seemed to walk like she was trying to hold a book on her head.

"Well, we'll definitely beat them," Lil said. "They're going to hate getting dirty."

"Don't count on it," Charlie said. "Vivi's gone to Mouratoglou for three summers."

"What is a Mouratoglou?" Kat hissed, taking the words right out of Lil's mouth.

"It's a highly competitive tennis academy," Charlie said.

Lil looked over at Vivi. Sure, she looked fit, toned—perfectly put together, even.

"I won't be able to outrun her," Sydney said. "I hate running."

Lil could see that. Sports might not have been one of Sydney's skills, but she seemed fiercely competitive in other pursuits. Surely that would come in handy.

"We'll be fine," Lil said confidently. "We all have skills. We'll just split up the tasks by strength."

"Hall B, Team B, you are with me at the opposite wall," Athenia said, indicating the wall to her right. Team B got up from the table. This included the girl with the wrapped blond hair. She didn't seem to be very motivated, Lil thought. She hoped that meant it would give them more of an edge.

"Hall C, Team C. You'll be working with Trudy," Athenia said, gesturing toward the third wall.

Trudy got up slowly. "Hup to, girls, lots to do," she said.

"That means we have Bente," Lil said.

"And last but not least, Hall D will go with Bente. Please meet beneath the fresco."

Lil handed her pen back to Charlie, who secured it in her case, and they all made their way to the fresco.

As she neared, Bente rose from her seat and they locked eyes. Lil tried to read her face. She thought the older woman squinted just the slightest bit. Her eyebrows lifted. It was nearly undetectable, but Lil could see the recognition. She stifled the flood of questions that rose in her. The questions she had been waiting all this time to ask. *Did you know my mother well? When did you meet? What was she like? Do you really think she . . .*

She forced herself not to reach into the pocket of her jeans and pull out the picture. Now wasn't the time.

Bente smiled and extended her hand to each girl. Lil took it in her grasp, feeling the firm squeeze.

"Lilith Bennette," Lil said, being sure not to hang on for too long.

"Very good," Bente said.

Lil moved to the side as the other introductions were made. Then Bente clicked her teeth and secured her hands firmly behind her back once more. "Team D. Tomorrow will be made up of a test of endurance, will and smarts. I suggest you not only make sure you are fresh for the morning, but also review what you know of Cretan history." Lil watched as Bente paced a few steps to the left, then turned and paced a few steps to her right. "This information may come in handy tomorrow.

"Second," Bente said, lifting a folded envelope from her back pocket and holding it out in front of them, "is this. Each team has a different clue that will tell you where to go first thing in the morning. Examine it. Figure out what it means. Be observant."

She looked from one face to the other as she placed the envelope on the end of the counselors' table and pulled a canvas jacket off her chair. She wrapped it over her shoulders. "If you decipher the clue correctly and make it to the location indicated, you will find me." She scanned the room. "The more prompt and alert you are, the more you work together, the more likely your team is to succeed. And it goes without saying, the more chances you have at winning the team scholarship at the end of the program." She looked from Lil to Sydney to Kat and lastly to Charlie. "I think it's clear that some groups need this scholarship more than others. Let's make sure the right team wins."

Bente walked away, without any departing words.

"She is so intense," Sydney whispered, looking at her for just a moment as she exited the dining hall.

"What did she mean by that?" Kat said. "That others don't need the scholarship?"

Charlie looked at the other groups. "It's not obvious? I guess they're rich."

Lil knew that the different dormitories had different fees. And she knew that she and her dad had picked the cheapest. That meant that Kat, Sydney and Charlie had all done the same. Vivi was right when she scoffed. They were in the servants' quarters, so to speak. Lil looked around at her group. Kat and Sydney both hung their heads, and Charlie fidgeted with the tattered leather strapping on her fountain pen case.

"Let's go and figure out our clue," Lil said. "We need to take every opportunity to heighten our chances of winning."

"Agreed," Sydney said, flipping her flashlight on and heading for the door.

W

e can use my room," Kat said, coming to the first door on the left, just across from Charlie's. Lil looked up at the top of Kat's door. Half man, half bull. She recognized the legendary Minotaur.

Kat turned the key in the lock and pushed the dormitory door open. As they piled in, a warm glow illuminated Kat's room. It seemed much cozier than Lil's, like she had taken the time to make herself at home. The stone had been decorated with a few colorful sarongs. On her desk was a set of knitting needles with a long section of ribbonlike yarn flowing from them like a river. But the most beautiful was the small tabletop easel with a charcoal drawing of a girl holding a puppy. Kat pulled a chair over toward the bench that ran along one wall as Lil stared at the picture. "This is beautiful. Did you do this today?"

"No," Kat said, coming to stand next to her. "I came in yesterday. It was so peaceful to work while the place was quiet."

"Who is it?" Lil asked as she stared at the large, round, yet sorrowful eyes of the girl in the drawing.

"This is Gabriela," Kat said, tilting her head to the side. "On Sundays, we hold an art workshop for the kids in Paraisópolis. Some of my friends from the International School come, too."

Lil tripped over the word. "Paris-opolis?" she asked.

"It's a favela."

Lil wasn't exactly sure what it meant, but she thought she'd heard that word before.

"What's a favela?" Sydney asked, lifting the charcoal from the table and setting it neatly into the container. She lined the charcoal up so that the tip was the exact same height as the ones next to it.

"A favela?" Kat paused. "A slum," she said, and then, shrugging, added, "but home to many. My aunt and uncle do programs with the kids there. I always bring art supplies from the museum and we have them draw their passions. Sometimes, their faces stick in my mind. Like Gabriela's."

"She looks sad," Lil said, taking in the large watery eyes. Lil couldn't draw so much as a stick figure.

"She is sad sometimes." Kat flipped the page, displaying a new piece of art. "Not all my pictures are so sad."

The next one was charcoal, but lit with colorful pastels. It was a woman with gray rags on one sleeve that melted into a beautiful flowing quilt on the other side. It expanded over her shoulder and twisted into a tornado of color behind her.

"A blank page is a place where you can dream endlessly." Kat picked up an orange pastel and moved it back and forth, filling in a little blank dot in the quilt.

"That's beautiful," Charlie said, joining them. "I'm sure the kids learn a lot from you."

"We don't make it too formal, but I love it." Kat set the pastel on the table and went to her balcony while Sydney placed the pastel back in its container once more. Lil watched her as she leveled the top of the pastel with the top of the others. When she turned, Kat was reappearing from the shadows of the balcony, holding a pitcher.

"*Chá*? Tea? Aestos let me borrow an infuser." She held it up.

"Yes, please," Charlie said, sitting down on the window seat.

Sydney pulled out the chair next to the desk and sat down on it, and Lil made her way to the window seat as well. They arranged the candles so that the space between them was well lit as Kat poured tea into mugs that she dug out of the bottom of her desk.

"Strange, isn't it?" Sydney said, accepting a mug from Kat.

"What is?" Charlie asked, pulling her notepad from her pocket. She looked around the room and started taking notes.

Lil accepted a mug of tea as well and took a small sip. It was still warm from the sun, and it made her think of her dad all of a sudden. She wondered how he was doing. If he was lonely. He'd sounded tired and slightly wistful when she had called him from the airport.

"What do you think?" Kat said, pulling her from her thoughts.

"It's delicious!" Lil said.

"No." Kat nodded toward Sydney. "What do you think of what Sydney said?"

Lil tried to recover, but Sydney had already jumped in again. "I said, don't you think it's strange that they only have stained-glass windows in a solar-powered building? I mean, I understand the eco-tourism experience requires self-sufficiency—that's part of it—but it seems like the building would be more modernized in some ways."

Lil glanced once more at the Minotaur. Like in her room, the frame was cast iron, ornamented on the right with a sconce. "I hadn't even thought of that. I thought it was just decorative."

"Weird décor," Sydney said. She yawned, but stifled it quickly with a wave of her hand. "I mean, wouldn't you want as much outside light as possible in a building that doesn't use electricity?"

"I don't know," Charlie said, shaking her head. "Perhaps this was some sort of holy building." She looked up at the stained-glass window as well. "You know how buildings have their histories. Our bookshop used to be part of a medieval prison."

"Where are you from again?" Lil asked, wondering how it was she had anything medieval in her town.

"Ah, Villefranche de Conflent. It is mostly a tourist town now."

"But your shop, do you think it is haunted?" Kat said, setting the pitcher down and joining the group.

Sydney rolled her eyes and picked at the chair momentarily.

"Margo says it's the floors that creak, but I know better," Charlie said. "When she's gone, the floors creak more. Like they wait for her to leave, and then the ghosts come out to play."

Lil felt a cool breeze slide in through the open balcony door, and she shivered in spite of herself.

"Actually," Charlie said, sitting up straight, "I did do a bit of research when I first got our packet. They said this building was originally an olive mill. Its foundations are from the seventeenth century, but the stones that make up the rest of it are even older. Culled from ancient villages, even. In fact, this quarter"—she indicated the dormitory around her—"is the oldest. My guess is the other dormitories probably aren't quite the same."

"Maybe we can investigate?" Kat said, lighting onto a bench. She crossed her legs pretzel-style and pulled her skirt over the top of her knees so it hung down to the floor.

"Speaking of investigations," Lil said, pulling the note card from her pocket. "We better figure out this clue before we have to turn in for the night."

"We've idled away our time. We have exactly ten minutes left until lights out," Sydney said, looking at her watch.

Lil peeled back the seal of the envelope and drew out a cream-colored note card.

At the top was a map of the manor and surrounding area. At the bottom was a simple riddle.

> *To the trail you'll head. In a timely manner go.*
> *Find the Minoans. Buried high or low?*

"The Minoans?" Sydney said. "Who are the Minoans?"

"Ancient people from Crete," Charlie said without blinking. "Though I'm not sure of the rest of it."

"What I would give for my iPad right now," Sydney sighed.

They all leaned in and looked at the riddle and the map once more. Charlie shook her head. "No iPad, but there *is* a library. Shall we take a trip?"

Sydney's head shot up. "The guidelines explicitly said that we need to be in our dormitories by ten o'clock." She looked down at her watch. "That's five minutes from now."

"What if we just go quickly," Lil said. "That'd make us the most prepared, and still well rested. We'll grab a book on Minoans and come back downstairs."

The girls looked from one to the other. Kat set her mug down. "I'm always up for a bit of adventure."

A mischievous smile crept across Charlie's face. "Sneaking through an old haunted manor at night? Absolutely."

Lil looked from the girls to the map. The alternative was to return to her room, to think about Mom. To obsess over the late hours. It would be nice to have a small distraction. "I'm game." She looked to Sydney. "We can always have just a few of us go."

Sydney rolled her eyes. "Oh, c'mon." She shook her head, stared at the ceiling, then looked back at the others. Then back at the ceiling and around again. "Okay, fine, I'll go. Let's just make it quick."

Lil jumped up and turned the note card diagonally, so the layout was in alignment with their position.

"So we need to make our way back downstairs to the foyer staircase, then take that up to the third floor. It looks like it splits Hall A and"—she squinted at the tiny print—"and the counselors' chambers."

"Oh, perfect," Sydney said. "Not only are we out of bed later than we're supposed to be, but we're actually walking straight into the counselors' quarters? What about this sounds like a good idea to you? What if we get caught? Could we get disqualified?"

They hesitated. Lil flipped the card over. No one had said anything about *when* they needed to solve the riddle. Nothing on the card indicated that they should wait, or would get sanctioned or be disqualified. "If it was off-limits until morning," Lil said, "why would we all have gotten our clues tonight?"

"Fair point," Charlie said.

"I think it's risky," Sydney said.

Kat and Charlie needed no encouragement, hurrying to the door. Sydney grumbled but pressed the button on her flashlight. The light went on for just a second and then flickered and died. "Oh, great," she said, rolling her eyes. "Macy—my little sister— must have unplugged my charger. Dumb kid."

Lil picked up a candle from Kat's desk, held the wick to hers until it lit and handed it to Sydney.

Then they entered the hallway, their candle flames the only light in the darkened manor.

8

L il carried the note card in her hand as they ascended the main stairs. In the silence of the hallway, Sydney's words itched at the back of her mind. Perhaps they would get in trouble, if not for looking in the library, at least for being out of bed past curfew.

She hadn't come for the scholarship, but, well, maybe the others had. And she had to admit, it couldn't hurt.

Lil looked down at the note card and hurried up the stairs, pausing as they came to the top floor. She lowered her light to the wooden panel next to the door. **ΑΙΘΟΥΣΑ Α (HALL A)**. Lil grasped the handle and pushed the door open, expecting to stare into another dark hallway, but as the door swung, Lil stared into a bright, moonlit hall. Beams cascaded in through skylights in the high ceiling. So this was why the different dormitories had different fees. They'd left an old olive mill and entered a palace.

"Whoa," Kat said, lowering her candle. They didn't need them now.

Lil looked from door to door. Instead of the short stall-like doors in Hall D, the ones in Hall A were large, arched at the top and white. Big urns sat in the corners at the far end, but they weren't the same type of clay-colored urns they had seen in the lower levels. These were more like marble, and they stuck out in a stark blue as if they held the moon under their stony skins.

"I see what Bente meant," Sydney whispered from behind. "I wonder why they're even competing."

A rustle erupted from one of the rooms, and they all blew out their candles. Sydney went silent, and everyone stepped back into the shadow of the doorway. Lil waited, ears alert, body tensed. When nothing moved, she stepped into a moonbeam and raised the note card in front of her.

"Straight down this hall. On the right," she whispered.

"Let's get a move on," Sydney said. "Just standing here is giving me the creeps."

They hurried quickly down the hallway, passing the moonlit urns. Lil looked behind them and gave a sigh of relief as they entered the shadows of the alcove. She peered down the hallway on the other side. It, too, was bright with moonbeams. That would be the way to the counselors' quarters. On that side, too, there seemed to be nothing but a wash of moonlight. She turned to the door and squinted to read a raw wood sign:

ΒΙΒΛΙΟΘΗΚΗ (LIBRARY)

Charlie grasped the door handle.

"Wait," Lil said, stilling her hand. "Just in case someone's inside. Slow and steady."

Charlie nodded and took a breath, then pulled the door open just a little, holding her eye to the crack.

"All clear," Charlie said, opening the door fully. Lil checked both hallways once again, then held the door open as the others spilled inside. She followed softly, pulling the door closed behind her, and drank in her surroundings. The library was even more elegant than the hallway. Large round windows on the ceiling let in the moonlight. Frescoes adorned the walls. They were bigger and brighter than the ones downstairs.

"Probably replicas," Kat said as if reading Lil's mind. They went over to the nearest one. Three women side by side, their hands raised in what might have been some sort of a dance or ritual, Lil thought.

"What makes you think they're replicas?" Lil asked.

"Well, they're so bright." Kat traced her fingers over the fresco. "Not like the ones that you find in ruins, covered in years of dirt and dust. Those you can barely see the lines to reconstruct."

"We don't have time for an art lesson," Sydney said, eyeing the door. "Let's get what we need and get out."

"She's right," Lil said, scanning the room for some sort of library catalog or a public access computer like they had at her local library. Her eyes fell on an upright cabinet with many small drawers that stood in the corner. She jutted her chin toward it. "It's a bit old looking for a future leaders' conference."

"You would think they would have something more up to date," Sydney said. Her nose crinkled up as if she had smelled something foul. "At least in a hall as fine as Hall A."

"You would think so," Lil said. They all circled the card catalog.

"Our riddle said Minoan, right? I wonder if there is a subject heading for Minoan," Charlie said as she scanned the small rectangular labels. She pulled out the drawer that said *L–M* and riffled through a stack of cards.

"Ah! Minoan—Society and Culture," Charlie said, picking up three cards. "Looks like they have a few books on it. All in the nine hundreds. Let's go with this one. Nine hundred thirty point one FIT." She closed the door and circled the library, staring at the bindings.

"I'm glad you're here," Lil said, unsure of the process Charlie was using to find the book.

A moment later, Charlie pulled a volume from the shelf and

moved back toward them. They stepped over to a large mahogany table next to a floor-to-ceiling window. *Minoans* by P. T. Fitzgerald. Charlie flipped it open, scanning the index.

"Minoan, Burial ritual, one hundred sixty-two," she muttered, then flipped the pages.

"Hurry, hurry, hurry," Sydney said. "It's ten twenty now."

"Relax," Kat whispered.

Lil was getting a bit uneasy, too, but a smile stretched across Charlie's face. "Right here. Minoans buried their dead in the gorge caves."

Lil heard a rustle. Her ears went alert. Her shoulders back. The hair on her neck seemed to stand up of its own accord. "Shh, shh." She waved a hand. There it was again, the light *tap, tap, tap* of feet on stone.

"You're kidding me," Sydney hissed.

A warm pool of candlelight eased under the door.

"Behind the curtains," Lil said, grabbing Sydney's arm and rushing around the table to the window. Charlie and Kat fell in as they dove behind the curtains. Lil and Sydney landed on one side and Kat and Charlie on the opposite just as a latch clicked free.

Lil heard a hinge squeak and yawn. She steadied the curtain with her hand and made sure to tuck her feet snug against the wall.

Tap tap tap—footsteps fell on stone, moving toward their side of the room. Lil held her breath, felt Sydney shaking at her side. She peered over to the other panel and could detect Kat and Charlie there in the shadows. Charlie was closest to her, just a few feet away, and she could see the reflection off her glasses as she looked up at Lil.

Lil's head snapped back up as a second pair of footsteps

joined the first. Maybe others had come searching for their clue before morning?

"My concern is not with Atticus or Aestos," a voice hissed. "What if the betrayal lies with one of the others? With one of us?"

Lil froze. It wasn't students. It couldn't be. She recognized the voice. Bente. A few steps more, and she could see she was right. The older woman stopped in front of the card catalog, her silver hair catching the moonlight.

"Where do you come by this suspicion, Bente?" a second voice asked. Lil inched slightly to her left and peered past the edge of the curtain. Athenia was with her. They each set their candles on top of the old card catalog.

"I have traced outgoing calls from the main phone. They go late at night. And they go to where I believe the Zephylite leader can be found."

Lil swallowed hard. Zephylite? It was an unfamiliar word to Lil, and yet she could see that this had nothing to do with the future leaders' conference. This was a conversation no one was meant to overhear. She looked back to Charlie and Kat. Kat was just a distant smudge in the shadows, but Charlie's pale face was easily read, and Lil watched her put her hand up to her mouth to muffle her breathing.

"And if they come. Do you know when they will arrive?" Athenia said, pulling out a drawer of the card catalog.

"I do not know."

Athenia nodded as Bente pulled out a second drawer. What were they doing? Lil wondered. Bente reached for two more and yanked them all the way out. A locking noise echoed throughout the stacks. Lil felt Sydney stop shaking next to her, and she leaned toward Lil. Lil shook her head, watching Sydney brush against the curtain as they both tried to see where the noise had come from. Athenia stopped. Looked over her shoulder. Lil grabbed Sydney's wrist, and they pressed themselves into the window. Had Athenia seen the movement? Lil pinched her eyes closed and waited. Waited for footsteps. Waited for the breeze of the curtain being pulled back. Waited to be caught. But nothing moved. Lil unglued her eyelids and eased back toward the edge of the curtain.

She watched as the card catalog unhinged from the wall. Bente reached to the side and swung it open like a door. There, embedded in the stonework, was a safe with what looked like the wheel of an ancient ship on the front of it. Lil stared, mesmerized, as Bente turned the wheel steadily one way and then the other. The turns and half turns worked to the right and to the left were impossible to count. Finally, with a *click* and a *zwooshpop*, the door slid free. Bente reached inside.

"You will secure the key in its secondary location," Athenia said.

"Until then it stays by my side." Bente raised her hands in the air, and Lil watched as a beam of moonlight caught the object. It twirled there momentarily hung on a thick cord, and Lil stifled a gasp, her heart making a new home in her throat. Surely she wasn't seeing it right. She leaned forward a bit more, her fingers curling around the edge of the curtain. The disk. One side a spiral with pictographs, the other a black labrys. It was about three times the size of Mom's. And not metallic. It looked old. Had Athenia called it a key? A key to what? Lil stood, stunned, as Bente lowered it around her neck and tucked it into her shirt so it was hidden.

Lil felt a pinch on her arm. She looked down to see Sydney grasping her wrist. She hadn't been aware of how far she had leaned in. She gave in to Sydney's pull, falling back into shadows.

"Try and get some sleep despite it," Athenia's voice whispered.

"Right after I do rounds," Bente said. Lil stared at the back of the curtain as the candle lights floated away, dulled. The footsteps retreated, then stopped. Had they made their way all the way back to the door? It hadn't seemed so. The candlelight was faded, but not gone.

"You were here earlier?" came Bente's voice.

"Yes, I was checking some facts in the special collection. Why do you ask?" Athenia said.

"Did you leave a book out?" Bente asked.

Lil's gaze darted to Charlie's and they stared at each other, not daring to breathe.

"I didn't." There was a pause. "In fact, I was in here a mere thirty minutes ago and the book wasn't there."

Lil heard Sydney's breathing pick up pace next to her and her heartbeat matched it, moving quickly and, she hoped, not as audibly as it seemed.

"Do you think someone was out of bed after curfew?"

"Perhaps." The candlelight slipped into shadows and the *tap tap tap* of footsteps retreated toward the door. "We should make an announcement about that."

The door yawned open and shut on its hinges. Lil held herself still, listening just in case it was a ploy. After several minutes had passed, Sydney pulled the other side of the curtain back the tiniest bit.

"It's all clear," she said. They pooled together in front of the window, an audible sigh of relief among them.

"What was that all about?" Sydney whispered, her face split by shadows.

"I don't know," Lil said. It was true. It was as if she had a handful of puzzle pieces from different puzzles. "The only thing I know is that it was not about the conference. Not at all."

"Something much bigger is going on here," Kat said, her face alight with worry.

"She said she's doing rounds," Sydney said, shaking her head. "We need to get back to our rooms. Now."

"Sydney's right," Charlie said. "They already saw our book." She gulped, raising a palm to her forehead. "I can't believe I left it. But they won't know it was us."

"Not if we get back undetected," Lil said, leading them to the door and down the stairs. Into the dark hallways they went without light, and slipped quickly into their rooms.

9

The revivalists have been trying to get this location opened up to them for spiritual rituals for the past ten years," Felice said.

Horatio laughed. The modern-day pagans were a joke. They didn't know the true history. But Horatio and Felice had known the truth of Zeus for a long time. They had studied the writings since they were children. Horatio could still see the old farmhouse, and the way Ares would come on Sunday evenings and read to them from the ancient scripts. There was no doubt in Horatio's mind that what his uncle had told him was absolutely true. The historical evidence was irrefutable. And now he, his brother and his sister would be the messengers of the Zephylites to the new world. They would seek the legendary Icarus Folio. They would be unrivaled.

Byron's voice cropped up from the shadows in the backseat. "Do you think they'll have any food at this meeting? I'm starving."

"Quit complaining," Felice said. "It's not every day you get sent on a holy quest."

Horatio smiled. Felice had always gotten it. Byron, not as much, but he tried to be good. Just as their mother had said. Byron was always trying to be a good boy, despite himself.

"Well, who goes on a quest without food?" Byron said.

"They'll have the traditional fare," Horatio said as he steered the car beneath the skeletons of old Venetian windmills. He squinted into the darkness, eyeing the tourist signs leading to the Dikteon Cave. Spotting a blue sign, he turned left and headed straight up a hill. Even without the sign, Horatio thought, he would have been able to find his way. The vibrations had changed. There was a great, ancient power here. He could feel it. That was why Horatio was the chosen messenger.

He pulled into the parking lot and eased the car into the shadows of the chestnut trees. There were only a few cars there, thankfully. Many of the others had arrived as tourists earlier in the day. Others would have walked over the western hill, and some would have carpooled. Horatio scanned the area for Giorgos: head groundskeeper, fellow Zephylite and gatekeeper to holy sanctuaries.

"Well, where the hell is he?" he huffed, sucking the life out of his cigarette and depositing it out the window.

"He's at your twenty," Felice said, pointing to the depths of the shadows.

Horatio smirked. Felice worked with a sixth sense of her own. Nothing but perhaps the silver side of a pocket pen was peeking from the darkness at them, but she had discerned it from the slivers of moonshine that escaped through the foliage. The shadow moved and morphed, and a moment later Giorgos was there beside them. Horatio rolled down his window. He hadn't seen the old man since he was a child, and he searched his face, now wrinkled with age.

"George? Is that you?"

"Sorry, we're closed," Giorgos said.

Of course. Horatio pulled the necklace from beneath his shirt, showing off the lightning bolt extended between the gold circle. He recited the blessing in ancient Greek. *"Athanate Dia, chaire. Chairete athanata tekna tou Dios. . ."* He kissed the necklace and raised it high, translating the words in his head. *To Zeus immortal, blessings. To his immortal kin, blessings.*

Giorgos' face broke into a smile. "Young Horatio, you have changed with age, child."

"So have you," Byron piped up from the backseat. "And I'm not talking about in a good way."

"And that must be Ronny. Good to see you, too."

Felice leaned toward Horatio. "Good day to you, Father Giorgos," she said, extending a hand. The old man smiled and accepted it.

"And Felice. As fast-footed and sharp-sighted as ever, I hope?"

"Even more so," Felice said.

"You will need it," Giorgos said. He turned toward the shadows. "When you are ready, we will proceed to the back entrance."

Horatio opened the door. "We have been ready for all the ages."

They stepped up the stone path to the Dikteon Cave, Horatio following Giorgos' sure footing. He turned at the top of the hill and watched the clouds roll under the moon, sending shadowy boats across the belly of the valley. His throat swelled with emotion as he thought of this day, millennia before, when Zeus had been born and hidden from his evil father, Kronos, in the cave of Dikte. The wind picked up, and Horatio lifted his face to it, breathing in the power. He raised his hands and felt the wind in his shirtsleeves.

A door squeaked on its hinges, and Felice punched Horatio in the arm as she passed. "Getting overdramatic," she said. "Let's stay focused on the task at hand."

Felice lacked the ability to enjoy anything with true feeling, Horatio thought as he dropped his hands by his side and stepped into the damp tunnel.

Giorgos struck a match, and a minute later a few torches were lit. He handed one to Horatio and another to Felice, and carried the third one on his own.

Horatio envisioned baby Zeus hiding here, in the belly of the caverns. The women snapped branches, and the warriors clashed their shields in the large chamber to hide the newborn's cries so that Kronos wouldn't hear him.

Horatio had visited this cave once as a tourist and once before as a Zephylite, so he knew about the hidden chamber, the one that no one could pay to see. The one where Zeus had been hidden so many years ago. It was less dramatic—no huge stalagmites or stalactites. No special LED lighting to make the fingers of rock loom gnarled and jagged. Just a back corner with a damp smell, removed from the rest.

Here, tonight, they stepped into the small alcove. A group of plain-clothed people held torches around a simple stone slab. Horatio nodded as he entered, recognizing many of the order's elders. There was Benedict and Francine. And there was Ares, his beloved uncle, the high priest.

Horatio led his brother and sister to the center. He was on one side of the stone slab while Ares stood upright and welcoming on the other.

"Shall we begin?" Ares said, his face awash with a smile.

Horatio dropped to one knee.

"Youngest first," Ares said. Horatio hesitated, then stood. He stepped back to watch, hoping Byron would do it just as they had rehearsed. He watched as his brother lifted the top of his leather satchel and extracted the decorative bronze vial. He unscrewed the cap and poured the contents onto the stone slab, then set the vial down, his head bowed.

"Thank you for your offering, messenger." Ares turned to a stone stool and lifted a leather thong with three charred shapes on it. "I bestow on you the three sacred symbols passed down for millennia as a token of luck and of Zeus' blessing on your voyage. The first, ash from the volcano of Thera that destroyed those who strove to destroy Zeus. This is the protection that Zeus offers you on your quest for immortality." He turned the band. "Next, a branch of ancient oak from the grounds where Zeus once lived. A token of shelter and safety with the lord." He flipped the band again. "Lastly, an eagle, sign of justice, but moreover to remind you that you carry a great message. May your flight be fast."

Horatio watched with zeal as Ares lowered the emblems into Byron's hands. Byron bowed, accepting the gift, and then stood.

Felice took his place in front of the stone slab and pulled a bunch of sagebrush from her pouch. She bent it to her torch and let it crackle until a steady line of smoke soared to the ceiling of the cave. She placed the brush on the stone slab and inhaled as the smoke permeated the room, then bowed her head.

Ares stuck his hand into the satchel at his side and pulled out a leather case. "Messenger, I bestow upon you an ancient cartograph drawn by Zeus' own son Minos. Written on stone tablets and preserved by the volcanic ash on Thera. It was found by our kin and translated here." He held out a leather scroll. "May its paths still be true to you, the chosen navigator."

Felice bowed her head and raised her hands, accepting the map, and then stood.

Finally, Horatio's turn had come, and he eyed the stone stool.

"Messenger," Ares said, his smile broadening.

Horatio grasped his satchel and pulled the top off. He extracted three large oak branches and laid them zigzag across the stone so that they resembled the lord's famous lightning bolt. "Father, I am here to serve," he said, raising his eyes to Ares.

Ares reached down and pulled Horatio's bag from his shoulders. What was he doing? Horatio wondered. It was common to receive a gift, not have one taken away. Ares lifted the final item into the air, and Horatio soaked in the beauty. There in his hands was a fine leather satchel, decorated from stem to stern with beautiful ancient symbols and images. He reached to place his fingers on the carvings.

"Messenger Horatio, I bestow upon you a sacred case for extraction and security of the Icarus Folio."

Horatio felt the weight of the remarkable satchel as it landed in his hands. "That is my task, my desire and my destiny," he breathed, happy to give up his tattered bag for this masterpiece.

A moan began around the circle as the torches swayed and the group began their ritual chant. Horatio felt the music, his voice climbing to join the others. For thirty minutes, they moved and chanted, and the room seemed alive with spirit and vitality. They honored the birth of Zeus with the passing of the wine and the banging of drums. And when the merrymaking wound to an end, Ares called the group together once more. Horatio sat bleary eyed, eager to see what lay ahead.

"We have not discussed retrieval of the key." Ares held up a picture of a double-sided disk with a labrys on one side and pictographs on the other. Horatio had seen it many times before in the writings of Hexalodorous. Book four, verse six, this crude illustration underneath. The key. "As you know, there are three entryways to the labyrinth, as indicated on your cartograph. Getting in is easy. But to get out, you require the key. You will need to find the Protector and *encourage* her to give it to you."

He extracted a large piece of cloth from beneath the table and laid it out in front of them, unrolling the package to reveal several weapons: a gun, a machete, a few pieces of explosives. A sword, more decorative than useful, Horatio thought. He scanned the others. There was a bronze blade and a few small daggers. Horatio reached for the machete, testing the weight in his hand. Yes, he thought as it balanced horizontally across his palm, it would do nicely.

10

When Lil had returned to her room, her mind had spun relentlessly. She had paced her small dormitory, stretched and tried not to stare at the symbols in the stained-glass window that decorated the top of her door. She had ruminated over the conversation in the library until jet lag and weariness eventually caught her and put her under around 2:00 a.m.

Now, as her watch alarm warned her that the day was going to begin, she reached up to silence it and opened her eyes. Five o'clock. She wobbled to a seated position, then yawned and stretched. How could she have wasted hours of much-needed sleep? She made her way up, got dressed and placed the picture of her mom and Bente into her pocket. Maybe, Lil thought as she went to a small sink in the corner and began to brush her teeth— maybe if she asked Bente about the picture, she might find out more information about the previous night. The question was, did she want to?

Lil spat in the sink and pulled on shorts, a T-shirt and a pair of socks and sneakers. As she tightened her laces, a knock came at the door. She hurried to it, opening the top half. It was Sydney. She was all dressed and ready for the day. Her twisty hair was pulled into two big puffs at the back of her head.

"I couldn't sleep a wink," she said, looking one way down the hall and then the other.

Lil opened the door all the way. "Me neither," she said, gesturing for Sydney to come in.

Lil yawned and dropped into the desk chair as Sydney started pacing her room.

"I mean, we're technically all cut off from the world," Sydney said. "Way up on a mountain 'retreat.'" She used quotation marks for the word *retreat*. "I mean, no cell phones, no computers? A solar-powered building with few communication methods at all? From the outside it looks like a wonderful off-the-beaten-path experience, but now I can see it's the perfect storm for a psycho-thriller horror flick."

The squeak of hinges followed by the sound of footsteps echoed in the hallway. Lil waved her hand, cutting Sydney off. Maybe it was a teacher making her rounds again. Sydney froze as Lil went and peered down the hall. Kat and Charlie locked their doors, spotted Lil and rushed toward her.

Charlie looked anxious as they neared. "Did you sleep at all?"

Lil shook her head, opening the door wide. Kat sat on the side of the bed, and Charlie took a position at the window seat. Lil closed the door tight, then dropped into the chair. She placed her elbows on her knees and clasped her hands together.

"So like I was saying," Sydney said, returning to her pacing, "this is the perfect storm for a psycho-thriller horror flick. We basically have no means of communication with the outside world. We're at the mercy of these 'counselors.'" She used quotation marks once again.

Lil's mind raced. Sydney seemed to think they were all dangerous. Surely a friend of her mom's wouldn't be dangerous. The symbol Mom wore, it couldn't mean something bad. Could it?

"I think you might be jumping to conclusions," Charlie said.

Sydney leveled her with a stare. "Jumping to conclusions? I don't jump to conclusions." She pulled a roll of papers out of her back pocket, went to Lil's desk and flattened them against it.

Lil stared down at the top sheet as Charlie and Kat came across the room. It was a meticulously drawn map of the surrounding area.

"Is that computer generated?" Kat asked, leaning closer.

"Like I said, no technology. I had to hand-draft it. I did my best based on my GPS."

Lil nodded, noting the homemade device attached to Sydney's hip.

Sydney traced the line of the road. "I drew it out to give you the whole picture. We're approximately one hour from Chania by bus. From there, along the national road just to the base of this mountain was eighty miles. Then"—she started tracing the winding road with the turnstiles up to where they were—"we had an additional ten miles up this road. The nearest house is—" Sydney's finger traced back down the mountain, straying to the main road they had come in on. Written in all capital letters in neatly slanted writing was a single phrase: *LAST SIGN OF LIFE.*

Lil tried to remember the ride up the mountain. She'd noticed the goats and sheep. She'd noticed that there were a few shepherds in the fields, but the houses? The houses, she remembered, slipped away into a tiny little model town in the distance. "No other houses for at least ten miles?" Lil said.

Sydney nodded and made a big, even-handed circle around the manor. "Farther in any other direction."

"So it's off the beaten path," Kat said, standing and crossing her arms. "We knew that coming here. You read all the reviews online. It's the premier Future Leaders International Conference. It provides a unique experience."

"Yes, but it's important to factor in that we are now in a new situation. We have gained knowledge." Sydney flipped her page to reveal a complex weblike chart.

"We're countless miles from home in each direction." She traced a thread. "We have very limited means of communication." She traced another thread to a Z inside a circle. "There is something called a Zephylite. I hope that's not like a Cylon. And lastly, they are coming for this thing." She traced a line to a picture of the disk with the labrys on it.

"The key," Lil heard herself saying. "I mean, they called it a key."

"A key to what?" Kat said.

"That's another valid question," Sydney said. "However, it's not as important as the one we should be asking—" She traced the thread to a huge balloon on the upper right where there were four stick figures. She had written in the counselors' names along with their credentials, circling the word *international* underneath each person. "Fairly high-profile figures. Working internationally. Hiding a key from some group that we have never heard of." She underlined the counselors' names. "Who are they, really?"

Lil's mind worked. Mom had started in the air force and then moved over to a job in the Department of Homeland Security. She had a habit of disappearing suddenly in the middle of the day. She was there for breakfast, but when Lil returned home from school, her plane would be missing from the airfield. She could always see the Longhorn, or the lack of the Longhorn, from the bus window as they circled toward the outlying farms.

"So are you saying," Kat said, twisting her bangle bracelets on her wrist, "you think this is some sort of a governmental conspiracy? An international spy ring—"

"That's just it," Sydney said, running the end of her pencil along the line to an empty bubble. "We don't have enough clues to come to a conclusion." She drew a big question mark in the empty bubble.

"We need more information," Charlie said.

Lil found her hand at her pocket again. Would telling them about the picture, about her mom and her mom's death, help them figure any of this out? Would it paint Lil as part of the conspiracy, too? Her fingers curled and uncurled. Maybe she could get some more information from the library tonight, and see what was really going on. Then she could share the rest . . . if it was necessary.

Lil and Sydney's watches started beeping suddenly. Lil pressed hers off. It was 6:00 a.m. "Let's think about it and talk more later. For now, we have a scholarship to win."

11

They reached the trailhead, and Lil wiggled her toes in her shoes. Her legs ached to run and stretch, and she pictured the days when she would run behind Mom, through the fields and into the trees. When she was little, she could never keep up. She would see the soles of her mother's shoes flashing steadily ahead of her. She'd lose her for a while, then around the next bend, spot her again. This path looked different from the wooded one she was used to, climbing up a slight hill and then branching off into four forks that rose ever higher, steeper and rockier.

The girls stopped in front of a sign with four directionals at the top of it, and Lil fought to make out the Greek letters. Some looked so much like the English alphabet, they were easy to identify—the *E*s, the *A*s, and the *K*s—but she got tripped up on the other letters.

"Ah, here," Sydney said as she rounded the other side of the sign.

They followed and looked up.

The top sign said **POCKET'S GORGE**.

The next said **HIDDEN WATERS**.

The third said **CAVE PASSAGE**.

And the fourth said **FUNNELS RAVINE**.

"Cave Passage," Kat said. "It has to be . . . where the Minoans bury their dead. In the caves."

"That's right," Charlie said. "Buried high, not low. That's undoubtedly our path."

Lil followed the arrow that pointed toward Cave Passage. The sun spilled down like melted butter onto the beginning of the path, then wound its way into shadows under the chestnut trees. The breeze picked up, and voices sprang behind them. A moment later Team A appeared. They all wore white shirts and white shorts lined with blue stripes. Their shirts said THE A-TEAM across the front.

"You have got to be kidding me," Sydney muttered. "When did they—how?"

Another group rounded the corner. They were wearing mostly khakis, and each had a red bandanna around her neck. It was Team B. Lil recognized the girl with the complicated braid that ran around her head like a piece of art. Each shirt said the wearer's name. Hers had HILDA written across it.

Lastly, Team C came around the corner. They were all wearing long capris and T-shirts—a combination that matched less, but somehow went together. Lil looked down at her running shorts and T-shirt. Then at the others. Kat's hair was pulled into a curly ponytail at the back of her head. She wore a bright, loose top and black pants that flared out in a bell shape just above her ankles, where a colorful, embroidered flower decorated the area above the hem. Charlie had traded her suspenders for a pair of khaki shorts and a collared shirt, and Sydney wore a pair of long shorts with a black shirt displaying the periodic table.

"Ah," Vivi said loudly so everyone could hear. "Looks like at least one team lacks team leadership *and* team spirit."

A few of the others giggled, but Lil noticed Team C shift their eyes away, giving Vivi a snide look. Apparently, Team D weren't the only ones who were sick of her attitude. Lil was about to retort when Aestos rounded the bend. He held a clipboard in the crook of his arm, and he surveyed the group and then made a few marks.

"What do you think he's writing?" Sydney said, leaning in. "Do you think he heard that? Do you think they are really going to take off points for fashion?"

"That has nothing to do with team spirit or leadership," Lil said, rolling her eyes.

"But do you think he's taking points off?" Sydney said again. She looked to Charlie and Kat.

"No." Charlie shook her head, the studs in her ears catching the sunlight. "She's just trying to get under our skin. She has no clue what the rules are."

"Attention, everyone!" Aestos hollered. "If you could all gather, I will give you the parameters of your race."

"Oh, great. Here we go," Sydney said as they wandered into a circle with the others. "I wish this were a building challenge or—basically anything else."

"It's going to be fine," Lil whispered. "There is nothing to running. You just move."

Aestos placed his foot up on a rock and leaned in. "Your mentors are stationed along the trails. Let's not make them wait."

The groups fell silent.

"This morning's task is a ropes course with a twist."

Lil's heart hammered. God, she hoped the challenges looked familiar. If they did—oh, Lil couldn't help but smile. She could do them in the dark. She could do them blindfolded. In fact, she could split the tasks up by skill level for optimum achievement.

"You have each received a clue," Aestos said, pulling her from her thoughts.

There was a flurry of hands as girls reached into their pockets and took out their note cards. Lil didn't bother to extract theirs. They already knew where they were going.

"This clue, if you have deciphered it correctly, will indicate which path to follow. If you reach the correct mentor, you have chosen the correct trail and may continue. If not, your morning task is over and your team will be disqualified. You will be directed back to the dining hall for other activities."

There was a murmur among them, and feet stirred. "When and if you reach your mentor, you will be following a series of challenges"—he paused dramatically—"and clues that we hope will test your knowledge of this beautiful island. Those who reach the final challenge have a chance to win the day and be in the lead for the manor scholarship."

He pulled a stopwatch from his pocket. Lil's legs tensed, and she saw Vivi jump up on the balls of her feet. She examined the other teams. Team B had two very strong-looking girls. One she thought she heard speaking Italian. Team C was definitely the least enthusiastic about what Aestos was saying. And Team A looked to be the most athletic, both with their attire and their long, toned legs. Vivi glanced over at Lil, tucked her tongue in her cheek and leaned forward in a runner's stance.

"Good luck, Team D," she said. "I hope the little one brought her inhaler." She jutted her chin toward Sydney.

Lil bristled.

"Don't waste your breath," Kat said, placing her hand on Lil's shoulder.

"Yeah," Sydney muttered, crossing her arms. "I stopped using my inhaler in middle school."

Lil couldn't help but smile. "All right, we can do this." She dusted her hands off on her shorts. "Besides, it's brains *and* athletics. We have a great team."

The others nodded, half confident.

"On your marks," Aestos began. "Get set."

They turned toward the Cave Passage trail, and Lil took a deep, full, delicious breath.

"GO!" Aestos shouted.

Lil sprang forward, digging up the dirt to rockier terrain. Her legs stretched out, working on their own, and she felt the breeze blow through her hair as they headed into the shadows of the chestnut trees.

Several yards in, they slowed. The terrain was pure rock, and they had to climb to stay on the path. Lil led the way, trying to see around the bend, wondering if the trail would flatten out again or if it would just rise this way, higher and higher.

"This seems extremely dangerous," Sydney huffed from behind her. "Shouldn't we be wearing ropes or something?"

"It's not that steep," Lil said. "Just keep your belly to it if you're nervous."

"Easy for you to say," Sydney panted. "You move like a lizard—a *hemidactylus turcicus*, to be precise."

Lil jumped higher and pulled herself to the last visible edge, peering down the path. It was still rocky, but it was also a steady grade. And off in the distance she could see someone standing, waiting. Someone wearing a brown shirt. She could swear she saw some slivers of silver in the person's hair across the distance.

"It evens out," Lil shouted, "right here. And I think I see Bente."

Kat crawled up next to her and Lil pointed. "I think you're right," Kat said, taking a deep breath and placing a hand on her shoulder. They pulled themselves over the edge and turned to help Charlie and Sydney up onto the trail.

Sydney stood, lurching onward.

"Do you want to rest for a minute?" Lil asked.

Charlie leaned her arm on an outlying tree root and pushed her forehead against it. "I should work out more."

"We don't have time for a break," Sydney said. "Team . . ." Her chest heaved. "Team A probably isn't taking a break."

"We'll be faster if we're fresh," Lil said. "Besides, we have no idea how long this will take." She took a quick sip from her water bottle and then handed it around. "It's better to go slow and steady than to waste all your energy up front and have none to push through to the end."

Charlie took a sip of the water, swished it around her mouth and spat it on the ground. Then she passed the water bottle to Sydney.

"I don't think so," Sydney said, waving her hand. She pulled a small water bottle from her pocket and took a sip. Charlie handed the other to Kat, who took a small drink, then handed it back to Lil.

"Okay," Sydney said. "Let's go."

Lil turned back to the trail. She surveyed the area, but didn't see Bente anymore. Maybe she had taken the time to sit down. Maybe she had moved. Maybe she was coming to them?

Lil hit the trail. She jumped from one rock to the other. It was just like running up Killies River. She and Mom had played this game dozens of times. Mom would time her to see how fast she could get across without getting her foot in the water. She would hop on one rock, then the other, waving her arms as she reached the ones that were unsteady and tried to buck her.

"Aim for the big ones," Mom would say. "Keep your movement fast. Even if you're on one that's unsteady, you won't disrupt it from its spot. Stay light. Let your feet fly."

The key was barely touching the surface, Lil thought. Just tapping it to know it was there and then moving away again. The gray rocks blurred as she ran, and she could see Mom just at the other end, coaxing her on, just like when she was five and six and seven. She jumped quickly, pulling herself forward like there was a line between them. Mom was always running out in front or standing at the other end. Lil was always following behind, trying to understand better, trying to figure out the mystery, seeing only the flickering soles of her shoes as she dodged around the next bend. Mom, both alive and dead, was always out of reach.

Lil took a wrong step and slid and twisted, letting out a shout as she careened into a rock. The sound of blood rushed to her ears for a moment, silencing the birds in the treetops. She pulled herself up, feeling her breath automatically slow as she surveyed the area. She had run across the rocks and had ended up on a dirt trail. Her ears cleared, and she could hear a brook. She turned and spotted the runoff, which was making the trail messy. She felt something drip down the back of her leg and turned to look. Mud. Up and down her calves.

Just like in the picture.

She could see her mother's legs, boots and leggings covered in mud. She reached toward her pocket, then stopped, peering behind her. She hadn't meant to leave everyone in the dust. She could see Sydney and Charlie and Kat teetering over the rocky terrain, arms out like scarecrows. All concentration. She had a minute. She yanked the picture from her pocket. Looked from the picture to the area. Mom and Bente were in a clearing. They had come out at the top of a mountain, a rocky vista behind them. The labrys was on the rock just to their right. Would she find the vista and the labrys at the end of this trail? She heard footsteps and breath behind her, and she folded the picture, replacing it in her pocket, making sure not to get it muddy. She shook her head clear. They were on a trail in the woods. Probably all of the trails were like this. She could hear Sydney's logical voice telling her not to jump to conclusions. Still, she peered down the path, wondering.

Charlie, Kat and Sydney huffed up to her, sweat streaming down their faces. Lil wiped sweat from her brow, too. She had to admit, the Cretan sun was hot, even this early in the day.

"You okay?" Kat asked. "I saw you fall."

"I'm okay," Lil said. "Do you need—"

They waved her on.

"Keep going," Sydney said. "We're almost there anyway."

Lil didn't need to be told twice. They charged ahead, twisting around a few more bends until they came face-to-face with Bente. Lil surveyed the scene. She was sitting on a large flat rock, and trees filled in the area behind her. No vista, no double-headed ax, just Bente. They ran up to her. Lil noticed the cord peeking out from her collared shirt as their feet pounded to a halt in front of her. She still wore the key.

"Well done," she said. "You chose the right trail, which means you will move forward to the next step."

As Charlie, Kat and Sydney circled, Bente pulled a shoulder walkie from a clip on her lapel. "Team D to checkpoint."

The radio crackled and Lil stopped to listen. "Team A likewise."

"We're neck and neck," Sydney gasped. "Where's our clue? We have to go!"

Bente looked to Sydney and reached for her pocket, but then the radio crackled again, and she tilted her head to listen.

"Team C right behind Team A. Wrong trail. Disqualified. Returning to dining hall."

"Team B at correct checkpoint," came another voice. "Moving forward with three teams."

Bente nodded and pulled the envelope from her pocket,

holding it out to the girls. Lil plucked it from her fingers and tore the seal.

"What's it say?" Sydney said.

Lil read the note card.

> *"Just ahead there's a fork in the road.*
> *Your job is to take the tale often told*
> *About an old man whose dreams were to fly*
> *But whose son flew too high in the sky."*

Sydney snapped her fingers. "Those people in the stained glass, on my window." She looked to Charlie. "What were their names?"

"I thought you said that wasn't applicable reading," Charlie said.

"Scholarship," Lil said. "We don't have time for fighting."

"Let's focus," Kat agreed.

"Daedalus and Icarus," Charlie said. They started jogging past Bente down the trail.

Lil turned and jogged backward. "Are you coming with us?" she shouted at their mentor.

Bente pulled a tube from her backpack and took a sip of water from a mouthpiece. "I'll meet you there. If you've chosen the right path, that is." She turned and darted through the trees.

Lil hurried to catch up with the others, and they moved steadily forward in a pack.

12

The trail forked, and they took a right, following a sign that said **DAEDALUS AND ICARUS**. They climbed higher and higher, and Lil figured that was why the trail was named for the famous mythological duo. Going up and up and up. Sweat pouring down, down, down.

Lil could hear footsteps and voices on the wind, but she couldn't tell if they were above, below or beside them somewhere in the woods. These paths, Aestos had said, would intersect, which meant one of the other teams was close. Probably Team A. They could be on top of each other at any second.

They huffed their way to another fork, where a wooden box sat in the middle of the two paths. Lil pulled the front of it open and extracted an envelope. She tore the seal and read:

> *"Cretan stories will tell you,*
> *Though they likely are untrue,*
> *A beast lived in the labyrinth.*
> *The beast was 'you know who.'"*

"The Minotaur!" they all shouted together. Of course, that was the most common mythological beast, Lil thought. Half man, half bull. Anyone would recognize it. They jumped up and ran forward down the path, moments later coming out in a clearing. Footsteps sounded around them, and Lil spotted a trail just below. She saw white shorts, white shirts. Blue stripes and bobbing ponytails.

Her heart jolted into her throat, and she stretched her legs long as the trail started to wind down the hill. The white shorts bobbed and disappeared behind a thicket.

"We can't let them win," Sydney said, suddenly right next to Lil.

"We won't," Lil answered through gritted teeth.

As they rounded the bend, there was another fork in the path. This time, the fork wrapped right and left into dark caves. They slowed to a stop, and Lil looked up to the sign that split the path.

HOME OF THE MINOTAUR, the one on the right said.

HOME TO DIONYSUS, the other said.

They all hurried into the one on the right, stumbling through the dark. Lil could see an arm of light at the other end. She tensed and moved forward, slowing only so as not to trip over the unsteady, shadowed ground.

"I can't see a damn thing," Charlie huffed.

Lil brushed past a stalagmite, her shorts catching on it. For a moment she was snagged back, but she pulled forward regardless.

Their footsteps and breath echoed in surround sound as they neared the domed end of the tunnel. She could see the silhouettes of the objects in her path against the ever-growing sunlight in the distance.

"Almost there. It's easier to see here!" She looked back, spotting Charlie and Kat right away. Sydney staggered forward, the white stripes on her sneakers the only part of her visible just behind them. Lil turned back to the cave opening as a thunder of footsteps joined their own and the white shorts and A-Team shirts flicked into view at the exit. Their paths were converging. Vivi turned and blew them a kiss as she shot ahead. Lil surged forward, her eyes somersaulting in her head as she went from the darkness of the cave to the blaring Cretan sunlight. She spotted Colleen, Bente and Athenia in the trailhead just in front of them, just out beyond Team A.

"Run ahead," Kat shouted. "Go get the clue."

Lil turned back for just a moment. They were together, mostly moving as a pack. Sydney nodded, and Charlie waved her on. Lil shot forward, letting her legs stretch to their full length. She laid her eyes on the feet of the person just in front of her. Oh, it felt good to let her lungs expand to their full capacity. To run and breathe and think of nothing else. She matched footfalls of the girl at the rear, and doubled them, tripled them. Overtook them.

The girl turned, startled as Lil strode past.

"Vivi, hurry!" the girl with dark hair shouted. "They're coming up on us."

Lil laid her eyes on Vivi. She was fast and fit, and had a head start. And as Lil ran toward her, Vivi picked up her pace. Her stride was practiced and unhurried. Lil relaxed her legs more, and they fled for her, taking her on their own. As she came up shoulder to shoulder with Vivi, she wondered if the girl had reached her maximum speed or if it felt like a light jaunt. They scrambled to a standstill in front of the mentors.

Bente held the envelope out to her, and Lil grasped the edge.

"When you have the answer, you must tell your counselor," she said aloud to both parties. "If you are correct, you move on."

Lil pulled the note card from within it. Her eyes wavered over the page as she caught her breath, trying to read the words.

There once was a woman, came across the sea
On the back of a bull, 'twas told in history.

A story of a woman who came across the sea on the back of a bull, Lil thought. Her mind flashed to the stained-glass window above Charlie's door. The picture of the woman on the back of the bull. That must be it, but what had she called her?

Team A surrounded Colleen and whispered as Lil read the note card over again. Charlie was the first to reach her, then Sydney and Kat together. She handed the card to Charlie.

"The woman above your door—what was her name?" she whispered.

Charlie read the note card, panting quickly and nodding. "Has to be that. Europa."

The others agreed, and Lil turned to Bente. Bente reached into her pocket and pulled out a green flag, her smile broadening.

"It's not always a bad thing to stay in the discounted housing, is it?" she whispered, winking. "Plenty of history there."

"And we have a correct one here as well!" Colleen said, holding up another green flag.

Lil wondered who had gotten the answer and how they had known. Did everyone here know all of the history of Crete?

"All right," Sydney said, clapping. "Let's get a move on."

Bente looked at Sydney, her eyebrows shooting up as she turned and picked up a large backpack full of what Lil could see was climbing gear. A rope hung down the outside in a figure-eight coil, carabiners hanging off the end.

"You set the pace," Bente said, stepping to the side. "I'll be right behind you."

Lil looked up at the sign and spotted the Europa trail. Up they would climb once more. She took a deep breath, wondering if Bente was watching her. Then she started the hike to the top.

"Welcome, Team B," Athenia shouted from behind them as

Teams A and D flew ahead. Lil lifted her head and planted her eyes on a distant patch of sun. Now it was a race.

A shiver ran up Lil's back. The trees here were different from Vermont, sure, but everything else was very similar to the ropes course behind her house. She stared at the cable walk and the rope swing. To the right was the swaying log, and to the left, the initiative wall. In the distance, she could see the raiders' bridge, cargo net, rock wall and zip line.

"All teams gather!" Bente shouted, and she blew a whistle that hung around her neck. "Congratulations, Teams A, B and D. You have made it to the final checkpoint. We will commence the ropes course. During this course, you will be critiqued on teamwork, team leadership, agility, endurance and, of course, brains. You may, I repeat, you *may* split up the tasks, but all members must do at least two stations together. I am in charge of the climbing gear for the high course and will prepare you on the ground for a safe climb. Colleen," she said, turning to her colleague, "will be stationed at the top of the rock wall to help you change carabiners and prepare you for the zip line. Athenia will help you from the zip line and distribute the final clue. You will not, I repeat, you will not, go ahead without a counselor's permission. Each team will go independently and be timed. When you reach the end of the zip line, there will be one final clue. In order to win, you must have the fastest time *and* the accurate destination. To signal your arrival at that destination, you will fire the flare gun. Only when we see that signal will the watch stop." She looked around as if to see if her instructions were sinking in. "We will proceed in alphabetical order in three minutes."

"I don't like the looks of this," Sydney said, wiping the sweat from her forehead.

"It's okay," Lil said as the others crowded around. "We'll split up the tasks by skill. Our entire group will do the easiest ones together."

Bente jotted a few notes on her clipboard. Lil hoped it was for leadership or teamwork, anything that would put them ahead of Team A.

Vivi's voice carried over to them as if she had heard the pen marking the paper. "All right, Team A! We can do this."

"I'm scared of heights," Kat said.

"Me too," Sydney said.

Lil looked from Kat to Sydney, then turned to Charlie. "What about you? How do you feel about heights?"

Charlie shrugged. "I work backstage at Charles de Gaulle Players on the weekends. I can do heights." She looked over Lil's shoulder. "Flying, though. Not my expertise."

"Okay." Lil got down in the sand.

"Have you done this before?" Sydney asked, scowling.

Lil nodded. "Many times." She placed a finger in the dirt and quickly laid out their plan. "We'll all do the rope swing. It's lowest to the ground." She scribbled a squiggly rope with a loop at the bottom. "Then we'll all do the balance log. The initiative wall is the hardest low-ropes course, but it's still close to the ground. If Kat and Sydney can do that one, Charlie and I could prep for the high course."

Kat rubbed her palms together. "I can do the initiative wall. My mother says I have strong hands and arms."

"I'll try," Sydney said.

"Nice," Lil said. "Charlie and I will have made our way over to the high course while you are doing this. You'll run to tag us, then Charlie." She drew big squares in the sand. "You'll climb and cross the raiders' bridge and roll down this cargo net."

"Okay." Charlie's nostrils flared as she took a deep inhale. "Then I'll tag you."

"Right," Lil said. "You'll tag me and I'll climb the rock wall and go down the zip line." She drew a long swaying line in the dirt. "Is that manageable?" She looked up at the others. "The problem is that this leaves me alone on the other side of the zip line with a clue, which I bet Charlie would be the most equipped to answer."

"Je suis désolée," Charlie said, staring at the zip line. "I don't—"

"What do you mean? You already know the final answer," Sydney said.

Lil looked over at her, confused.

"One minute, teams!" Bente said from the center of the three groups.

"You heard Bente: she said that there is often an advantage to staying in Hall D. All that history. The only myth we haven't covered yet is . . ." Sydney scowled as if working out a math problem. "The one above your door."

"Ariadne," Lil said. "Of course."

"But what if it's not?" Kat said. "What if the relation to our dorms has been coincidental?"

"Ten seconds, people!" Bente shouted.

Sydney shrugged. "Is anyone else going to fly?"

The others shook their heads.

"Then it doesn't matter, does it?" Sydney said.

"And let's move!" Bente shouted, blowing her whistle. "Team A! You're up!"

13

That's exactly six minutes and fifty-seven seconds," Sydney said, staring at her watch. "Is that a good time?" she asked, turning to Lil.

Lil watched as Vivi disappeared at the end of the zip line, landing perfectly and running out of sight into the trees. "It's good," Lil nodded, gulping. Good? It was nearly flawless.

"She still has to answer the riddle correctly and get to the right destination, remember?" Charlie said.

They waited, the wind shifting through the trees, making the flags on the course billow and flap. Just then a green flare went up, and the rest of Team A started cheering. Bente, who was standing at the base of the rock wall with her belay on, clapped and then sent up a whistle by sticking two of her fingers in her mouth.

"Nice work, Team A!" She leaned into her walkie-talkie and then turned back to the others. "Seven thirteen is the time to beat. I hope you still have your legs, ladies!"

Lil's mouth went dry, and the sun felt hotter now than when they had been running up the hill. She pulled her water bottle from her waist and took a long sip.

"Team B, you're up!"

Lil watched as they prepared themselves for the rope swing.

They had the same technique that Lil would use, hooking a knee to keep all appendages off the ground.

"Watch closely," Lil said, leaning toward Sydney and Kat. "We want to do that exactly."

They nodded and watched.

"They're not all fast," Kat said. "But Sudha"—she jutted her chin toward the girl with brown skin and dark hair who had just come to land on the other side of the gauntlet—"we arrived together. She is a good runner. She plays field hockey, so she is in great shape."

Team B finished the rope swing and darted toward the balance log. This one would only work if everyone worked together, lifting one another up and arranging their weight along the log until it balanced evenly. Then they would have to make a pendulum swing to land in the right place. Sudha was up first, her side of the log swinging dangerously close to the ground. The one with a complicated braid and HILDA written on her shirt jumped onto the other side, evening the log out for a moment, but then she lost her balance and dropped off.

"Yes," Sydney muttered.

Lil took a deep breath in agreement and eyed Bente. She was watching intently as Sudha encouraged her to jump up again.

"They're already lagging ten seconds behind Team A," Sydney whispered. "If they want to win this, they are going to have to really step it up."

Hilda tried to climb onto the log again, and again it swung erratically, bucking her off.

"You can do it!" Kat shouted, clapping her hands so her bangle bracelets hit together.

"Are you kidding me?" Sydney hissed.

"What?" Kat said. "Good sportsmanship must count for something. Plus, they deserve to at least get to the other side."

Sydney rolled her eyes.

Apparently encouragement was all that Hilda had needed, because the next time she jumped, she landed, balanced and spread her feet so that her weight was evenly matching Sudha on the other side.

"Nice work," Sudha shouted. "Next up!"

The other two had it easy, just jumping onto the center and balancing their weight so no one else could fall. Then they got into a rhythm, swinging the log until they jumped off the right side one at a time, adjusting in between every time the log swung. They hurried toward the initiative wall and climbed, then struggled on the high course.

"They're looking at at least nine fifty, maybe ten. *If* they even get to the destination," Sydney said.

"You know what?" Charlie said. "You're very competitive right now. I would hate to come up against you in your area of expertise."

Sydney gave her a smug look. "Google Science Fair finalist two years in a row."

"Only two?" Lil said, joking as she watched Sudha reach the other side and head toward the trees.

"Supply budget. You know how it goes."

"But don't you get scholarships for that?" Kat asked.

Sydney dropped her wrist. "Yes, other things had to be paid for, thank you for asking."

Like what? Lil wondered, but before she could ask, she saw a smoky flare fly up into the blue sky. It was green.

"They made it!" Kat shouted, clapping. Sydney groaned.

"Team D!" Bente shouted. "You're up, ladies. Seven minutes, thirteen seconds is still the time to beat!"

Lil grasped her watch and placed her hands on the timer button.

"Get ready!"

The rest of Teams A and B gathered at the edge of the course.

"Get set," Bente shouted.

"You know what our plan is," Lil said.

Kat, Sydney and Charlie all nodded.

"Go!" Bente shouted. Lil pressed the button on her stopwatch and ran.

14

They swung across the gauntlet, and Lil glanced at her watch. Thirty seconds. Then they darted, in a pack, toward the balance log. Lil hoisted herself onto it, grabbing the ropes and spreading her feet out wide to get it as parallel to the ground as she could. Charlie jumped up second, doing the same. Kat climbed on more cautiously, and Sydney centered herself between Kat and Lil.

"Everybody ready?" Lil said. "To the right."

Sydney's eyes popped wide as the log jerked to the right, but she maintained her footing. "Oscillations frequency," Lil heard her whisper. "Galileo Galilei."

Lil wondered what she was talking about as she said it again. "Oscillations frequency. Galileo Galilei."

Whatever it was, it was helping her get a steady rhythm. Keeping the log in motion, they disembarked one by one.

"One minute," Lil warned as they hit the initiative wall. It shot straight up with a rope hanging down to aid the climbers. Kat dove for it, grasping the rope in her fist and planting a foot at the base.

"Climb high and climb fast!" Lil shouted as she and Charlie darted away to the ladder of the raiders' bridge. Charlie stopped at the ladder and eyed the flimsy bridge above. Bente appeared with a harness and quickly helped Charlie into it as Lil continued alone to the rock wall. As she reached it, she checked her watch.

One thirty. Kat's hands came over the top of the initiative wall, and she watched her scramble down the other side.

"C'mon, Sydney," Lil shouted. "You've got this!"

She couldn't see the opposite side of the wall from this angle, and it seemed a century as she waited for Sydney's hands to grasp the top edge. A few Team B members clapped and shouted. Bente landed next to her once more, checked her stopwatch and scribbled on the clipboard in her hand. "C'mon, Sydney, you can do it!" Lil shouted again. She glanced at her watch. Two fifteen . . . two thirty. Sydney's hands finally appeared over the wall, and Lil let out a breath. Sydney yanked herself up and tumbled down the other side, landing awkwardly on the ground. Kat reached down and helped her to her feet.

"Over here!" Charlie shouted from the bottom of the ladder. They ran to her, Kat reaching out to tag.

"We're at three minutes!" Lil shouted as Charlie grasped the ladder and started climbing. Sydney collapsed against the bottom of it.

"Good climber," Bente said as Charlie reached the top. Yes, she was a good climber, but Lil couldn't help but feel a little pang of jealousy at the words. She wondered what Bente had on her clipboard about her, if anything. Charlie snapped her carabiner to the safety line and began to make her way across the wooden planks.

"Harness up?" Bente said, peeling her eyes away from Charlie long enough to hand Lil a green harness. Lil jumped into it, pulling it up around her waist. She adjusted the strap and accepted the rope that Bente handed her.

"Close time," Bente said as Charlie wavered midway across the bridge. "Three forty-five. Nearly neck and neck, in fact."

"We're doing good!" Lil shouted. She could make up the

time on her own, as long as Charlie could get to her. She was sure of it. She watched as Charlie regained her balance and continued a bit more swiftly over the next half of the bridge. When she reached the end, she unclipped her carabiner and tumbled down the cargo net.

"Nice!" Lil shouted. Charlie raced toward her and, a moment later, tagged Lil. She turned toward the wall.

Bente dropped her clipboard. "On belay," she shouted.

"Climber ready," Lil said, grasping a handhold.

"Climb on."

"Climbing," Lil said.

And then just as she started to step away, she heard one more line. One line that was never in the climbing commands. *"Zeis tolmira,"* Bente whispered.

Lil faltered only for a moment at her mother's phrase. Then, as if lifted by it, she shot upward. The hand- and footholds were close compared with what she was used to, her stretch never reaching its max. She didn't have to swing or jump to awkward positions. It might as well be a ladder, Lil thought. She heard Kat and Charlie and Sydney cheering from below as she reached the top. Colleen's short hair swung into view as she climbed over the upper edge.

"Very well done," Colleen said, unclipping Lil's carabiner and securing her to the removable trolley. "Here's your brake if you need to slow down," she said, gesturing to the outer edge of the T-bar. She clipped everything back to the line. "Ready to fly?"

"Neck and neck," Sydney shouted. "We're only three seconds ahead!" Lil grasped the T-bar, making sure not to squeeze the brake.

"Ready," she said to Colleen. Colleen nodded, and a second

later, Lil was off the rock wall, flying into the treetops. She curled tight, willing her weight to make the line move faster. She felt the breeze getting stronger, the leaves and variety of greens blurring around her and below her. She glanced up and laid her eyes on the end of the line.

"Go, go, go," she heard Sydney shout from below.

She neared the end. She saw Vivi. She saw Sudha. And Athenia. Then just a flash between the trees. Barely noticeable at all. A rock, a cave opening, a double-headed ax, the labrys. But she was past it so quickly. She craned her neck. Had she imagined it? Her eyes searched the terrain, body twisting. The line suddenly ending. The wind being knocked out of her. Her feet scraped the ledge, and she bounced back, treading the wrong way. She felt her face flush as everyone behind her went silent. She tried to still the wobble in the line and push it smoothly forward. Athenia grasped a rope and pulled her. She stumbled onto the ledge and ripped the carabiner from the trolley. Athenia handed her the envelope and she tore it open, trying not to see the time on her watch tick by. Maybe, just maybe, if she was a faster runner. Her mind skittered away and her eyes involuntarily flicked to the hillside. She couldn't. Not now. She had to focus. She blinked and read the swimming letters.

> *In the labyrinth dark and deep*
> *A lonely girl did often weep.*
> *She knew every path ahead*
> *And lent her love a guiding thread.*

Athenia gestured to the signs. One read **ARIADNE** and the other read **PASIPHAE**. Of course, the thread. Sydney was right.

She scrambled up the hillside to the Ariadne cave. There, she grasped a box of flares that was sitting next to the flare gun. She grabbed a flare and jammed it into the chamber, snapping it securely into place. Trying to steady her hands, she aimed it high and pulled the trigger. It flew, a tail of smoke choking her as it climbed.

"Seven minutes, fifteen seconds for Team D," Athenia shouted. "Valiant effort. Second place."

Lil crumpled, the extra flares spilling across the rock. Team A erupted in cheers, and Lil looked away as Vivi shrieked. She couldn't look over to Sydney and Charlie and Kat down below. She took a deep breath. The day was so hot now. If they had started earlier or— Her eyes flicked to the path on the right. Had she really seen it? The same spot as in the picture. She stood up, feeling the outline of the photograph in her pocket. Perhaps she had made it up. There was only one way to know for sure. She stacked the flares back into the box, checked over her shoulder— Athenia was busy making marks on her clipboard—and darted up the path.

15

Lil pulled the picture out of her pocket. The scenery was nearly unaltered. The cave the same, the vista the same, the rock showing the labrys only slightly faded. Of course, no Mom. But that symbol. Here on the rock. On Mom's neck, and—Lil pictured Bente in the library—on the key. The wind picked up and shuffled her hair, shifting a cluster of flowers at the base of the rock at the same time. Lil tilted her head as the wind moved the other way and pushed the flowers back. But she had seen something there. An etching. She moved to the flowers, knelt and lifted them to the side. Her eyes landed on the bottom of the rock. May 21. She knew it. Not a birthday, not an anniversary and not a death day. It was Mom's name day.

Every May 21, Dad would get up early and make the bread. Lil helped out with the dough, shaping the small leaves to decorate the top. Mom slept in—the only day of the year that Lil knew her to sleep later than 7:00 a.m. Some people, Mom said, spent their name day as a Sabbath, others, celebrating with friends. It was all part of a religious background that Lil hadn't quite grasped. A religion which she had never been taught. And she knew Yiayia and Papou didn't approve of Mom's unfaithfulness. And so they never came and visited and Mom didn't go home to Greece because of it. Not even when Yiayia passed away. Not even when Papou slipped away, too. Lil guessed they were disappointed in America, and in Mom's choice to marry Dad, too. So instead of celebrating Saint Helene in a traditional way, Mom's name day had evolved into a family outing. By noon, they would be on a picnic at Crobs Pond. Mom and Dad would lounge and sip wine while Lil chased dragonflies and caught salamanders. Then they would all come together to eat olives and *za'atar* with the special bread and, if Dad was feeling really ambitious, snails with rosemary and olive oil. By nightfall they would burn candles, watch the stars and gaze at the west field as it turned silver by the light of the moon.

"Ah, I see you found your mother's favorite spot."

Lil jumped, pushing her hand against the rock to balance herself. She turned. Bente.

"You knew her?" Lil said, realizing she was still holding the picture in her right hand.

Bente sat down on the rock adjacent to her and put her hands on her knees. "Of course I knew her." She lifted her hand out toward the picture, and Lil stood and gave it to her. The older woman smiled, lines creasing the sides of her eyes. She looked up at Lil. "She was one of the most spirited mentees I ever had. Driven, fast." She stared at Lil with a look Lil knew well. The one people gave when they were trying to separate you from your parents. Discerning if the nose was your nose or someone else's. Trying to figure out the formula for creation.

"You have her stride," Bente said, handing the picture back.

"You know, she—" Lil paused, thinking of the best way to phrase it. "She died."

Bente nodded, looking at the ground, then up and over Lil's shoulder. Lil turned and looked at the vista. Trees peeled toward rock and plunged into a gorge in the distance.

"The day she died, I came up here. I etched her name day into the rock. It was her favorite spot. Before you were born, she would come by when she was in the region on assignment. And if I happened to be here, too, and couldn't find her, I'd run out here and she'd be sitting on this rock, looking at this same view."

Lil stared at the ledge cutting into sky. She looked at the sun, rising toward noon now, hanging like a pendant against the blue backdrop, and she imagined her mom right there with her. And she could see why she liked it. Not only was it beautiful, but it was high enough for a balmy breeze. The air was savory with the aroma of herbs from bushes below. Birds outnumbered people. Mom had always liked that, preferred time to reflect over time to talk.

"I don't think she killed herself," Lil said, her thumb creasing the picture. She turned from the view back to Bente.

Bente shook her head, straightening up. "No, not her style. Your mother was not one for an easy way out."

But then what? Lil wondered. If not suicide, then murder. There was no middle ground. No natural causes when you find your mother—

Footsteps sounded, and Lil looked up to see Sydney, Charlie and Kat round the bend.

"Athenia said you were up here," Kat said. "We were starting to worry."

Lil struggled for words, trying to pull her head from the past.

"Ah, everything is fine, fine. Just a rough ending to a good race," Bente said, recovering.

"Sorry, guys," Lil said.

"You did great," Kat said.

"I could have gone faster across the bridge," Charlie said as they reached her.

"And I couldn't get my feet to plant on that stupid wall,"

Sydney admitted, shaking her head as if she had never been so disappointed in anything in her entire life.

"It wasn't you," Charlie said, reaching out her hand and clapping Lil on the shoulder. "You climbed like a—" She turned to Sydney. "What did you say she climbed like again?"

"*Hemidactylus turcicus*," Sydney said. "It's a gecko."

"Like that," Charlie said. "Way faster than anyone else."

Lil saw Charlie's eyes land on the picture in her hand. Sydney's followed and then Kat's. She curled it quickly and put it in her pocket.

"We'll get them tomorrow," Lil said, trying for distraction, but Charlie's eyes were already darting to the symbol on the rock and then to Bente's neck.

Bente scowled up at her, then stood, adjusting her collar so it covered the cord. Lil's heart lurched.

"We'd best be getting to lunch. We don't want Aestos waiting on us," Bente said. She turned to the trailhead.

"Hey, Bente?" Kat said, turning toward her as she went. "What does the symbol on the wall mean?" Her eyes flicked to the others and then back as she hurried on. "Since I want to be an art history major, I was wondering—"

Bente turned, and Lil's heart rammed into her throat, but she wanted to know the answer, too. What was the symbol Mom wore?

"The double-headed ax?" Bente asked.

Kat nodded.

"The Minoan labrys," Bente said. "In ancient days gone by, this land was filled with large communal structures with winding passages. Visitors to Crete would often get lost in their confusing hallways. These buildings were the inspiration for the mythical labyrinth. The labrys was a directional tool. The wall would be marked with it to indicate a correct path to the main quarters." She leveled her eyes on Lil and continued. "A guide. A compass. A clue, if you will."

The breeze picked up and wicked the sweat from Lil's back, sending a sharp shiver up her spine. A clue. What did she mean, a clue? All she had was clues.

"Oh," Kat said, turning back to the rock.

"But that one," Bente said, "that is no artifact. Probably put there by a tourist who wanted to give others something to wonder about." She smiled. "You can't expect everything in Greece to be a key to the ancient past."

"Oh, that's fascinating," Kat said, pulling her hair around to her shoulder. "Thank you."

"Aestos. Lunch!" Bente looked from Lil to Sydney to Kat to Charlie. "You still seem fresh. Let's run it. We're late!"

They fell into step behind the older woman, trying to keep pace.

16

L il looked for a time for them to talk, but they had arrived late to lunch and ended up eating with Bente in the kitchen. Aestos hurried from one area to another, tossing bowls, breads, salads and cheese onto the counter.

"I said don't be late," Aestos said. "The one thing I said was that I have other duties to attend to and not to be late!"

Bente leveled him with a stare. "We got caught up. I apologize."

"Eat whatever you want," Aestos said, taking a cloth wrap and pulling it across his head until he had affixed it like a hat. "Fresh tomatoes in the garden. I'll see you at dinner." He walked out the large doors into the garden, then turned. "Don't be late," he said.

Charlie, Kat, Sydney and Lil talked idly while they inhaled the food. Avoiding all talk of the labrys, they discussed only the race and its implications, including other ways to win the scholarship.

"It's already time for afternoon workshops," Bente said over a mouthful of bread. She looked down at her clipboard. "Team D," she mumbled, "is with Trudy first. To the science lab."

They finished their meals quickly, and Bente escorted them past the dining hall to a section they hadn't visited before.

"You're there, and then you'll go to the studio with Athenia," Bente said.

"I know where that is," Kat said. "I got a chance to explore it earlier."

"And then you will end up in the library with Colleen."

Lil glanced over at Charlie and locked eyes. Maybe then they could do some snooping. Maybe then they could at least talk about what Bente had said about the labrys. She could explain about the picture.

Bente swung the door open, and they entered a cool stone room on the back of the building. It was surprisingly state-of-the-art, with walls decorated with test tubes and counters equipped with Bunsen burners. Everything was pristine except for the desk behind which Trudy sat.

"In and fetch a lab coat, please!" Trudy said, waving them in the door and indicating a series of lab coats on the wall. Lil pulled hers on and took a seat.

"Since tomorrow will be your science challenge, I wanted to begin with something light," said the Irish woman. "We'll be making mulberry gumballs this afternoon." She pulled a bottle of liqueur from her apron and then collected a set of beakers from the side counter. "Candy is chemistry."

By the time they had each combined their ingredients, Charlie had created a slime that clung to both the inside and outside of her beaker. Lil had managed to make one gumball, but when she tried it, it was the consistency of a gobstopper.

Kat picked up the pale sphere she had created and popped it into her mouth. "Tastes like plastic," she said, spitting it quickly back into her hand.

"And that is what happens when we forget to add the flavoring," Trudy said, eyeing the still-full eyedropper on the other side of the beaker.

Sydney held out a handful of perfectly shaped gumballs. "You can have one of mine," she said with a smile.

"Well done, Ms. Bennington," Trudy said, selecting the

largest gumball from the pile. Lil took one, too. It was soft and chewy and full of a berry flavor.

"Seriously, guys," Sydney said. "Grade school." She turned back to Trudy. "Do you have any information on tomorrow's challenge?"

"I can't give away too many details, but the challenge will be based on renewable energy," Trudy said.

"Fantastic," Sydney said. She stepped toward the door. Then, as if a thought had just hit her, she turned back. "Do you know anything about neurological disorders? I would love to pick your brain about causes of epilepsy and potential treatments and cures."

Trudy's eyes went wide with surprise.

"Interested in epilepsy?" She looked down at her clipboard, then mused, "No check box for that." She turned back to Sydney. "Why the interest?"

Lil was eager to know as well.

Sydney steadied her with a stare. "My sister suffers from it. I'm going to find a cure."

Lil made herself busy cleaning the lab supplies while she listened some more. This was a side of Sydney she hadn't seen yet.

"Lofty goal," Trudy said, thumbing her clipboard. "I know a bit, but I can find out more. Let's meet after the challenge tomorrow."

"Great," Sydney said, joining the others at the door.

By midafternoon, they were working clay with Athenia. Lil tried to shape hers, but it was unwieldy: either too hard or too soft, but never in between. The stuff seemed to mold like magic under Kat's hands. By the end of the session, she had whipped one lump of clay into a Grecian-style urn and had started to design the outside of it.

"Very nice, very nice," Athenia said as she looked over the work in progress. She stopped in front of Lil. "And what is this, Lilith?" she asked, examining it from every angle.

"It's supposed to be a cow," Lil admitted. She had never been very artistic. Athenia's eyebrows went up, and then her eyes softened. "Of course, I see it now."

"Yeah, right," Sydney whispered from beside her, showing off a perfectly shaped clay sphere.

"And what is yours?" Lil asked.

"It's a proton," Sydney said. "Obviously."

"You have no appreciation for good art," Kat said.

"And you have no appreciation for foundations of our known universe," Sydney retorted.

Athenia looked from one to the other. "Interesting." She made a few notes on her clipboard before moving on to stand in front of Charlie. Lil watched as she tried to press a handle onto a poorly shaped clay cup.

"Mine is a pen holder," she said as she secured the handle and lifted it. The handle broke free, and the clay landed on the table with a *clumph*. Lil couldn't help but laugh. At least she wasn't the only one who sucked at art.

"We'll work more tomorrow," Athenia said cheerfully as Charlie picked up the mashed remnants of her masterpiece. "I don't want any of you to be disappointed. We'll be doing more directed projects later this week. For now, you are headed to the library."

They all looked at one another.

"That's up on the third floor between the east and west wings," Athenia said as she placed the tools they'd used on the clay into cups.

"Between the east and west, was it?" Lil said, wanting to make it clear that they had never been there before.

"That's correct," Athenia said, waving them on.

They left the lab and ascended the stairs.

"We need to look for the name Zephylite," Charlie hissed as they climbed.

"And we need more information on the labrys," Sydney said.

"And probably information on the significance of the labyrinth, too," Kat said as they reached Hall A.

Lil wondered if there would be any house records, something that might have information on her mom.

"No matter what," Lil said as they reached the top of the stairs, "we can't be too obvious about it."

"Right," Sydney said.

"Ladies!" They all jumped, and Lil grasped the railing as Colleen appeared from the shadow of the doorway.

"I was thinking we would take our lesson in the plateau garden, instead of the library." She smiled. "It's far too lovely a day to be stuck inside."

"It's really hot," Sydney said, leaning against the stone, "and kind of gross—"

Colleen raised her eyebrows. "We'll sit in the shade, then," she said, handing each of them a notebook and a pen. "Shall we?"

"Teachers always say that," Sydney whispered as they turned and started back downstairs, "as if it were actually a choice."

They exited the building and made their way up the stone staircase that hugged the outer edge of the west wing. Lil looked around as they reached the top. It was beautifully landscaped with stones and benches, urns overflowing with flowers and a few potted trees giving the shade a hint of emerald.

They settled in and, for the third time that day, they sat muted. Their first instruction was to write their observations about their experiences thus far. Lil scribbled thoughts on the page about the manor, the food, the trip to the top of the mountain. She scribbled notes about the remote area. She didn't write a single word about their midnight trip to the library, or her talk with Bente on the hillside or her search for how her mother died. Or the symbol she saw everywhere. Her pen dug into the paper, and she lifted it, looking to see if Colleen had noticed, but she was intently scribbling in her own notebook a few feet away.

"Wrap up and we will start our session," Colleen said.

Charlie raised her hand. "Are we required to use this notebook for the duration of the stay?" she asked.

Colleen shook her head. "Not if you have come prepared and have other means of taking notes."

Charlie nodded and drew out her sling of fountain pens and a bound notebook from her back pocket.

"I prefer this one to keep my thoughts in," she said. Lil watched as she unrolled the fountain-pen holder, ran her hand along several of the pens and selected a short one from the end. She pulled the cap off and put it on the other side so it was the size of a normal pen.

"Quite the collection," Colleen said.

"It's only half my collection," Charlie said. "I couldn't bring all of them."

Colleen smiled. "Always prepared to record something? The mark of a good historian." She turned to the others. "For today, we will be talking about both history *and* mythology."

Lil watched the bees collect pollen from a nearby foxglove and then dip heavily around the side of the building as Colleen once again spoke about the flight of Daedalus and Icarus, the thread that Ariadne gave Theseus, the death of the beastly Minotaur by Theseus' sword and finally the bull guise which Zeus had used to woo Europa and carry her across the sea to Crete.

"I don't get it," Sydney said, waving her hand. "Why would Europa fall in love with a bull? Is she some sort of idiot?"

Colleen paused in her lecture. "Well, you have to remember that these stories were handed down to the Greeks orally, and some classics experts would posit that they changed from their original forms during that time, essentially warping myth and history. Others may say that the literature of humankind has always had a bit of fact and a bit of fiction—room for both reality and imagination."

Lil's attention faded in and out as Sydney tried to grapple with the number of love affairs with animals in the mythological stories, until she realized she was tuning in to another conversation. Her ears perked up as she heard Bente's voice somewhere to her right. She was about to turn and look, but there was something about the tone. A whisper, but one slightly more audible than intended. She tilted her head. It was coming from a window to her right. One that she could see was open just a crack.

"I will deposit it tonight," Bente said. "This schedule is so busy."

"You were practically there . . . ," another voice said. Lil recognized the accent of the grand counselor. It had to be Athenia.

"I was in the vicinity . . . Lilith was . . . You saw her. She wanted to know . . . mother."

"What did you tell her?"

"I didn't . . ."

"So she doesn't know . . ." The voices faded away.

A lump formed in Lil's throat. Bente knew more than she was saying. Much more than she was saying. Bente knew everything.

"Lilith, are you all right?"

Lil snapped her head up as Colleen stepped in front of her, her small figure blocking the sun.

"Fine, sorry," Lil choked.

"All right, I can see you are all tired from your long day. Our session is almost over. Tomorrow we will discuss how Ariadne ended up on Naxos, abandoned by Theseus."

"Abandoned?" Kat said. "After everything she did for him? What a *palhaço*."

"So it would seem," Colleen said. "Off to the dining hall with you. I will see you tomorrow for more fun!"

Lil rose to her feet. Her legs felt like Jell-O, and it was a struggle to move them forward. They had made it halfway down the stone stairwell before Kat looked behind them and then to Lil. "What is the matter? You look like you've seen a ghost."

"I—" Lil's hand went to her head, then to her pocket and then back to her head. "I overheard—" Words seemed to evade her. Her thoughts wouldn't stop spinning. Did Bente and Athenia know everything because they had been part of it? Had they killed her mother? She shook her head. No, Bente had said her mother was one of her favorite mentees. She seemed genuinely fond of her. But—

"What's this about?" Sydney asked. "Is this about the symbol?"

Lil reached for her pocket once more, and pulled out the picture.

"Have you been here before?" Sydney said, reaching for the picture.

"No," Charlie said, curling Lil's fingers closed around the photograph. "I think it's about her mother," she said through gritted teeth. "Put that away for now. Incoming."

They reached the bottom of the stairs, and Lil was blinded by white shorts and shirts.

"Oh, look, Team D. I noticed you were absent at lunch to-day," Vivi said as she went by. "We had wanted to congratulate you on your near win. Good effort." She stood straight up and smiled at Lil with her stunningly white teeth. "Not good enough, of course. But don't worry: even if you don't win the scholarship, maybe there are some charities or something that could help your type out. Maybe we could put up a collection."

Lil bristled, lurching forward.

"We'll see you later," Kat said. "Good job. You're really great. Congratulations." She pushed Lil past them, and a moment later they ducked back into the office and headed into the cool of the dining hall.

"What did you hear?" Charlie said as they rounded the corner.

Lil turned toward the others. "Let's eat dinner fast and meet in the dormitory. We need to discuss this. In private."

harlie flung her balcony door open and pulled a chair out for Lil. "Sit down. You look like you're going to be sick."

Lil collapsed into the seat. "I don't know what to think," she said, her foot accidentally upending a pile of books.

Charlie reached down and righted the stack, then went over to her desk. She opened the drawer and drew out a squat bottle of ink and a large green pen with gold lettering on it.

"What are you doing?" Lil asked.

"I'm refilling my fountain pen," Charlie said as she unscrewed the top of the pen and submerged the writing end in a glass of water. The water ran blue as she squeezed the top. Then she deftly wiped the end with a handkerchief and submerged it into the bottle of ink.

Sydney bowled through the door with the roll of papers she'd had that morning, and Kat appeared with her pitcher of tea and a ball of yarn.

"Are you knitting?" Charlie said, tightening the casing back on the pen.

"It helps me think," Kat said, setting the pitcher down.

They each took a seat. Kat unraveled some yarn from her ball. Sydney flattened her diagrams out in front of her, and Charlie opened her notebook as though she were taking dictation.

Lil leaned forward, pulling her picture from her pocket. She unfolded it and glanced at her mother's smiling face.

"She looks just like you," Charlie said.

"Looked," Lil said. "Past tense."

Sydney gulped, twirling her pencil between her fingers. "Sorry," she said quietly.

Kat paused with the yarn extended over her left hand. "How did she die?"

Lil flapped the photograph. She hated talking about it. Really hated it. Hated thinking about it, reliving it and reseeing it. But it was so clear to her, from start to finish, an unstoppable movie that played over and over and over again in her mind.

Lil knew the smell of lentil soup at midnight. It had been a regular routine at her house, just as some families had Sunday breakfast, or went to church or met for ice cream on Friday nights. In Lil's house, Mom made lentil soup at midnight. Smelling the garlic and thyme, the caramelizing onions and rosemary, Lil would rise from her bed, pulling Binky, her brown bear, from the pillow, and go to the kitchen. Mom always stood on the opposite side of the counter, knife blade moving quickly across carrots and celery, chopping them into tiny pieces.

"Are you okay?" Lil had asked over and over as she sat down on a stool on the opposite side. "Mom, are you okay?"

And Mom's eyes would flit to Lil, and over to the cedar cabinet that held a smiling picture of her dressed in her air force attire and then over to the pot. Sometimes, her hand would find its way to her necklace. Always to the labrys, and then she would flip it to the alternate side. The side that coiled and spiraled. She would run her thumb along the pictographs, pressing the shapes with her fingertips. And then, as if the aroma of garlic and onions and the feel of a favorite piece of jewelry could heal, her eyes would clear. "I'll be okay," she'd say. Twisting a tomato from its stem, she would roll it onto the cutting board.

"Nightmares?" Lil asked.

Mom's eyebrows furrowed. "I suppose so," she said. Lil had wondered how you could suppose you had had a nightmare. She always remembered hers very vividly.

"And you, *boubouki*?" Mom would say as she pulled a piece of bread from a loaf. She would press it into the bottom of the hot pot. When it came back out, it glistened with oil and garlic and herbs, and she would hand it over the counter. "What are you doing up in the quiet hours?"

Lil would accept the bread, taking a bite of the midnight snack.

"Not tired," she would lie. But once her belly was full, Lil would sit down on the little bench near the cedar cabinet and fall softly to sleep, only to wake up as she was being carried to her room. Lil's eyes would flash open, watching Mom's necklace bounce as Mom climbed the stairs.

"Good night, *boubouki*," Mom would say, setting her into her bed. "*Kalinixta*."

"Night night," Lil would answer as she sank back into dreams.

But the week of the tragedy had been different. The week of the tragedy, Mom seemed flustered. Up at odd hours. At ten, and two, and four and six. And Lil had slept through most of it, unable to acclimate to the new schedule.

But on that day, it wasn't until after midnight that Lil rolled out of bed. That Dad had met her in the hallway, worry in his eyes. They had raced down the stairs.

"Stay here," Dad had said as they reached the lower landing.

Lil had peered across the room from the banister. The kitchen was empty. Garlic skins were littered on the tiles leading toward Mom's study. The door was half open. And Lil knew something was wrong. Not because she could see beyond the door. Not because of Dad's strangled cry, but because the pot on the stovetop was sending up a steady signal of black smoke.

It wasn't like Mom to let the soup burn.

"The police said it was suicide," Lil said. "No questions asked." She shook her head.

"And she had this necklace?" Charlie said, scribbling in her notebook.

Sydney extended her hand for the picture. Lil passed it over to her. "And she knew Bente," Sydney said, circling Bente's picture on her own chart.

"Before we arrived on the rock," Kat said, her knitting needles clicking, "you were talking to her. Did she give any indication of knowing what happened to your mom?"

"That's just it," Lil said, pulling her feet up onto the chair. "She said it wasn't like my mom to commit suicide." She paused. "My mom had this saying. She said it was an old Cretan adage. *Min zeis aplos. Zeis tolmira.* 'Do not just live. Live boldly.' Bente must have known this, because she said it to me before I started climbing the rock wall."

"That's weird," Sydney said.

Lil continued. "But when we were sitting out in the plateau garden, I heard Athenia and Bente talking. Athenia asked her . . . I think Athenia asked Bente if she had told me how my mom died."

"Do you remember her exact words?" Charlie said.

Lil thought for a moment. It had all happened so fast. They weren't talking loud enough. She shook her head. "Not exactly. But they did talk about that key." She snapped her fingers. "That's why they were talking about me. I think Bente was supposed to leave it somewhere up there near the labrys rock. She said she couldn't because I was there."

"That's interesting," Sydney said. She drew a new circle on her diagram. "What was your mom's name?"

"Helene," Lil said, watching Sydney scratch her name into the new circle. "I just wonder how Bente knows. Or why it would be a secret."

"Well, that's just it," Charlie said, tapping her fountain pen on her paper. "We have multiple secrets here. We have a secret key, a secret hiding place."

"A secret group," Kat said, swinging her yarn around a needle. "The Zephylites."

"And a secret death," Sydney said.

A knock came at the door and the girls jumped into motion. Sydney piled her papers and flipped them over. Charlie closed her book and slid her special fountain pen into the desk drawer. Kat knitted more frantically. Lil pocketed her picture, reached the door in two strides and swung the top half open. Bente. Her name died on Lil's tongue. Had she heard? Before she could stammer out an excuse, Bente held up a tray.

"I noticed you left the dining hall in a hurry. Before sweets."

Lil glanced at the tray. Several spoons lay across it. Some with what looked like honey-covered walnuts, sugar-glazed strawberries, cherries and what was it? Lil examined the glistening orange wrap held together with a toothpick. A citrusy aroma wafted toward her. Candied orange peel?

"You don't ever want to miss Aestos' spoon sweets. I said I would deliver them and check on you. Is everything all right?"

"Fine, uh, thank you," Lil said, accepting the offering over the door.

"We're just strategizing for tomorrow," Sydney said. "Renewable energy challenge in the morning."

Bente nodded. "Actually, you missed the guidelines of the challenge. Athenia was wondering where you were, but I defended you, explaining that I made you run back from the ropes course today. I assumed you were overtired." She pulled an envelope from her pocket. "Here are the details. Breakfast is at six o'clock. I will meet you there."

"Thank you. Thanks again," Lil said, accepting the envelope. Bente moved back toward the stairwell. Then she stopped and turned.

"Lastly, it was mentioned at dinner that some students were out of bed last night."

Lil's heart did an upswing to her throat, and she struggled to maintain a neutral expression.

"Against the rules," Sydney said from behind her. "They should probably be sanctioned."

"We are making a manor-wide announcement that curfew is for your safety." She paused and stared at Lil. "I cannot stress this enough. When in Melios Manor, you are in our care. And the rules are in place for a reason."

Lil gulped and nodded. Then without mention of anything more, Bente turned and made her way down the hall. Lil waited until she saw Bente round the corner to the stairwell before she pressed the door closed. There was an audible exhale.

"Okay, she definitely knows we know something," Lil said.

Sydney took the envelope from Lil's hand and pulled the note card from it. "Well, actually, the simple fact of the matter is that we know nothing. We have no conclusions." She looked at the guidelines for the renewable energy project. "Oh, micro-hydro, should have known."

"Listen," Charlie said, pulling the note card from Sydney's hands. "We don't know anything now, but we need to figure out more. We have to go back to the library."

Lil nodded. "Last night, they made the rounds at ten thirty. Maybe we wait a little longer."

"I am not disobeying the rules again. If we get caught, there's too much to lose," Sydney said, yanking the note card and guidelines back. She picked up her pile of papers and lined up the edges.

Lil looked to Kat and Charlie. They would go—she knew that they would go. Just like the night before. "Well." Lil looked down at her watch. It was nearly nine forty-five already. "If you don't want to go, you don't have to," she said, looking up at Sydney, "but we have time to convince you otherwise."

Lil looked toward the western horizon and watched the leaves flip over, revealing their soft bellies in the dying light. A massive cloud muted the greenery, and as if grabbing the warmth from the air with its presence, a breeze blew in, riffling the papers in Sydney's hand. Cold. Inordinately icy, Lil thought. Charlie grabbed a match and laid it to a twig in the preset fireplace as outside their dormitory window, rain set to its eternal work, whittling away at wood and stone.

18

Fog descended on Melia Mountain like a noose dropped from heaven's gallows. Horatio lifted his face to the sky, feeling its cool hand over his skin.

"Brother. Sister. This is what we've been waiting for."

He saw the light flash across the faces of his younger siblings as another shudder of lightning crackled through the night. He felt the electricity in the air. Everything was coming together. "This is what we're meant to do. And our rewards will be everlasting."

Felice grasped her pendant, hidden under her shirt, and Horatio watched the rain run over her fingers.

"Do we know where to find Bente? So that we might force the location of the key from her?" she asked.

Horatio smiled and shook his head. She still had so much to learn, his little sister. "No need to find the Protector. She will find us. She must already know we're on our way." He paused, weighing the machete in his hand. "I suspect she is already afraid."

"You think she's afraid?" Byron laughed. "Has any Protector ever been afraid?"

"Let me handle her," Horatio said. "Felice, secure the key. Byron, you keep a good look out. And make it quiet. We don't want any of the others knowing of our arrival."

"Yes, sir," Byron said.

"If one of us should fall, the others must carry on as we have vowed."

"Without fear," Felice said.

Lightning crackled. Bony arms of trees and jagged rock protruded from the shadows. Horatio could feel his god's presence all around. In the darkness, in the electricity in the air, in his skin. "We are also protected, and by something far greater than a mortal with a few combat skills," Horatio said. "There is nothing to fear."

He fell to his knee, genuflecting here on the mountain where Zeus had lived and died. Felice and Byron joined him. He put a hand on each of their necks for one final blessing.

"For the great father. And for our mother, who made our dreams bigger than hers. We are the messengers, and we will see our obligations through," Horatio added.

"Ma ton patera dia, tha ginei," Felice said.

They made the sign of the great father, marking a jagged line from right shoulder to left rib, then tapped their hearts twice. They pulled their pendants from the folds in their shirts, kissed them hard and held them to the lightning-splintered sky.

19

il blinked her eyes open, and her hand automatically dropped to the edge of her bed, feeling for her sneakers. When they weren't there, she realized where she was. Her mind took a moment to let go of dreams and fast-forward to reality. She jolted up in bed and checked her watch: 11:55. She grappled for the matchbox and candle on her bedside table, struck a match and held it to the wick. It crackled to life, and Lil forced herself from bed, pulling on a dark T-shirt and a pair of jeans. She deposited the box of matches into her pocket in case she needed to relight her candle later and yanked her sneakers on, tying them quickly. She went to the door, opened it and looked out into the hallway, first one way and then the other. She heard a shuffle and a crash. Charlie must have upended a chair—or Kat dropped something? Lil eased out of her room and shut her door behind her. She crossed the hall and knocked lightly on Sydney's door. They hadn't exactly had any luck getting Sydney to agree to come, but she hadn't directly said no, either. Lil waited for a few seconds. Drew up her hand again. There was another muffled crash from Charlie's room. Or was it the kitchen? Lil peered into the shadows beyond her candle, searching the darkness.

The door in front of her swung open and Lil jumped, nearly dropping her candle. She struggled to regain control and righted it before it sputtered out. Sydney appeared in front of her. "I told you I was *not* coming."

"But you're awake?" Lil said.

Sydney rolled her eyes. Hinges squeaked and they both looked down the hall. Charlie came out of her room, holding a candle in one hand and smoothing her hair with the other. Kat entered from the other side of the hallway. They had all decided to wear dark clothes, and Kat was in her black pants with the embroidered legs. She pulled a black cardi-wrap over her arms and secured it at the waist. Charlie adjusted the sleeve of a cabled black sweater over her right shoulder.

"Were you moving furniture down there?" Lil hissed as they walked toward her.

Charlie frowned. "Moving furniture?"

"Yeah, the clothes aren't going to conceal us if we make a big racket just getting out of bed."

Kat and Charlie looked at each other as they stopped in front of Lil. "What are you talking about?" Kat asked.

As if on cue, a louder crash echoed up from the kitchen. Sydney's eyes shot wide, and she disappeared back into the shadows of her room.

"Oh," Lil said, her voice just a wisp of what it usually was. "It wasn't you?"

A clatter erupted from below, like pots and pans had spun off their handles and smashed along the stone floor. Lil stepped between Kat and Charlie and headed for the end of the hall. Could it be Atticus or Aestos? No, there was something else, some other noise barely audible over the rain on the rooftop.

"It's probably just—" Kat began, but a muffled yell sounded from the same area. A low strangled cry.

"Back, back, back," Sydney hissed from behind Lil.

Lil stepped toward the stairwell. The light of her candle stretched, an orange pool overtaking shadow in a smooth sweep. It inched its way up the wall, hugging the corners of the stones, and curved toward the top stairs. And as the light climbed down the first step, her voice caught in her throat. Glistening with blood was a hand, shaking and reaching, as if asking for help before it fell loosely against the stairs. Fingers splayed as if releasing a soul.

Lil ran forward, candlelight spilling down the other steps. There in front of her was a figure, lying prone, neck twisted strangely.

"Are you okay?" She lowered the candle to survey the damage and gasped when it illuminated the side of a face she didn't recognize. She drew back her hand, startled, and someone grabbed her shoulder. She whirled. It was Charlie.

"Peut-être que nous devri—"

Lil lifted the candle, the light shaking in her hand. She heard a grunt and another crash. She backed up, the sound of her heart pulsing into her ears.

"Hide," Charlie whispered, her eyes wide and searching.

Lil nodded, catching Kat's frozen expression in the shadows.

Footsteps came toward them and Lil turned, her candle wavering in her shaking hand. A stooped figure rounded the corner and staggered up the steps, lurching over the body. Lil fell back, but the silver hair. The tawny limbs.

"Bente?" Lil whispered, pulling free from Charlie's grasp. She ran toward her. God, Bente. She had told them to stay in the dormitories. She had stressed that it was for their safety. Lil caught her as she staggered forward.

"What's going—?" Lil started, but before she could finish, Bente covered her mouth, heaved herself off the wall and yanked

Lil away from the stairs. Lil stumbled, trying to keep her footing. She could see Kat and Charlie by her side as they ran. Was she dreaming? Bente stopped in front of Lil's door, and Lil hurried to extract her key. She jammed it into the lock with shaking hands.

"Inside," Bente hissed. "Everyone."

Sydney darted out of the shadows of her own room as they all dove into Lil's.

"The door," Bente wheezed.

Charlie slammed it shut while Lil moved Bente to the wicker chair, lowering her into it.

"What's going on?" Sydney whispered from the bed, where she and Kat now huddled.

Bente pressed her fingers to her lips and reached for the candle in Lil's hand. She blew it out. She gestured to the others to do the same. They plunged the room into shadows. The only light came from the embers of the dying fire, and Lil wondered if she should rush to smother them, but before she could move, footsteps echoed in the distance.

Lil strained to hear the words being spoken, but despite her best efforts, she couldn't understand them. The footfalls stopped before they reached her door and Lil heard a pounding fist on the door of another room. Was it Kat's or was it Charlie's? Would they duck into one of those instead of pursuing them?

Bente slid down to the floor and Lil dropped onto one knee.

"What's going on?" she whispered, barely audible. "Where are you hurt?"

Bente reached for her stomach, and as Lil squinted in the dim light, she saw the dark color staining Bente's already dark shirt. She reached down, felt her fingers grow sticky with blood.

"She's been cut," Lil said to the others, her heart kicking at her ribs.

"Listen," Bente said, pushing her hand away. Sydney, Kat and Charlie appeared next to her, and Charlie pulled a handkerchief from her pocket, trying to stop the blood. "Listen to me," Bente said, stilling her arm. "They'll come for me in just a moment . . ."

She sucked in a shuddering breath and grabbed Lil's shirt, knotting it into a ball in her fist.

"You must be gone . . . Take . . ." Her hand drifted to the cord at her throat, and with shaking hands Lil helped her lift the key from her neck. It swung for a moment in front of her as Bente gasped and Lil's eyes blurred, seeing her mom there for just a moment.

"Wha-what is it?" Lil said.

Bente coughed and sucked in a breath, inhaling a wisp of gray hair that hung around her face. She locked eyes with Lil. "Climb out the window . . . Go and alert Athenia and the others. Go quickly. Tell her there . . . are two left."

Lil's arms shook.

"Use the bedsheets," Bente whispered.

The footsteps echoed on stonework once more and Lil froze as she heard them come to a standstill outside her door. Her hair stood on end.

"We'll, we'll get—get—get the bedsheets," Sydney said, voice shaking. Charlie tried to stop the flow of blood that continued to erupt from Bente's stomach. Bente pushed her hand away. "It is no use. You must go. They will not spare you."

An angry fist banged on the door, and Lil watched the latch quake against the frame.

"They're here," Lil whispered, her body feeling as though it were full of needles.

Bente grabbed her wrist. She sucked in one final time and Lil could see the old woman strain to speak.

"He-He-Helene," she gasped, and she squeezed Lil's arm with bloody fingers. Lil's heart nearly stopped at her mother's name.

"Bente, Bente, what is this—"

But Bente's hand dropped away and her head rolled to the side, hanging loose and lifeless.

"She's gone," Charlie said. "That's all." She got up, shaking her head. "We have to go."

Sydney and Kat hurried to the balcony door with a bundle of sheets. Lil heard glass break, and turned to see pieces of stained glass fly from above the interior door. A hand with a machete clutched in its fist followed. Lil scrambled to her feet, placing the disk around her neck just as Bente had done, and hurried to the balcony where Kat, Sydney and Charlie were pulling sheets together.

"It's not even remotely long enough," Sydney said. Her hands were shaking as she tied a knot between the blanket and a sheet.

Another crash echoed inside, and Lil looked back to the door. She shook her head, trying to clear it. "We have to buy some time."

She looked to Charlie, who deposited the bloody handkerchief into her pocket. The timbers of the door strained and cracked. "Dresser? Desk?" Charlie asked.

"Both?" Lil said. They sprinted back inside, grabbing the desk by the corner. Lil pushed while Charlie pulled until it slid in front of the door. She felt little pinpricks of glass fall down around her shoulders and pierce her skin as the machete reappeared in the window. Her shoulders stung with small cuts, and all of a sudden Lil's mind became sharp. If they had killed Bente for this disk . . . had they killed her mother, too? She felt her breathing go ragged. Lil spotted candles on the floor. She picked them up, reaching momentarily for the matches in her pocket, but decided that the embers in the dying fire would be faster. She placed the wicks to them.

"What are you doing?" Charlie whispered.

"Well, it's not like they don't know we're here," she said through gritted teeth as the wicks lit. She moved back toward the door, watching the bloody knuckles dance along the glass.

Sydney raced into the room. "We need T-shirts and pants, whatever you have."

Lil pointed toward the duffel bag, then climbed up onto the desk chair. She steadied herself against the wall as she brought the candle flame to meet the hairy knuckles above her. The hand withdrew with a start, but she pressed her lips together and moved the flame closer. A snarl echoed outside and the machete swung. Lil arched back, the blade just missing her jaw. She felt her foot tip on the chair, tilt away from the wall. The dresser quaked as a body hit the door.

"Harder, Felice. You must hit it hard," a deep voice growled.

Lil, trying to keep her balance, reached for the iron sconce that decorated the wall next to the stained glass. She fell back. To her surprise the sconce loosened in her hand and tipped down-ward. The window frame flipped, landing upside down with a *thwak*. A yanking sound, like roots being torn from earth, came from behind her. The smell of soil filled the room, and Lil turned to see Kat and Sydney freeze—arms overflowing with clothes. She followed their gazes to a gaping shadow on the opposite side of the bed. Charlie reached up, taking one of the candles from her. Lil released the sconce and leaped off the chair. The dresser bucked again and tumbled, nearly clipping her heels as she hit the floor.

"Yes. There," the deep voice growled again as another crash echoed from behind her.

Lil sprang up. Sydney and Kat were already dropping the clothes. A breeze tore into the room as the door behind them opened. Kat, Charlie and Sydney jumped over the bed, into the hole in the wall. Was it a second exit? Was it a panic room? Why hadn't Bente sent them that way? Lil grasped the disk that hung around her neck as a shadow loomed over her. She dove through the doorway, following the others into the darkness. She ran a few feet, pivoting to see behind her. Her foot caught on something. The candle flew from her grasp. She clutched the disk to her chest. The room dipped. The floor shifted. And they were falling.

20

The disk jammed into Lil's ribs, knocking the air from her lungs, as she tumbled head over heels. She collided with roots and limbs, and gasped for breath as she held the disk tightly. She crashed and slid and finally came to an abrupt stop, elbow erupting with pain as it ran into something hard. She tried to stumble up, only to be thrown back down by the others in the chute. As she sprawled sideways, her face met the ground, and pain ricocheted through her jaw. The taste of dirt filled her mouth. She let the disk swing free as she propped herself up on hands and knees, spitting.

"I-is everyone okay?" Lil sputtered, wiping her chin with a shaking hand. There was a moment's pause, and she only heard shifting around her. Someone coughed and another person moaned. Lil strained to see, opening her hand in front of her face and closing it. It was nearly pitch black.

"Is everyone okay?" Lil asked again, reaching out.

"I'm okay," came Kat's voice from in front of her.

"Me too. Just bruised up," Sydney said.

"Charlie?" Lil said, trying to detect her in the shadows.

"Ah, *oui*, okay. Can anyone see anything?" Charlie asked.

"I have no idea where my candle is," Kat said.

"Me neither," Lil said.

The sound of squeaky hinges echoed above them. Then voices and the dull glow of a distant flashlight wound its way through dirt and dust, like a ghostly, swirling hand reaching toward them. It illuminated the spot where they had landed just enough for Lil to see. Kat, Charlie and Sydney's faces appeared, dazed and dirt-covered in front of her. The ground they sat on was dirt, the walls around them stone. Lil peered past the pool of light into the yawning dark. There was no way to tell how far it went in either direction.

The beam brightened in the shaft.

"Well, we're going to have to move." Lil got to her feet. "They're coming after us whether we can see anything or not."

Sydney looked both ways. "I think the mountain is to our left and the front of the building is to our right."

"Then we should go right," Charlie said. "Maybe this tunnel leads into the basement or out to one of the caves."

The disk weighed heavy on Lil's neck. Too many unanswered questions swirled in her head, but she forced them back, watching the shaft of light get brighter. A booted foot appeared in the tunnel, loosening dirt that rained down as their predators began to slide toward them. Lil grasped Sydney's hand and pulled her up. Kat and Charlie leaped up, too.

"Okay, let's go to the right." Lil put her left hand against the stone wall. "Keep one hand on the wall," she said, plunging into the darkness.

"And the other out in front," Charlie said from behind her.

They moved as quickly as they could. Lil and Sydney stayed close, and Lil could feel Sydney shaking against her arm beside her.

"Maybe if we get closer to the outside, we'll see a light," Kat said.

The sound of a mini landslide caught Lil's ears, and the passageway brightened. They were coming. Lil stumbled as the girls' shadows spilled out in front of them, the beam of the flashlight hitting their backs.

"'Ratio, over here," the woman's voice called.

Lil could see in front of her as the flashlight beam bounced. There was a turn, just a few yards away. "Around this corner!" she shouted.

Her hand caught on something sharp, jamming it flat into the wall as she rounded the corner. As if a switch had been flipped, light flooded down the passageway in front of them. Torches fired to life, filling the black passage with pools of orange.

"Whoa," Charlie gasped.

Lil watched the torches stretch endlessly ahead. Where were they?

"In here!" Kat hissed.

Lil swung to the right. There was a small wooden door. It was low and arched and had cast-iron strapping for hinges. Lil ran for the door, helping Kat push it open. She winced as it echoed loudly. They dove inside and pulled the door behind them.

This chamber was only lit by one torch, and Lil grasped it from the wall, spinning around. They needed something—a barricade, anything. Her eyes landed on a huge pile of rocks, with a large boulder at the base of it just to the left of the door.

"Quick!" She hurried over, pressing her shoulder into it. It was big and heavy and felt unmovable. Kat, Sydney and Charlie ran over and gave it a heave along with Lil. The boulder groaned free of its spot, and they rolled it in front of the door. Sydney came back with a branch in her hand and wedged it hard between the ground and the edge of the rock, locking it in place as the door shook with a thump.

"Damn it!" a muffled voice said from the other side.

Lil gulped, looking around. She wasn't sure if they were all shaking or if it was the effects of the torchlight, but the whole room seemed to tremble. She tried to still her breathing.

"Do you hear that?" Sydney asked, inching toward the pile of rocks on one end.

Lil couldn't hear anything over her breathing.

"It's rain," Sydney said.

She stepped onto the pile of rocks. Lil heard it now, too. There was a sliver of diffused light shining in the crevices between rocks in the enormous pile. There was the smell of mountain soil. Lil reached the torch up to light Sydney's way as she climbed. A ribbon of fog had found its way to them.

"Yes!" Kat said, readjusting her cardi-wrap, which had loosened and come untied during the fall. She joined Sydney on the hill of rocks. "We just need to move . . . all of these."

Charlie reached up, dislodging a small fist-sized rock from the space. A few others skittered downward.

Lil heard a shuffle from outside, and then the boulder jammed against the stick. There were only two attackers, and it had taken all four girls to move that boulder, plus Sydney had wedged it in place with the stick. Lil was pretty sure it would hold, but she moved back to the entrance just in case. The two seemed determined and, though Lil had only seen them for a moment before she fell, they were bigger, older.

"I'll guard the door," Lil whispered, hoping she could at least keep an eye on the branch while the others moved the rocks. Her torchlight stretched to the other side of the small chamber as she made her way to the boulder, and Lil caught her breath.

She squinted. Had she seen it right?

She lifted her torch and stepped forward. Bente's words from that morning on the mountaintop echoed in her ears: "The labrys was a directional tool. The wall would be marked with it to indicate a correct path to the main quarters. A guide. A compass. A clue, if you will."

There, in the center of what she now saw was an old stone door, was a double-headed ax. A labrys.

Lil moved to it as if pulled by an invisible thread. The marking was indented. A perfect sphere. She looked down at the disk that hung around her neck. A perfect fit. A long, smooth, rectangular slab next to the door caught her attention. She reached out and brushed her hand across its surface. Dust filtered from beneath her fingertips, unveiling a large plaque, the top etched with symbols. Most of them were new to her, but some of them looked familiar. In the very top line was a skull and next to it a few squiggly lines side by side. She yanked the disk to eye level, looking from one to the other. Many of the symbols were the same. What did they mean? She glanced back at the plaque, wiping her hand downward, shuttling more dirt to the ground. There was another script, something that ran in lines like tally marks. Next was Greek. Next perhaps Italian? And at the very bottom, she found words she recognized. She knelt down in front of it, pulling the torchlight to her. Her breath loosened the remaining dust from the crevices as she read the familiar English.

> *Those who seek knowledge, knock*
> *At the door that lies herein,*
> *But only ones with fierceness*
> *Will find a common kin.*
> *Beware folly and weak footfall.*
> *Beware your mortal sins.*
> *A simple word of advice*
> *Before you do begin:*
> *Everything you think you know*

Abandons you within.
And if you do not let it,
Then you will find your end.

Lil squinted at the final line. It was written in Greek, but she could read it. It was the one phrase she could recognize. She twisted the torchlight lower, her breath catching in her throat.

Min zeis aplos. Zeis tolmira.

She could hear her mother's voice echoing through the chamber, saying the phrase over and over again. First in Greek. Then in English. Her mind spun. There it was on the playground. Before a test. At a soccer game. When Lil was afraid to try the ropes course for the first time. *Do not just live. Live boldly.* The phrase was the embodiment of strength, the embodiment of her mother.

Lil's throat tightened, and she backed into the wall behind her. Why would her mother's favorite expression be here? Why would Bente bring her the disk? Had her mother been beyond this door? Were there answers in there, about how a woman who lived her life so boldly could give up? Could end it?

Lil spun around with the torch in hand. "I have to go this way," she said, sparks flicking down around her as she waved toward the group.

"I think we can clear this," Charlie said. "We should be able to climb out once we figure out how to move the bigger boulders."

"No," Lil said, shaking her head. "I'm not—I can't go that way."

Kat and Charlie stared at each other, looking confused. Sydney dropped the rock she was holding and hurried toward Lil.

Lil swallowed hard. She gestured toward the indentation. The symbol. "I have to figure out what this means."

Charlie's eyes went big as she saw the indentation and inscription.

"Didn't Bente say it was a guide?" Kat said in a hushed voice.

Lil nodded.

A crash came from the opposite side of the door, and a gruff voice followed. "Shoot it, Felice. Shatter the rock."

"It's a bit narrow . . . if it ricochets—" a voice replied.

Lil's heart kicked. Whatever they were going to do, they had to do it quickly. "Well?"

Sydney shook her head. "No, this is irrational. We need to keep dismantling that pile. We need to go and get the police."

"We don't even know if we'll be able to move those stones. They're huge," Lil said. She held up the disk. "And I have to know what this means. Where it goes."

Lil pictured Bente, dying to protect it. Had her mother died to protect it, too?

"I just think it might be a clue," she said. "To my mom. To what happened . . ."

"There's got to be another way for you to figure this out," Sydney hissed.

Lil saw Charlie's eyes land on the disk and flick to the wall. "You have to admit that it appears to be an artifact with an interesting history," she whispered. "One longing to be discovered."

"Listen," Lil said, stepping away from the others and pulling the disk from her neck. "You three can work on that pile, figure out how to move the rocks. Tell Athenia. Call the police. Let them know someone's in here and that we've trapped the people who killed Bente behind a boulder. I need to do this. I need to know."

Kat shook her head, a long dark curl coming loose from her ear. "We stick together. It's safer."

Charlie nodded. "We're a team," she said.

Lil took a breath. "You don't have to. We have no idea what's in there." She knew she had to do this, but she didn't want to endanger everyone else. She was used to going it alone. She could handle it.

The boulder barricading them in shifted and groaned, but stayed in place.

"I highly object to this," Sydney said. She cast her eyes toward the stones, as if calculating their size, then peered at the labrys on the wall, then back at the stones. "We have no idea—there's no way of—" She let out a breath as the branch jolted and shuddered with the compressed weight of another push on the exterior. "Fine," she said.

Lil looked at all three girls. They met her gaze. "You really don't have to . . . ," she said as she lined up the labrys on the disk with the labrys in the door.

"I'm sure," Charlie and Kat answered at the same time.

"I said fine, didn't I?" Sydney said, pushing her glasses up on her nose.

"Then here we go." Lil pressed the disk into place.

The door swung, noiselessly craning open like a mouth filled with rotted moths. A breeze blew toward them, old, soft and decomposing. And Lil looked in. The passage was dark, shadowed and littered with stones, and though she knew her eyes were playing tricks on her, she could swear she saw the flash of the soles of her mother's feet flicking off into the distance, her black hair aswirl, disappearing down the passage. Ahead and away from her, always. Even if there was just a chance of finding out more—somewhere in the shadows—she had to try. Lil retrieved the disk from the door, took a breath and stepped into the labyrinth.

21

As the door closed behind them, wooden arms moved and flint clicked. *Pop, pop, pop.* The passageway came alive with pools of light, glowing out of rounded stone cups that protruded from the walls. Roots hung from the ceiling, draped down above them like extended arms—knobby, withered fingers reaching, begging for help. Rocks hobbled up from the ground, stretching to extract themselves, as if every bit of life longed to escape this place.

"This was a terrible idea," Sydney said through gritted teeth. "I can already see this was a terrible idea."

Lil jumped over a loosened stone and ran forward, her eyes searching. She wasn't sure for what exactly, except that the path would be guided by the labrys. She knew that, and she knew they had to keep moving. When they came to the first corner, Lil looked to the left, then to a tiny passage on the right.

Sydney reached to her waist and unclipped her device. She flipped it on. "Maybe we can see it on satellite. Commence trilateration," she said into the gadget. She held the device between them and worked at clearing her glasses with her other hand.

NO SIGNAL flashed across the screen. Sydney shook her head, sighing loudly.

"That was a good idea," Kat said, patting her shoulder.

"Please do not patronize me," Sydney said, rolling her eyes as she placed the device back in her pocket.

Lil waved the torch back and forth, searching the walls. Some of it was covered with a sticky slime. "Do you see it?" she asked.

"I think here," Kat said, rubbing the wall to her right. A moment later, the labrys appeared from the dirt covering that had shielded it.

"Good eyes," Charlie whispered.

They hurried down the hallway, and Lil wiped away the cobwebs that filtered down from the ceiling. Something skittered in the shadows, and she wondered what types of animals had made their home down here. The tunnel narrowed as she peered into the darkness, pushing the torch ever forward.

As they rounded the next corner, she spotted three doors. They each had a dark strip of cast-iron metalwork splaying out in a wedge shape from their hinges.

"Here it is again," Lil said, raising the torch. This labrys, more obvious than the last, was drawn on the face of the center door.

Kat placed her fingers to it, rubbing them together. "Feels like charcoal."

Lil ran the torch to the right and to the left. No handle. "How do we get in? No latch."

"Of course there's a latch," Sydney said. "Up there."

Lil straightened, lifting the torch to the root-clotted ceiling. A massive spiderweb caught and sizzled like a hot coal. And behind it was a stained-glass window, dimly lit, covered in soot or dirt. This one, unlike the ones in the manor, was small and circular, and the image inside it was the head of a bull. The edges of the horns seemed to be decorated with flecked gold, sparkling despite the dim light of the hall. Lil flicked the torch to the right and saw the unlit sconce wrapped with roots. She reached for it.

"Wait, wait, wait, wait," Charlie said, grabbing her wrist.

"But the labrys," Lil said.

"Ah, *oui*," Charlie said, her eyebrows rising, "but look." She gestured toward the wall. Just to the right of the door was another inscription. Like the previous one, it was set up like the Rosetta stone: different prints at the top leading down through languages of the world. Lil squatted as Charlie moved a root to the side.

"See," she said, pointing toward the last verse.

Lil read the English out loud.

> *"Follow to the Minotaur,*
> *Son of Minos, full of lore.*
> *Choose right and walk that way,*
> *Or accept your death today."*

"The Minotaur," Lil said.

"Are you reading the same thing I'm reading?" Sydney said, looking over her shoulder. "'Or accept your death today.'" She swallowed hard, the twists in her hair bouncing on their own.

"Take a deep breath," Lil said, trying to stay focused on the subject at hand. It would all come clear, she told herself. She hadn't been impulsive. Bente had called this a clue. And Lil knew. Lil knew beyond the shadow of a doubt that she would learn something more here. Something important.

Charlie pulled her notebook from her back pocket. She gripped a pen cap between her teeth and yanked the pen free, copying the passage quickly. Lil reached up, grabbed the sconce and tugged.

The wooden door swung open, but not silently like the other had done. It creaked, and then a low moan sailed toward them from the shadows, bristling the hair on the back of Lil's neck. It was a cry that descended into a whimper. A human voice, full of mourning.

22

oratio pushed against the door, but the boulder stuck hard.

"Fe, help me," he said, his shoulder aching.

He dug in his heels with all his strength as Felice pulled her satchel from around her shoulders. She swallowed, placed her gun in the back of her pants and met him up against the door. Horatio felt the boulder give, his feet moving forward an inch.

"We're losing them and we're losing the key!" he shouted, his body surging with rage. "We will never find it!"

"Stop," Felice said, calmly pulling the ancient scroll from her bag.

He stepped away from the door, trying to clear his head. "Right, right. We must think. We must use what we've been given."

He clutched his gold pendant, trying not to picture Byron, still lying on the stairs. He had retrieved the gift given by Ares that hung around his dead brother's neck. And reached into his pocket, now, to grip the lava rock. Remembering Ares' words. ". . . ash from the volcano of Thera that destroyed those who strove to destroy Zeus. This is the protection that Zeus offers you on your quest for immortality."

"We are protected," he said quietly, as he sent a silent prayer to the lord.

"Are we?" Felice said, unrolling the cartograph.

"Don't, sister," Horatio said, his voice coming out deeper and more menacing than he meant it to. "Don't lose your faith. Not now."

Felice fell silent as she surveyed the cartograph, but he saw her jaw working. His mind raced despite himself. How had things gone wrong so early? How had the heathen woman wounded his brother so easily, especially since he was the one carrying the symbols of protection? Poor Byron, poor, poor baby brother.

"He's at peace now," Felice said, as though reading his thoughts. "Perhaps his role, his destiny, was to fall so that we could continue."

Of course. "You are correct," he said, realizing that she was right. They all had a purpose.

Felice looked away, then pressed the cartograph flat against the wall. Horatio panned the beam of the flashlight over it. The lines were faded, of course, from being so old, but they had the benefit of being burned directly into the hide.

Felice traced a line. "Do you see it, 'Ratio? There is one other way to get up to the first passage," she said. "This crosses the Minotaur chamber, and we don't need to move the boulder to access it."

"Let's go," Horatio said.

Felice rolled the map quickly and placed it back into her satchel, then swung the satchel over her shoulder.

"Wait!" Horatio stood slowly. "We meet them there, we take the key. Continue to the chambers on our own. No loose ends, just as Ares would have it done."

"I am not Ares," Felice said.

Horatio studied her face as Felice looked to the side. He

pictured Byron lying dead on the ground, killed without remorse by the Protector. He felt a tug at his heart.

"They are not the same as us. Even the young ones. They are not family like we are. And they will not spare us." He reached out and squeezed her shoulder. "I need you with me. Clear-headed. Precise. Just as Ares says. They are a small sacrifice in the greater arc of destiny."

Felice paused, but a moment later pulled her gun from her belt and nodded.

"Fine, but not for Ares," Felice said. "For Byron."

"Indeed," Horatio added.

They moved swiftly down the hall and headed for the Minotaur chamber.

23

The girls stepped inside the chamber. Lil went first, holding the torch high with a trembling fist. They circled in the pool of light, which seemed to dim with each step they took, diminished by the darkness around them. The door creaked and shut behind them, and the cry began again. This time it was louder and much closer.

Mmmmm—mmmmm—mmmmm.

Lil spun, searching, trying to see past the torchlight.

"Hello," Kat said, her voice quiet. "Is someone in here? Are you all right?"

No answer came. As they circled, Lil spotted a protrusion on the nearby wall. An identical one marked the opposite side of the door. They looked just like the wells that they had seen in the outer passage that had burst with fire. Were they oil wells? She swung the torch, dunking the flame into it. A river of fire coursed around the wall. When it hit the corner, it split, sending a path vertically along torches while the other half traveled toward the next corner. Lil could see it raced along a narrow trough, and as it did, the room was revealed. The angry face of a bull loomed out of the shadows. She jumped back, careening into Charlie, who clutched her arm.

"It's not alive," Charlie breathed.

Mmmmm—mmmmm—mmmmm.

The cry rose up again, and Lil turned, searching. It was coming from the other side, wasn't it? It seemed like it was everywhere. She searched, scanning more bulls' heads across the far wall.

"Over here," Kat said from the opposite side of the room.

Lil hurried to her, stopping midstep as she looked past the largest bull to a man. Her body tensed, and she felt as though she had been drenched in ice.

"Be careful," she said, grasping Kat's arm and pulling her back.

Mmmmm—mmmmm—mmmmm.

Lil watched his shoulders shake as the cry circled the chamber once more.

"It's okay," Kat said. She leaned forward and touched his shoulder. The figure didn't move. Just continued to weep. Lil stepped closer. He was tall, standing about two feet over her, and as she neared, she could see up into his face. His cheeks had tracks running down them as though he had been crying inky tears. And in the wavering light, Lil thought he trembled.

Mmmmmmm—mm—mm—mm.

The moaning echoed again, and this time the man's shoulders jolted. One of his hands went to the urn next to him while the other pressed his cheek.

Mmmmmmm—mm—mm.

His shoulders trembled, then his hands jolted back to position by his sides, and Lil expected him to look up at her. He was so real, and yet the way he moved—he was not human.

Sydney stepped past her and knelt down next to him. Lil grasped at her. "Careful."

But Sydney lifted his right foot as he trembled again. The moaning started and then stopped as Sydney pressed one of her hands into his knee. "This is an automaton," she said. She jerked her hands away, and the moaning started again. She wiped her hands along her shirt. "A very old and disgusting, greasy one.

Let me see that," she said, gesturing toward Lil's torch. Lil handed it to her. "See?"

Lil and Kat got down close as Sydney pulled the torch toward the floor. Lil could see a small bellows underneath the automaton's foot that led back into the wall. Hiding behind the automaton was what looked just like an organ pipe. As the foot pressed down, the air went through the pipe, and a second later the familiar moan started.

"Gross," Lil said, tentatively touching her fingers to the skin. It felt greasy and firm against her fingertips.

Sydney pushed her hands into her sleeves. "I'm assuming it's made from wood with some sort of animal hide over it to cover the joints. We must have triggered the mechanism when we opened the door." She swallowed as if trying not to gag. "It's— it's an interesting design."

"Yeah," Lil said. "Interesting." She felt only slightly relieved.

Lil grasped the urn and pulled herself up as Sydney handed the torch back to her. As she did, she noticed the automaton's hand descending to its resting spot on the lip of the urn. His fingertips were covered in soot. Kat leaned over the opposite side, reaching in. She pulled out a piece of ash and stared at it quizzically.

"Charcoal?" Kat said.

Lil stepped toward the center of the room to have a broader look. The walls were dark. She'd assumed it was the color of the stones, but at a second glance, images seemed to take shape before her eyes. Sooty images, drawn on thick. Lil tried to connect the dots. The bulls' heads were the most obtrusive parts, but she hadn't noticed that their bottom halves were sculpted out of stone, chipped into shape from the wall itself. There were multiple variations. Some had the legs and body of a man that rose into the head of a bull. Some became a bull at the torso, leading up to the bull face. Some were all bull on the right and all man on the left. Lil's eyes fell to a hammer and chisel in the corner. It was resting on the floor, handle leaning against the wall as if an artist had just completed a project.

Besides the bulls, the room was fairly simple. There were embellished urns in each corner, and there was a simple stone desk where Kat and Sydney now stood.

"These must have been for different pigments," Kat said, running her index finger around the inside of what looked like a very old mortar and pestle.

"What do you think of that?" Sydney asked.

Kat looked to another small stone bowl and then a third. "See how this one has a red hue?" She tipped the closest one so they could see. "It's barely visible, but this looks to me like sinopia— red ochre—"

"Ochre?" Sydney said. "Like iron?"

"Exactly," Kat said, looking up.

Lil squinted to see the red hue. It matched the faded color of the paintings on the walls.

"They would have crushed it and mixed it with water to make paint," Kat said.

"And what's this?" Sydney said, holding up a bull's horn. Kat took it and scrutinized it. She studied one side, then flipped it and studied the other. Then she went back to the urn next to the automaton, pulled out a piece of ash and slid it into the end of the horn. As if it was made to fit, it lodged there, making a writing utensil, like a pencil but bigger, thicker.

Kat gestured toward the walls covered in charcoal. "It's like an ancient art studio."

What would an art studio be doing in the underground

labyrinth, and why was it in a room with hideous bulls' heads attached to the wall and a crying man next to them? Lil wondered as she scanned the chamber once more. It was as if the room was split between grotesque and beautiful, trying to balance itself somehow.

"That's all very interesting," Charlie said, uncrossing her arms. "I mean, you know I like old stuff as much as the next person, but"—she eyed the door through which they had entered—"what does this have to do with the inscription? The Minotaur?" She gestured toward her paper, popping the cap of her pen on and off quickly.

And what does it have to do with Bente and Mom? Lil wondered. "Read it again, would you?" she said.

They circled to the center of the room.

> *"Follow to the Minotaur,*
> *Son of Minos, full of lore.*
> *Choose right and walk that way,*
> *Or accept your death today."*

"Well, what do we know about the Minotaur?" Lil asked.

The girls rehashed their lecture with Colleen. Charlie had, naturally, been paying the most attention.

"The story goes that the Minotaur was half man and half bull." She gestured toward the bulls' heads. "That he was created when Pasiphae coupled with a bull."

"Oh yeah," Sydney said, scowling. "I tried to delete that from my memory."

"It's mythology," Charlie said. "Anyway, he was exiled to the labyrinth and eventually killed by Theseus."

Lil stared down at the paper. *Choose right and walk that way, or accept your death today.* "Well, there are multiple Minotaurs here," she said, eyeing the bulls. "We have to choose the right one. How do we differentiate?"

"The Minotaur is depicted in a few different ways, but generally with a man's body and a bull's head. I think we can rule out these," Charlie said, pointing to the ones that were half bull on the right or the left and half man on the opposite side. She stepped to the right, standing in front of the bull with a human body. "The Minotaur is usually depicted like this in paintings and stories."

"It does seem like the most obvious," Lil said. Then she watched as Kat drifted down the line, placing her hand on each animal's face.

"Yes," Kat said, "but why is this room filled with art?"

"Well, someone had to create these," Charlie said. "Maybe they just left their tools."

"Maybe this is just a haunted house," Sydney said. "And no one created these at all."

"They do look authentic, though," Charlie said, picking up an urn.

Kat nodded and stepped in front of the automaton. "You know, one time, we had a Greek mythology exhibit at the museum. And every time I looked at the Minotaur paintings, all I could see was Theseus attacking an innocent animal. Minotaur did not hold a weapon in any picture I saw of him. He just stood with head bowed, a dagger at his brow. Ready to die."

Lil looked at the automaton. "But *he's* not a bull. *He's* a man. If the myth says choose the Minotaur . . ."

"What is the English word *lore*?" Kat mused. "It's story, made up, right?"

Lil cocked her head to the side. "Yes, fable or story."

"Son of Minos . . . ," Kat said. "Full of lore." She reached toward a string around the automaton's neck.

"But doesn't that work for all the stories in Greek mythology?" Charlie asked.

"It just seems to me," Kat said, peering up into the automaton's tear-stained face, "that if anyone has reason to cry, it would be the Minotaur. He's not accepted by Minos. He's exiled to a dark labyrinth. People are sent to destroy him."

"But he's a monster," Charlie said.

Kat shrugged, grasping the string and pulling it forward. A hood at the back of the Minotaur's neck rustled, and Kat lifted it. "Perhaps he's a man, turned into a monster in story."

Lil's mind spun. "At the entrance," she continued, "it said, 'Everything you think you know, abandons you within.' Maybe Kat's right. Maybe the Minotaur was a man, not a monster."

Kat lowered the hood so it landed on the crown of the Minotaur's head. Lil could see it was a headdress. Kat adjusted it so that the horns wavered and settled.

"Are you suggesting," Charlie said, her eyes twinkling in the candlelight, "that we are supposed to abandon the writings handed down from the Greeks altogether? There is nothing about the Minotaur being a man."

"Let's not be hasty. I'd rather not 'accept my death today,'" Sydney said, quoting the last line of the riddle. "If we choose wrong, we die."

"But Kat's right," Lil said, joining her in front of the automaton. Kat adjusted the eyeholes. The animal hide popped forward an inch, securely hugging the cheekbones of the automaton. There he stood, topped with the ornamental headdress. He fit along the wall better now, crowned with the hide and horns, blending more naturally with the other minotaurs. His hand came down on the urn once more. A loud sound echoed through the chamber like a rope being yanked through a pulley. The bull statues spun away, revolving into the shadows, replaced by stone from ceiling to floor. The automaton dropped to one knee. A string unwound at the nape of his neck as he descended. A warm breeze blew back the girls' hair as a dimly lit stairwell formed and locked into place behind him.

Lil gulped and stepped over to the stairwell. A stone at eye level jutted open like a drawer. And there, nestled inside, was a wooden charm about the size of Mom's necklace. Lil's mouth went as dry as ash as she pulled it from the shadows. It swung free on a leather thong, revealing two horns, crossed at the points.

"Oh," she said, disappointed.

Kat took the necklace in her hands and examined it.

"I think I hear footsteps," Sydney said, racing over to the others.

Lil glanced at the door, heart kicking into her throat. Could Bente's murderers have moved the boulder all by themselves?

"Look," Kat said, pointing toward the casing where the pendant had just been. Lil lowered the torch. There in the inlay was the faint, sooty imprint of the double-headed ax.

A bolt of hope drove through her.

"It's the right way," Charlie said.

The footsteps came again, louder this time.

"Hurry." Lil turned toward the stairwell.

Three shots rang out behind them, and Lil heard the stained-glass window shatter and fall to the ground. The girls dove into the passageway, and Lil scanned her body, wondering if a bullet had met its mark. Her thoughts flashed to the gun and to the machete and to Bente and to death and to the horn symbol, which she had never seen before. A thousand puzzle pieces, with no way of sticking them together. And imminent death at their heels. She hurried forward, pushing Kat, Charlie and Sydney onward. She peered behind her as the automaton started his low hollow moan once more as they plunged deeper into the labyrinth.

24

L il ran harder than she had ever run before. Headlong they ascended into a snake-shaped passageway, nothing but breath and footsteps between them. Lil watched doors slip past on either side. She swung her torch to the right and the left, searching for the next labrys, the next clue. Finding nothing.

"Does anyone see the battle-ax?" she whispered as she tried to still the disk that swung at her side.

"I don't see one," Charlie said from right behind her.

"We're going to have to go somewhere," Kat said from the back of the line. "I can see their flashlight."

As if on cue, the flashlight flickered like a stark strobe, casting their shadows in front of them.

"We have to go faster," Lil said as they rounded another corner.

"We have to hide," Sydney said.

The flashlight beam turned the corner and licked at their heels.

"Right there!" a voice behind them shouted, and the chamber echoed with a blast. Lil covered her head as rock ricocheted from the wall and sprayed on them like shrapnel. She searched the shadows, hoping beyond hope that there was an archway, a tunnel, maybe an invisible door like in her dorm room—anything that could free them from certain death. She heard a footfall falter. Now was not the time for unsteady steps, she thought as she grasped Sydney's arm.

A door loomed on their right, and Lil could make out a cast-iron handle at the center of it. She jammed to a halt, and the others slid to a stop behind her. Lil tried the latch. The door easily gave way. She held her hand to her lips, gesturing for quiet, and prayed as she pushed the door. It slid open as though the hinges had been recently greased. They ducked inside. She grabbed the bolt and slid it into place. A click echoed through the chamber. Lil took a deep breath and let it out as silently as possible as she squatted down, leaning hard against the door.

Footsteps stomped and voices echoed past.

"Do you see them, Fe?" the man hissed.

"They must be up ahead," the other voice said.

Lil clutched the end of the torch, her knuckles white as the footsteps faded into the distance. She swallowed, trying to catch her breath, her vision wavering in the torchlight. She told her racing pulse to still, and in doing so felt a second pulse against her skin. She looked down at her arm. How long, she wondered, had Sydney been gripping it? She looked up into Sydney's face and then shifted her position to follow Sydney's gaze into the interior of the chamber.

A shockwave of fear buckled Lil's muscles, sending her knees onto the floor. She stifled a scream. Three doors led out of the chamber. Against the one on their left, three corpses were pinned as if they had met their fate while trying to exit. Three arrows pierced their backs. Lil stared at the one closest to her. A strange-looking necklace had come unclasped and lay on the stone floor. It looked to be a circle with a lightning rod through it. She scanned the rest of them. Three sets of large rubber-soled boots hung from three sets of thin-skinned ankles. Three heads rested together in a dying embrace.

Lil turned back to the door, placing a hand over her mouth, trying to stop herself from retching. She listened as the footsteps faded in the distance.

"Let's get out of here," Lil said, voice wavering.

Sydney squeezed her forearm. "Don't." She nodded to a rope that extended from the bar on the door.

Lil's eyes followed it as it ran from the end of the bolt into the wall, where it disappeared behind the stones.

"Up there," Sydney said, pointing toward the ceiling. Lil raised the torch high, spotting three giant bows with oversized arrows protruding from the shadows. Stone arrowheads, filed to fine points, winked in the candlelight.

"It's a trap," Kat whispered, exhaling.

"I guess that is why we follow the labrys," Charlie said.

"We didn't have a choice," Lil said.

The others nodded silently.

"I think if this goes slack," Sydney said, noting the rope once more, "those are going to fly."

Lil gulped and looked over to the bodies on the far wall. They had met the same fate.

"Maybe we could leave the bolt in place but cut off the part that bars the door? Cut the latch?"

"That might work for a minute," Sydney said, "until we open the door. Then the rope is going to withdraw into the wall anyway. Same result."

"Plus, what are we going to cut the bolt with?" Charlie asked.

Lil looked from corner to corner.

"Where do you think the other doors lead?" Kat said. "That

one"—she pointed toward the one with the corpses pinned to it—"has already been opened."

The door swung slightly on its hinges, like an open fence gate that had been loosened by the hands of time. Lil shook her head. "I don't want to find out." The hinges moaned and bent against themselves like they might break away any second. "But maybe—"

"What are you thinking?" Charlie asked.

Lil looked from the broken hinges, to the hanging door and back to the others. "I might have an idea."

25

il ripped a corner of her shirt away and secured the fabric around her face with a knot behind her head.

"I'm going to need some help," she said as she walked over to the corpses. Kat and Sydney shrank back, but Charlie groaned and went forward. She pulled a clean handkerchief from her pocket, unwrapped it from an extra fountain pen and tied the kerchief around her face.

"What are we doing, Lil?" Charlie's whisper was muffled by the fabric.

Lil knelt down by the first body, choking back the urge to gag as the torchlight illuminated the leathery skin. "We need to move the bodies and remove the door," she said.

"I wouldn't disrupt a resting place," Kat said, getting up from her spot.

Lil looked from the bodies to Kat and back again. "I don't think they're at rest," she said. "I don't think they were ever at rest here."

Kat's eyes brightened with tears.

"Maybe we could set them peacefully to the side," Lil said.

"I would highly recommend not touching them at all," Sydney muttered. She pressed her glasses up her nose and pulled her sleeves down over her palms, kneading them with her fingertips.

"It's our only way out of here," Lil said, turning her attention back to the corpses.

"I hope you know what you're doing," Charlie said, pulling the sleeves of her sweater over her hands.

"Here," Kat said, untying her cardi-wrap from her shoulders and holding it out to Lil. "Sydney's right. You can't touch them. You're going to get sick."

"Thank you," Lil said, accepting the soft material. Kat took the torch as Lil wrapped her arms, and then she reached over the first body and grasped an arrow. It stuck for a moment and then popped and released, sending the corpse onto the ground. She saw a shoulder bone give way at the joint and turned, hearing the scrape and clack of it hitting the stone. She pressed her eyes closed as someone behind her threw up.

"I don't have the stomach for this," Sydney groaned.

"Me neither," Charlie added.

"We have to do this," Lil said, feeling a sense of revulsion building up inside her. "We'll end up just like them if we don't get out of here. You realize that, right?"

She swallowed and grabbed the second arrow. Charlie took a deep breath, sucking the kerchief in around her cheekbones as she grabbed the last arrow.

"Just close your eyes," Lil said. She pressed her eyes shut and pulled the arrow from the wood. The corpse dropped onto Lil's foot and she jerked back, smacking her shoulder into the wall.

She set down the arrow and watched as the door creaked and swung on the weak joint. As Lil opened her eyes, she stared into the black interior. The torchlight seemed to die in the face of the darkness. It was unable to go farther. The only thing detectable was the frayed end of a rope, tucked in the corner of the door.

Lil felt a grip on her shoulder and turned. "Let's keep working," Charlie said.

"All right. Let's get the door off the hinge," Lil said, trying not to gaze into shadows.

Charlie reached in and grasped the outer edge of the door and yanked on it, testing the remaining hinge.

"It's pretty secure," Lil said, watching the bolt catch. She handed the cardi-wrap back to Kat and took the torch, lowering it to the hinge and held it there until the wood started to catch on fire. Then she lifted her foot and kicked at the flames several times. Every time she kicked, the fire seemed to wrap farther into the grain, to dig a little deeper. She hit it quickly, just feeling the tiniest bit of warmth beyond the edge of her sneaker. The wood cracked around the bolt. She gave it one final kick, jarring it from its place. Lil grabbed it at the top as it lunged free, balancing it on her shoulder while holding the torch in her opposite hand.

"Let's lift it and throw it into the center," Lil said hurriedly as the remaining flames climbed toward her fingers. "Put the fire out."

Lil, Kat and Charlie hoisted the door above the corpses and tossed it into the center of the room. Lil jumped on it, stomping the flames. Fire dissipated to smoke and peeled away from them, twirling toward the darkness and disappearing in the opposite tunnel.

Lil reached down and grasped the edge of the door again.

Sydney came forward, too, and they all pushed their fingers under the wooden edge.

"What's the plan?" Kat said.

"Let's stand it up," Lil said. They hoisted the door to an upright position.

"I see; we're using it as a shield?" Sydney asked.

Lil nodded. "When they tried to leave"—she looked over her shoulder—"they just darted outside. We need to protect our backs. We'll hold this up like a shield when we open the door."

"The rope will withdraw," Sydney said, looking at the door, "and fire the arrows, but we'll be protected."

"And we'll head back into the hallway. Is everyone clear?" Lil asked.

Charlie, Kat and Sydney nodded.

"On three, lift," Lil said.

They hoisted the shield up, positioning it so that they were sandwiched between it and the exit.

"Now," Lil said, grasping the outer edge with one hand to prop it up more securely, "we need to keep it steady while we open the door." Charlie grasped the outer edge on the opposite side and Sydney and Kat bore the weight in the middle.

Lil held the torch with her free hand, feeling the weight of the door stretching her forearm muscles on the other side. "Sydney, can you grab the latch?"

"Anything to get us out of here," Sydney said, stepping away from the shield and lifting her hand toward the door.

Lil tightened her grip on the outer edge, praying that this would work. Sydney reached for the latch. "Wait," Lil said. She turned to Kat and Charlie. "Just make sure that the shield is covering our necks and backs. If it slips, we—we want to make sure we get hit . . ."

"In a nonvital organ?" Sydney finished.

"Right."

They nodded and Sydney reached for the latch once more.

"Ready?"

Lil took a deep breath. If this worked, they would be back on the path. The path to finding out what happened to her mother. A shiver ran up her back and into her hair. If it didn't work, they would be dead, just like the people already entombed here. She felt the weight of the disk on her neck. Eventually the man and woman would circle back around and retrieve it from her lifeless body.

"We're going to have to go quickly once we're in the hallway," she heard herself saying. "In case they're out there. In case they smell the smoke."

"Right," Kat said.

"This is getting heavy," Charlie whispered from the opposite side.

"Okay, on three, Sydney."

Sydney grasped the latch.

"One . . . two . . ."

"Keep it high," Kat said.

"Three," Lil whispered.

Sydney pulled the bolt. The rope zipped as it yanked back and spun into the wall. The door swung open.

Lil felt the *thunk, thunk, thunk* as the arrows sliced through the air, embedding themselves in the wood. The force threw the girls forward, and they collapsed into the hallway. Lil felt a sharp sting in her back.

"Is everyone okay?" Lil whispered, hand tightening around the torch. She reached over her shoulder with the other hand, feeling a small cut where the tip of an arrow had pierced her skin.

"*Oui, et toi?*" Charlie said.

"Okay," Lil answered. "Just a scratch. Let's get this off."

The wood slid against stone as they pushed it off, then Lil grabbed the handle of the door and pressed it closed with a sigh of relief. She turned to the hallway, eyes scanning. It seemed clear in both directions.

"Let's go quietly. And watch for the labrys," she said.

They turned and hurried as quickly as they could, down the corridor.

26

Horatio fingered the fleece and buckles on the special bag he had been given to hold the Icarus Folio. He saw the opportunity to use it, to fill it, slipping from his grasp.

"So this is the way to the nebulous chamber," Felice said, running her hand along the map.

Horatio felt a bolt of rage fill him. "What is the purpose of going forward without the key?" he said, pulling his hand from the bag. "We can't get out. Right now we don't need directions, Felice. We need to pursue and retrieve."

His sister stopped, her eyes flicking to him and away. Horatio felt his face heat up. Was she judging him? She always had a way of doing that. He was too emotional, too illogical, she would say. But now, here, he was the only one *with* any logic.

"We need to find the key, not the nebulous chamber," he said. "We need to find the keepers and take the key back."

"I understand that—"

"Then do something," Horatio bellowed. "You're the one who's good at navigating. That's your skill, isn't it? Where are we?"

"The cartograph predates this section," Felice said, rolling the map up. "The rooms—I don't see one they could have slipped into. So"—she turned looking at three paths that split off in front of them—"the question is, which way did they go?" She stepped forward and perked up her ears, then turned back the way they came. "And yet, I hear something behind us."

Horatio stared at her. "Let's retrace our steps," she said.

Horatio looked both ways. He grasped the pendant around his neck. He didn't hear anything. Not behind them, anyway. He listened closely to the corridors. He listened to the hum of the labyrinth. He listened for the songs of Zeus walking through the passageways, ruling over his tribe.

He heard a skitter. Felt a footfall? Felt the pull, the tingle of energy, and turned toward the far right passage.

"I think that passageway ends there," Felice said. "Let's turn back. That won't take you anywhere, brother."

"Your doubt blinds you, Fe," he said.

"I am confident I hear something," Felice said. "Back toward the outer passage."

The problem with Felice, he thought, was that when she was the least confident, she overcompensated by acting overly confident. Horatio felt the pull of the lord calling him on.

He took another step and placed his hand on his satchel. He closed his eyes and invoked Zeus' presence, picturing the god walking the chambers of this labyrinth long, long ago. The lord could lead him straight to them. He stepped into the darkened hallway, the flashlight illuminating a narrowing passage. It would be a perfect place for them to hide: no sign of oil wells to lay flame to. No light to guide their way. They could snuff out a torch and blend into the shadows quite comfortably. Horatio walked along it, trying to see into its depths, but too entranced by the curve at the far end, he hadn't notice the lack of stonework below. He hadn't noticed the large hole. Not until his foot curled over a loose edge. He fought to stay upright, but the more he scrambled, the more the floor disappeared from beneath him. His hands reached out, but caught nothing. And then he fell, down, down, down, onto hard ground, the flashlight flying from his grasp and burying its light in the wall.

27

The girls hurried down the hallway, Lil taking the time to run the torch over every door, sending crackling cobwebs fleeing toward the stone.

They took a left, and Lil spotted a labrys. This one seemed to be constructed of pebbles and shells, layered on top of one another. Above the door was a stained-glass window. It showed a picture of a woman along with a ship boasting a flag that held a set of bull horns.

Lil lowered her torch, revealing several tablets hanging from leather thongs. Each of the tablets was a rectangle about the length of a forearm and twice as wide. They followed the same pattern as before, and Lil scanned quickly to the bottom, where she saw the English.

Charlie pulled her notepad from her pocket and began scribbling as Lil read aloud.

> "Here lay Europa, Zeus' stolen bride,
> Carried forth her brother's trade, just to stay alive.
> Find Europa's story, patterned side by side.
> Finish what is started in the oldest archive."

Lil raised the torch, looking for the sconce in the wall. It was broken off, but there was still a metal piece protruding from the stone. Lil reached up and grabbed it. It was jagged against her palm, but she wound her hand around it and yanked it down. The wall to their right opened, the bricks spinning and twisting over one another until they came to rest in the shape of an archway. The room sent a chilly breath over them, bending the torchlight as Lil forced herself inside. There was something eerily pleasant about this chamber, though. An unmistakably sweet smell emanated from it. Something like honey and flowers.

"What is that?" Sydney said as the torch illuminated the room. Lil knew what she was talking about right away. There, a few feet in front of them, was a large, knobby growth, as though a tumor had bubbled up from the floor. She stepped toward it tentatively, peering at it from every angle, bending the light to it with a shaking hand. As she circled, she feared what she might find on the other side. But the only thing that stared back at her was more of the same. It wasn't moving. Lil reached out to it, ran her fingertips along the hard coating. The honey scent was stronger now. And as Lil took her hand away, she realized that it wasn't bubbling up from the floor. It was sinking into it.

"Wax," she said, feeling it on her fingertips. "It's a giant candle." It smelled just like the candles upstairs. Beeswax, Lil thought. She placed the torch to the wick, and it burst to life. The archway behind them closed. The bricks spun and swiveled back into place until there was no way of telling that a door had ever been there at all. Lil's body coursed with adrenaline as her eyes surveyed the dark room. Forward, the only way to go.

"More light," Charlie said from the shadows. Lil moved to her. There in the corner of the room was another candle, sliding its way down the wall. She placed the torch to it and then worked her way clockwise, lighting one after another, her eyes widening as each candle revealed the chamber more.

Stone shelves rose from floor to ceiling. They were striped

with what could have been mistaken for the bindings of books but were the stone ends of tablets. Between each set of shelves stood an arched alcove, giving the room the air of a library with reading nooks. Lil saw that there were candles within the alcoves themselves and as she lit them one by one, she saw that little benches occupied each space beneath fading wall frescos.

"This one's different from the others," Lil said as she reached the far end of the room. She held the torch aloft and looked into it.

Instead of a bench there was a bed. It was made of stone from foot to frame, but with a topping of matted fibers. She pressed her hand into it momentarily, then jerked it back, wondering what animal might have decided to take refuge in the hay.

"It's an archive," Charlie said from behind her. She turned to see Charlie select one of the tablets from the wall. "An actual archive. What is this script?" She looked from corner to corner. "It's almost as if this room was used as a study." She pressed the tablet back into place. "A long, long time ago." Then she looked from one alcove to the next. "These urns, these benches," she said, shaking her head. "You wouldn't see them so well preserved even in a museum."

Lil looked at her. She looked at the artifacts. She thought about the Minotaur chamber, and now Europa, an eerie feeling coming over her. "Are you suggesting that Europa lived here?"

Charlie nodded. "I don't know. Someone did. Didn't Colleen say that myth and history had intersected because it had all been handed down orally? Maybe Europa was real. Maybe she stood here?"

Lil's back bristled with nerves.

"You're joking, right?" Sydney said. "They didn't exist. It was mythology. Fake by definition."

Kat stared at a tapestry that seemed woven from reeds

between two of the alcoves. "'Everything you think you know, abandons you within,'" she whispered.

"Indeed," Charlie said, talking faster now. "Archaeologists didn't believe that Troy existed before Schliemann uncovered it below a modern city. They knew the story, they had the *Iliad*, but they thought it was mythology, folklore, until they found the artifacts."

"Then why wouldn't this be uncovered? If this is real, wouldn't it be important to have in a museum?" Sydney said, shaking her head in disbelief.

"Well, that's just it," Lil said, her mind spinning. She clutched the disk. "Maybe no one wants it to be. Whatever's down here must be important"—she glanced at the door—"for people to die over it. To hunt us for it."

Charlie spun. "History revealed?"

"Treasure?" Kat said.

Secrets? Lil wondered.

Charlie looked down at her paper and surveyed the room once more. She stopped as she glanced over Lil's shoulder. "Over here," she said, walking to the other side of the room.

There was a nook that they'd missed. One right next to where they'd entered. Lil followed Charlie, ducking into the musty alcove. This one had a desk in it. A simple one, built into the stone wall. A candle sat atop it and Lil set the torch to the wick, lighting the scene with a fiery glow. From the center of the desk rose what looked like the inner workings of a broken typewriter, but old, made of stone and wood. Instead of keys, it had just six levers. Six little catapult-type arms that lay against the table. Each arm was topped with a round wooden holder. The first three holders already held what looked like stone stamps. The second three were empty. And in the top part of the mechanism, where a piece of paper might be on a typewriter, sat a rectangular wooden frame. It was filled halfway with clay, and imprinted in the clay were three symbols, marked there by the stamps in the first three holders. Lil peered at them. A shell, three parallel squiggly lines and then what looked like a yoke. She immediately recognized them. How many times had she traced them as she stared at her mother's necklace? The disk at her side was just a replica of the same. She lifted it, comparing the two. What did one have to do with the other?

Charlie pulled the seat from beneath the desk and sat down. She took a deep breath and set the notepad in front of her. "'Here lay Europa, Zeus' stolen bride . . . Carried forth her brother's trade, just to stay alive.' Europa's brother was Cadmus. He was known for introducing the alphabet to the Greek world."

Kat picked up one of the stone stamps from the top of a pile at the edge of the desk. She tilted it between her index finger and thumb. She lined it up with one of the levers at the base of the old typewriter. "It's as if these are letters or characters. Except you would have to switch them out regularly depending on what you are trying to write." She scrutinized the symbols. "Which would make sense if Europa was, in fact, a scribe. But was she?"

"*Je ne sais pas,*" Charlie said, tilting her head to the side. "They didn't talk much about Europa in the myths. I only remember that she was enamored with a bull, Zeus in disguise, who carried her across the sea on his back to Crete. But this is different. Perhaps this is her true story?"

Lil stared down at the riddle. "It says, 'patterned side by side.'" She scanned the desk. "I don't see a pattern. Do you see a pattern?"

Sydney leaned over the pile of stamps as Kat placed the one she was holding back at the top. "Not particularly."

Lil stared at the incomplete tablet. She looked at the disk.

Perhaps when they had said the disk was a "key" they meant it was a key to a puzzle. She saw the yoke. She spotted the three squiggly lines. She saw the shell on the outer edge, but none of them seemed to line up. It was like using a code to decipher a code.

"I don't see a pattern, either," Lil said, dropping the disk to swing around her neck once more.

"But the shell—" Charlie said, touching the indentation with her fingertips. "Didn't we just . . ." She spun toward the interior of the chamber. "There."

Charlie pointed over Lil's shoulder. Lil turned.

"Where?" Lil said, searching the first fresco. There was Europa. She was standing under a tree, smiling.

"See?" Charlie said, pointing at the keystone above it.

They crossed to it and Lil lifted the torch higher. As she did, she saw a shell imprinted on it.

"That's the first symbol," Lil said.

If they were supposed to finish her story, and that one was the first symbol on the tablet, then it must be the beginning. She perused the scene. "Before she is taken by Zeus. She must be home? On this beach?" She moved toward the next fresco.

"Then," Charlie said, "she gets abducted by Zeus in the form of a bull and carried across the sea."

"This is where your story falls apart," Sydney said, "the human-animal love affairs." But as they peered into the alcove, Lil could see a man—not a bull—standing by a ship that boasted a flag with bull horns.

The keystone above this alcove showed the three squiggly lines.

"The lines depicting their journey across the water?" Kat said. "But instead of on the back of a bull like Colleen was telling us about, it was on a ship."

"Maybe," Charlie said, snapping her pen cap on and off with vigor. "Crete is known for its bull worship and bull history. I remember reading that when they had earthquakes, they blamed it on the bull within the ground, shaking his horns in a fury."

"So it wasn't an animal-human love affair after all?" Sydney said.

"Perhaps the story was confused when it was handed down because Cretans were simply known as bulls," Charlie explained.

Lil considered the fresco and the story. It was easy enough for a story to change in a single afternoon around town. How much would it change through time? It sounded possible. More possible than the mythology.

"That actually makes me feel a little better," Sydney said.

Charlie moved to the next alcove. Lil looked up at the yoke on the keystone and below at the fresco. Europa was standing, her bound wrists raised to the sky.

"The third symbol," Charlie said, scribbling in her notebook. "It looks like a yoke . . . Must symbolize her captivity."

"But I thought she fell in love with Zeus as a bull?" Kat said.

Charlie shook her head. "Depends who you are reading. The romantics would say 'fell in love' or 'wooed'; other sources would say 'abducted.'"

"That's a little different," Kat said.

Lil watched Europa's face in the flickering light. It seemed to twitch with pain. If these old frescoes were telling a true story, it was an awfully sad one.

"That's the last symbol in the wooden holders," Sydney said, moving back to the desk. "We have the shell, the lines depicting water and the yoke depicting captivity. What is the next part of the story? What is the next symbol?"

Lil saw her spread the stamps out and examine them before she, Charlie and Kat moved to the next alcove.

The keystone showed a circle around a figure of a woman. "Birth," Charlie said without hesitation. "She bore Minos, one of the most famed figures on Crete."

"What is the symbol exactly?" Sydney said from across the room.

"A woman in a circle," Charlie said.

"Got it!" Sydney said, picking up one of the stone stamps. She hesitated, the stamp hovering over the wooden arm. Lil could read her thoughts. What would happen if it was the wrong choice? Was it engineered like the automaton? Or like the arrows in the trap?

"What if—" Kat started.

"I don't know," Lil said. "It has to be the right answer."

Sydney nodded. "We don't have many other options and this makes the most sense."

"Go ahead and put it in," Charlie said, scribbling on her notepad as she made her way to the next alcove.

Sydney took a deep breath and placed the stamp into the wooden arm. Lil couldn't help but brace herself as it clicked into place, her eyes darting around the room, waiting for something to happen, to spring out at them, for the walls to start moving, for javelins to come piercing up through the floor. When nothing changed, there was an audible sigh of relief among them. They hurried to the next alcove.

Lil shivered as she looked at the fresco within. It was dimmer than the others, both the torch and the wall painting. On the upper right-hand side was a yellow-and-tan drawing of a large building. A variety of pictographs littered the sky and ground. And below was a picture of Europa, her right arm extended with nothing but a stick in her hand. She looked, for a moment, like a little kid drawing her name in the sand.

"A hand with a pen," Charlie said, staring up at the keystone.

Lil looked down at the disk around her neck.

"Perhaps symbolizing her invention of the language? Her role as scribe?" Kat said as she traced a pictograph of a bird with outstretched wings.

"Got it," Sydney said from across the room as the next stamp clicked into the next wooden arm.

"Just one more," Charlie said, moving to the final alcove.

This one was darker still, barely lit by the candle within. Lil poked the torch inside, straining to see. Her voice caught in her throat. The wall was covered in black flames. And in the center of it were two people. They lay sleeping. Or they lay dead, holding tight to each other's hands between them.

For a moment, Lil's mind flashed to Mom in her coffin. She shook her head, trying to banish the thought. "Death," she said softly.

"The final symbol," Charlie said. "It's an urn."

"I have it!" Sydney said.

Lil hurried away from the dark alcove as they all crowded around the desk once more. Charlie placed her notepad back down and accepted the final stamp from Sydney. They all looked at one another.

"Here goes," Charlie said.

Lil's body stiffened as Charlie placed the stamp into the sixth and final lever. She pressed it and it snapped into place with a satisfying *pop*. For a moment there was only silence. For a moment nothing moved. For a moment the look of tension slid from the girls' faces.

But only for a moment.

A heartbeat later, a small door began to open to the left of the desk. Then it picked up speed, stone grinding so swiftly against stone that it let out a banshee scream. A burst of flame erupted from its belly. They doubled over, shielding their faces as a hot blaze jumped toward them.

28

L il stared into the fire. The blaze was sucked back like it might be contained inside the wall, but then it snaked out, climbing into the ceiling in fiery paths.

"Do you think that's supposed to work like that?" Lil said as she watched the reed tapestry light, curl and fall off the wall. A billow of smoke filled the air, and she covered her nose. She searched the room for an open door, another passageway leading out, but the mechanism hadn't opened anything else.

"No, I don't think so," Kat said, doing the same with the top of her cardi-wrap.

Lil's heart raced as she watched the fire continue, grasping cobwebs and lighting debris. They were going to be smoked to death. She turned toward Charlie.

"Any ideas?" she shouted. "We're in an oven."

Charlie was half off her seat, staring into the flame and then back at the other side of the machine.

"It's a wood-fired oven of some sort!" Sydney shouted, indicating a long-handled paddle leaning against the wall. "My uncle built one of those in his backyard for cooking flatbreads." She yanked the collar of her shirt over her face, too.

"No, no, no," Kat said, shaking her head. "It's a *forno*— how do you say it in English—you fire the sculpture to make it strong?"

"A kiln?" Lil coughed.

"Yes," Kat said, nodding. "It's a kiln." She turned and gestured toward the tablets on the shelves. She pulled the nearest one off and held it out, flicking the corner. "See their colors? See how hard they are?"

Lil stared at the tablet. It was black and charred. They would be just like that if they didn't start moving soon. They had to douse the flames, put them out. She stared around the room, toward the bed. But there were no blankets, only hay. No fabric, anywhere. The path of flame scattered ash down to the floor as it sailed toward the outer alcove.

She turned back toward Charlie, her gaze landing on a spout to her right. A shelf of urns sat above it. She rushed around the desk, twisting the handle. A landslide of muddy water descended, splashing into the large urn at her feet.

"We have to put out the fire," Sydney shouted. She grabbed a small urn from the shelf while Lil filled another and handed it to Kat.

"Of course!" Charlie shouted as Lil filled yet another to the brim and threw its contents at the nearest patch of fire. The flames hissed and sizzled back, then regrouped. More smoke billowed up.

"Of course what?" Sydney wheezed, filling her urn and doing the same.

Kat flew across the room to a spot in the corner where the flame seemed to be attempting to light stone, dousing it, stomping on it. Lil went after the flames that hung in the ceiling like an upside-down grill.

"It's only partly a kiln. This whole thing is one giant machine. Don't you see?" Charlie said. Without hesitating, she reached over Lil's shoulder, thrusting her hand into the base of the urn that was secured to the floor. "It's a printing press!" She yanked and pulled until her hand came up out of the abyss with a loud *schlaaap*. "It's clay," she said, mashing the clay into the frame, completing the tablet. Without hesitation she hit the fourth lever. It burst forward, slapping into the wet clay, then came away, leaving the symbol etched into the glossy surface. Charlie hit the next key, embedding the fifth symbol in the tablet, and then the last. She cranked a lever as Lil exchanged urns with Sydney, handing her a full one and taking an empty one.

"I don't think it's helping!" Kat said as she reached them. She held her elbow over her nose, her eyes circled with red. Lil watched the flame as it stopped momentarily, then danced toward the alcove with the small hay-filled mattress.

"Hurry!" Lil shouted, sloshing half the water onto the ground as she handed an urn to Kat and turned to Charlie.

Charlie cranked the lever on the side and the frame flipped up, depositing the tablet on a revolving paddle. It slid toward the fire as the frame settled back into place.

Lil glanced around the room, looking for a door. Looking for the secret passageway.

"It's still not doing anything!" Lil shouted as smoke billowed toward her. Her eyes burned as she tried to see Sydney in the distance. She heard a cough and a gasp. Charlie swiveled to look into the room, shielding her face with her arm. The flames tore steadily now, diving into the alcove with the bed and causing a patch of fire to erupt along the mattress.

Lil's mind raced. Her throat grew raw and strangled. Her eyes blurred and her head buzzed. "Everyone get down low!" She coughed.

Charlie was on the floor next to her, clutching the tablet. Her eyes darted from corner to corner. "Maybe we need to archive it? Put it on the shelf."

"I can barely see anything," Kat said.

"I can barely breathe," Sydney wheezed.

"Look for spaces on the shelves," Lil said. "We're running out of time." She looked up, counting spaces in the wall in front of her where the tablet might belong. There were perhaps eight.

"I have one, two, three," Sydney said.

"I have several," Kat said.

Lil turned, surveying the walls. "There are over two dozen empty spaces, at least," she shouted.

"Too many options," Sydney coughed.

"Over here," Charlie called to them from the final alcove.

Through gasps and coughs, the girls made their way to the opposite side of the room. Lil could just see Charlie by the blaze of the mattress fire.

She could hear Sydney, her breath a strange whistle.

"Where?" Lil shouted frantically.

"There," Charlie said, pointing to the other side of the bed.

In the wall on the other side of the flames was a rectangular indentation. One that would allow the tablet to fit perfectly.

"Oh God," Kat said.

"I can get to it," Charlie said, grasping Lil's shoulder and pushing herself up before Lil could object.

Charlie landed on the other side, but the flames were hot. Surely they would burn her. The flickering flame, Charlie, the bed and Sydney and Kat began to fade around her, almost like she was seeing them through a tunnel.

"Hurry!" she gasped as Sydney fell into her.

"Oxygen deprivation," Sydney wheezed. "We have three . . . minutes . . ."

Charlie embedded the tablet into the indentation. A grinding noise rose from the chamber, and a door in front of them opened. The smoke was sucked forward like a thick zephyr around them. The flames on the bed blew back, for a moment decreasing. "GO!" Lil said, pushing Sydney. She lurched forward, tripping over the mattress into the far wall. Kat dove next, and Lil jumped up last, grabbing for the wall to steady herself.

"Hurry!" Charlie took her hand as they stumbled into the stairwell.

"Wait," Lil said, reaching back. There was the brick, jutting out just as it had in the previous chamber. Like a little drawer that had been hidden in the wall. When Lil bent over it, she saw that this time it contained a different charm. She grasped the leather thong, pulling it from its resting place. A miniature rectangular tablet hung from the end of it.

Underneath it she could just see the symbol of the labrys through the encroaching cloud of smoke. "Okay," she said, her voice coming out hoarse now. "This is right." Though nothing about it seemed right to her at all. She threw the talisman to Charlie, and they ran into the shelter of the tunnel.

29

Horatio scrambled for his light. It couldn't have been a draft. His ego, his elbow and his heart were bruised as he clutched the gold pendant of Zeus. The lightning rod, poking from the edge of the circle into the palm of his hand. Perhaps Zeus was trying to teach him the lessons of humility? Perhaps before one can gain eternal life, he thought, he needs to be humbled. He kissed the pendant and told himself to be patient. Then he reached for the flashlight, dusted it off and sent the beam to the trapdoor many feet above. Felice's face appeared over the edge.

"Throw me the rope," Horatio shouted, grasping at the wall. Why wasn't she getting it out already?

"Are you all right, 'Ratio?"

Horatio groaned. "Fe, do you think I would be asking for the rope if I was hurt? Please just throw me the rope and get me out of here." He felt the heat rising to his head. "It's getting late. We're going to miss them."

Felice pulled the rope from her satchel. "If you had listened to me and turned back to follow the noise, you wouldn't be in this predicament, so don't be mad at me about it."

Horatio slammed a fist into the wall, grasping a nearby root and strangling it. She was always the first to point out his mistakes.

"Hurry up!" he shouted, his chest forming knots. "Hurry up."

The rope descended into the pit, whipping his shoulder as it appeared.

He grabbed it.

"Not yet," Felice shouted. "Let me tie it off on this root."

She disappeared from the edge for a moment, and Horatio flipped the flashlight off and placed it into his satchel. He counted to ten, waiting for her to hurry. His fingers ran over the Deus Maxima beads that he always had at his side. They clicked against one another as they ran swiftly between his fingers. Ares had given them to him when he was a child and he kept them in his pocket to this day. When he felt as though he might lose his temper, he would run them through his fingers, counting individually, then by twos, then by fours, then by sixes. Just pressing his fingers along the wooden spheres made him calmer, somehow. Made his mind work better, strengthened his intuition. Listen to Felice, it was telling him. Do not be too prideful.

"All right," Felice said, reaching the edge once more. "Climb away."

Horatio deposited his beads back into one pocket, and jammed the flashlight into his other as he grasped the rope. He planted his feet and moved quickly up the wall, pulling himself over the top.

"Do you still hear them?" he asked as he yanked the end of the rope up from the abyss.

"Yes," Felice said. "Back the way we came."

Horatio handed her the ropes and wiped the dirt from his body. He wouldn't argue with her, not this time. "Lead the way," he said.

Felice lifted her head like a hound on a hunt, and they stalked back the way they had come.

30

The torchlight cast a warm glow around them, and Lil felt a surge of energy as they moved forward. This passage was larger, wider. The ceiling was higher. There was more space. More air. Less death.

Lil glanced at her watch. It was two o'clock in the morning. Seven p.m. in Vermont. Dad would be eating dinner soon alone, his mind spinning with unanswered questions as night was falling. And here was Lil feeling the bounce of the disk by her waist. With the labrys leading the way, surely she was coming closer to answers. What they were she didn't know.

"If these are all ancient artifacts," Charlie mused, "then this place—this labyrinth—is a treasure trove. Archaeologists would die to see this stuff."

"It just doesn't make sense," Sydney said. "If Bente and the others knew this was down here, why not just turn it in and make money?"

"Put it in museums," Kat said, coughing. "Why hide it?"

Lil shook her head. "I don't know." Her throat was still raw from the smoke, and she automatically reached for her hip, as if her water bottle holder might be there, but her hand came up empty.

The sound of a flag tossing in the wind flapped overhead. She looked up, holding the torch high. She spotted a large, winglike sail. Ten feet farther, she could detect the corner of another.

"I think this is it," Sydney whispered.

Lil jerked to a stop. She was so busy looking at the sails, she hadn't even noticed the door to their right.

"See," Sydney said, moving a large root to the side, revealing the labrys. Unlike the dark and multicolored rocks that made up the passageways, this labrys was made out of white sandstone. As the light radiated over it, she could see the surface was rough with what looked like fossilized leaves.

Lil panned the torchlight over the door until the glow landed on a dusty old plaque to the right. The English, at the bottom, was covered by twigs and sticks, and Lil reached down and pulled the debris away until they could see the inscription.

> *Daedalus—the first to test flight,*
> *Great inventor, miscalculated height?*
> *And his boy would meet a sorry plight.*
> *If only they had flown at night.*
> *Creation to destruction bends*
> *Despite a father's wish to make amends.*
> *Select the tool he used to mend*
> *And a helping hand do lend.*

Charlie quickly scribbled the text into her notebook, flipping the page and proceeding to the next. Lil looked both ways down the hall, tapping her foot.

"All set," Charlie said, nodding.

Lil looked up at the sconce by the window. "Would you like to do the honors?" she asked, looking to Sydney.

Sydney scowled. "Not particularly."

Lil reached up and pulled the sconce. As the door opened, a small switch flipped at the hinge and the chamber lit with a soft glow. They stepped inside and the door closed, bolts locking into place.

The room was round. And as Lil peered inside, it took a moment to realize what she was seeing. Lamps popped to life all around the walls, springing out like little glowing toadstools of varying colors. Candle flames hooded by stained glass. Malformed and thick stained glass, but stained glass, nevertheless. They were all different, as if each were a useful experiment but not yet perfected.

The rest of the room was a mess. A rough-hewn desk sat against the far wall. Tablets were scattered from the desk to the floor. Chisels and daggers, cudgels and arrowheads hung from hooks on the walls. One corner was a resting place for a large, floor-to-ceiling labrys. Other hooks were vacant, their tools scattered on the floor. A sculpture loomed to the right, a half-formed face emerging from the rock. Next to it sat a long bench with tablets covered in fossilized leaves. The plants that had made the prints had long since disintegrated.

The strangest piece was the wheel protruding from the left wall sitting parallel to the floor.

"And there are the wings," Charlie said, looking up. Lil glanced toward the ceiling.

There was fabric stretched over thin wooden frames. Some had tapered edges, others rounded. Some were shaped like dragon or bat wings, others like the long, smooth wingspan of a blue jay. There was one pair, hung just above the others, made of feathers, and it loosed a few quills to the ground as they stepped toward the center. The girls crowded around Charlie, who turned her notebook back to the beginning of the riddle.

"'Creation to destruction bends,'" Sydney said. "I don't like the sound of that."

Lil swallowed, surveying the room. "Do you guys see anything obvious?"

"Just the wings," Kat said. "The wings Icarus used were ones with wax, right? They melted in the sun?"

"Right," Charlie said, "but that's what we *know* as the story. That may not truly be the case." She tapped the barrel of her pen on her notepad. "The traditional story says that Daedalus built wings to escape from the labyrinth. He was imprisoned there"— she gulped—"here, by Minos."

"'If only they had flown at night,'" Sydney said, shaking her head. "Ridiculous."

"What do you mean?" Lil asked, looking at the quills lying at her feet.

"I mean, the poem—" She took the notepad from Charlie and read aloud. "'Daedalus—the first to test flight,/Great inventor, miscalculated height?/And his boy would meet a sorry plight./ If only they had flown at night.' He would never have tried to fly with wax wings in the daylight," she scoffed, handing back the notepad. "Wax melts in the heat, anyway. They would have melted before they even left the ground. Like I said, that story is ridiculous. I mean, if we're going with this ludicrous theory that we need to untangle myth from history. Well, if he was a great inventor, he wouldn't have made that mistake."

"Sydney's right," Lil said. "Daedalus can build a winding labyrinth, but he can't figure out that he shouldn't fly in Crete with wax wings?"

"Valid point," Charlie said, scowling and putting the end of her fountain pen to her lip.

Sydney smacked it out of her hand. "That's disgusting. Are you trying to get typhoid?"

"Well, what if they had limited resources?" Kat asked, sidling up to the half-completed sculpture. "What if wax and feathers were all he had?"

Sydney looked up at the canvas wings. "I have a feeling they had a lot more than wax and feathers. Even the earliest inhabitants of the earth created technologies." She nodded toward the arrowheads, daggers and battle-axes. "You employ your resources. They had bronze and gold and wood and stone, and they had ships manned by thousands with giant oars. They had tools and fabrics." She tugged on one of the cloth wings.

"Well, if it isn't the wings, then what?" Lil said.

"In the other rooms, there was something that seemed different from the rest," Charlie said, picking up her pen and wiping it off on her pants.

"The sculpture is different," Kat said, looking into the one completed eye. "Art, not technology."

"Well, it's not really that different," Sydney said, going to it. "Art and technology are both created. The wings were a creation. The axes were a creation. The labyrinth, a creation. They share creation."

"The lamps were a creation," Lil said, accidentally knocking one of the glass tops to the ground. It hit the stone and shattered at her feet. She jumped back as the splintered glass skittered toward her legs. She held her breath, waiting for the walls to move or the room to go up in flames, but nothing happened.

"'Creation to destruction bends,'" Lil said, backing away from the wall. "We need to find something that causes destruction."

"But that's the point," Sydney said. "All of this causes de-struction—or is destroyed." She went to the other wall. "You cre-ate an ax, it can be used to slice off someone's head. You create an arrow, it can be used to cut straight through organs." She moved to the sculpture and picked up the hammer and chisel. "You create a sculpture by destroying its original form. They're inter-twined. You can't have one without the other. It's cyclical." She set the hammer and chisel down and stared at the wooden wheel.

"Like nature," Kat said.

"Right," Sydney said, leaning over the spoked wheel. "Cy-clical." She tentatively placed her finger to a stopper, flipping it forward.

For a moment, nothing happened. Then the wheel turned. The sound of water rippled through the walls, and the wheel spun faster. A rush of wind swooped into the room. The stained-glass lamps were snuffed out. Lil was blind, hunched over the torch, trying to protect it from the same fate. The wind changed course, sending the flame hungrily up her arm. It bit at her skin, and she batted it away, dropping it from her hand. The torch clattered on the floor. Someone screamed behind her. Was it Charlie? Was it Kat? Lil turned to see. To help. But the chamber dissolved into darkness.

31

Lil's skin smarted as she reached into her pocket with the opposite arm. She yanked out the box of matches, glad she had thought to grab them to go to the library earlier that night. The wind slowed to a modest breeze and she lit the match, holding her hand around it to protect the flame. She spotted the torch first. Just two feet away. She shuffled to it, relit the top and held it aloft.

She spun. The sound of water still rushed somewhere unseen. As she looked back to the center of the room, she saw a large gaping hole. She leaned over to examine the opening. It was perfectly round, like a sewer drain.

"Help!" Kat's voice rose up from the dark. "Charlie's hurt!"

Lil's heart catapulted into her throat.

She bent the torch in, trying to see how far down it went, but it only lit the opening with a hellish halo.

"Over here, Lil, please!" came Sydney's voice.

Lil looked up. There across the way, Sydney was leaning hard against a cog in the wheel, but it pushed relentlessly on, dragging her toward the wall.

"It's a turbine!" Sydney shouted, her face straining.

Lil ran to her, trying to understand.

"Water propulsion," she said. "I opened the door. I can't stop it." She shifted as she reached the wall, pressing her back into it and extending a foot against the wheel.

"Help! Something's coming!" Kat screamed, and Lil heard a rush of water below.

Lil slammed the torch into the hand of the nearby statue and sidled in next to Sydney.

Planting her feet against the wall, next to Sydney's shoulder, she winced as a cog pushed into her ribs. With her feet planted, the wheel seemed to jolt and give. Then with another gush of water, it redoubled its strength. She'd never in her life felt something so powerful.

"I don't know if I can hold it," Lil gasped.

"It's too much," Sydney said. "It's going to crush us."

Lil fought for breath, her muscles straining against the wheel.

"Please!" Kat shouted. "Throw down the fabric. Or something. Please!"

"The water's rising!" Charlie shouted.

Lil stared at the wall in front of her, trying to remember how many wings were on the ceiling. Would there be enough to reach Kat and Charlie if they tied them together? "We're not going to be able to stop the water," she said, the wheel's cog biting between her ribs. "Maybe we can get a sail and send it down the chute."

She sent all her strength to her legs.

Sydney squeezed her eyes closed and nodded. "We just have to move without getting crushed."

"You go first. Let go and duck under my legs," Lil said.

"You sure?" Sydney gasped. Lil saw her legs quake.

Of course, she wasn't sure. Would she be able to hold it on her own? But Kat and Charlie needed them, and they needed to, somehow, get out of this.

"Yes," Lil said, bracing her feet an inch farther apart. "Go now!"

Sydney dropped and rolled out of sight. The wheel dug into her back, and Lil could feel herself breaking under the weight. She took a deep breath, pushed and dove to her left, crashing hard against the floor. The wheel snapped into a fast spin above her head. She stayed low, sure it could easily break her neck if she got it caught between the spokes. Lil could hear the water gushing in the walls and in the chamber below. Faster now.

"NO, nonononono!" Sydney shouted.

Lil looked up. Her vision wobbled. But she saw Sydney scramble across the floor. She saw a circular lid sail across the opening. Sealing Kat and Charlie inside.

Sydney looked up at her. "They're going to drown!"

Lil leaped up and tore the torch from the sculpture's raised hand. Then she landed next to Sydney, trying to find the seam. As she felt for the corners, her fingers scraping against the hard stone, she paused. The top of the door was changing before her eyes. First, a small rectangular plaque holding three wooden objects revealed itself. Next a little door opened and something began to appear.

"It's a hand," Sydney gasped. It was lifelike, but wooden, like the automaton had been.

Lil bent her head to the seal. The sound of rushing water seemed to be louder. She could hear Kat—or was it Charlie? The voice was too muffled to discern. Her heart pounded against her rib cage, her mouth going dry. Her mind raced, trying to think of what to do. If she could pry open the door. Send something down. But her fingers bent against stone, more likely to snap back on themselves than to accomplish anything.

"Okay," Sydney said, pushing the arms of her glasses firmly back behind her ears. "This is a puzzle, just like all the others." She nodded. "We do this right, we open the door. It's going to be okay."

"We can do this," Lil said, wiping some sweat from her upper lip.

"We need to remain calm and think," Sydney said. "It's just that I don't remember the riddle."

Lil's mind raced, trying to recall what it said. "Something about a tool he used to mend."

Sydney's eyes shone with tears, and Lil watched her eyelids flicker fast as she tried to blink them back. Or was she trying to remember the details of the riddle that was now with Charlie, far out of reach?

"What tool is used to mend?" Lil asked, looking down at the three objects next to the hand. First, a wooden compass. Next, a small set of wings. Third, a crossed hammer and chisel. And one empty spot at the right. What if the answer had been there? Now it was gone. Then they wouldn't be able to open the door. Lil banished the thought from her mind. The only thing she was sure of was that one of the objects was meant to be placed in the hand. But which? All of them seemed to be equipped with a handle that would match the fingers. How did it work? Did it detect a variation in weight? Did it detect the width of the object's handle? They all seemed to be slightly different sizes.

"So we choose the correct tool and place it into the hand and it will open the door," Lil said.

Sydney nodded, grimacing. "If the pattern so far in this place is correct, we ignore the common story," she said, scanning the items. "We know the wings are out. They didn't mend anything. Instead, Icarus died by them."

"Right," Lil said.

Sydney rambled on. "The compass, a tool used to measure, not to mend."

"HELP!"

Lil shuddered as the voice jumped toward the door. The water must have been high now, pushing Charlie and Kat closer and closer to the ceiling. Closer and closer, and yet there was no way to reach them.

Sydney gulped and placed her hand on the compass, then retracted it. They both looked from one tool to the next.

"None of these are used to mend," Lil said.

"Maybe the chisel? Could you mend something, anything with a hammer and chisel?" Sydney said, moving her hand to the chisel.

"I don't think so," Lil gasped. "It seems more like something you would use to break things apart."

"So?" Sydney said. The water below gurgled, and Lil jerked back as a thump came from the other side of the door.

"They're near the door. They're going to run out of air any second," Lil said, scraping across the stone with her fingers. Her nails screamed and then bent back on themselves. Her fingertips throbbed.

"What do you think was in this spot?" Sydney said, looking at the empty place. "What if that was our key?"

A scream came from below them, but it seemed to fill the room, to bounce around the walls. To echo in Lil's head. Lil heard a gurgle, and a small stream of cold water washed over her fingers. She jerked her head up.

"We're out of time," she shouted.

Sydney scanned the tools once more. "What else did the poem say? There was another line." She muttered a few words under her breath. "'Select the tool he used to mend.'"

"The compass?" Lil shouted. "We're out of time."

Sydney's head snapped up, her eyes going wide and clear. "That's what's missing. 'And a helping hand do lend.' 'Select the tool he used to mend/And a helping hand do lend.'" She held up her hand, palm extended, and then slammed it into the fake hand. The wooden fingers popped and closed, clamping down hard.

"Ahhhhhhhhhh!" Sydney shouted, her face filling with regret.

Lil reached out to pry the wooden fingers, but they released before she could move them. The room shook as the seal peeled back. Rolling water spilled into the chamber. Lil scanned the top, trying to see beyond the black bubbles. Cold water soaked her legs. She shoved her hand into the abyss. As she held her torch high, trying not to let the light go out again, her other hand grasped at nothing. Were they too late? She searched frantically, blindly. No hands, no hair. Nothing but age-old water. Its musty rankness climbed into her nose, making her gag.

Sydney grasped around frantically, her legs and arms soaking. "I don't see them!" she shouted.

Lil leaned farther. Water rolled over her arm for what seemed like an eternity. Something slipped past her fingertips. Was it Kat's hair? She grasped at it, but it disappeared as quickly as it had come.

"Oh God, we lost them," Sydney shouted, her hands coming to her face. "We were too slow. We lost them!"

Lil stared as the water frothed out of the opening like saliva from a hungry mouth. Was it true? An eternity seemed to pass. Her heart started to sink down, down, down, a heavy throb working its way into her stomach. How could this— A hand grabbed the edge of the hole, making her jolt back. Then all of a sudden there was Kat, sputtering up out of the water. A moment later, Charlie came, too, gasping and reaching for something to hold onto. Lil grabbed her and pulled. Kat and Charlie both convulsed, spewing water, drinking in air. For a few moments everyone sat there, breathing, panting as the water flooded the room. Lil collapsed next to Sydney.

"Nicely done," she said, squeezing her shoulder. "Hands can mend."

"We need to get out of here before the water rises more," Sydney said, through gritted teeth. She pushed herself up and pulled Kat with her, pointing toward a stairwell that had opened behind the desk.

"Take . . . to the high . . . ground," Charlie wheezed as she pushed herself to her feet. She reached for the wall, one foot held awkwardly.

"You're hurt," Lil said, positioning herself under Charlie's arm.

Charlie winced, her short brown hair now matted to her head. Her cabled sweater, twisted and torn. *"Un petit peu.* A little." She wiped the water from her face. "I'll manage."

The water surged, licking at the backs of Lil's knees. She fell into step behind Kat and Sydney, helping Charlie to the door. They stopped at the brick that extended from the wall like a small drawer. Lil's eyes found it fast now that she knew what to look for. There, lying in the center, was another charm. Sydney raised it by the leather thong and stared at the symbol that swung from it: hands held in the shape of wings, the thumbs latched together at the center. Sydney draped the pendant over her head as Lil peered into the base of the brick, happy once again to see the labrys. One more clue. One step closer. She pictured her mom carrying her upstairs to bed on that night before she lost her, and she hurried onward, determined to find her again.

32

Horatio followed Felice through a very narrow corridor. As the walls seemed to shrink to crush him, his faith in her was waning once again. Why had she chosen to come this way? They had stalked through three different passages. Each time he tried to question her, she lifted her hand as though she were listening to something, but here they were, as far as he could tell, lost again and in a very tight predicament. If it closed off any more, he would have to find another way around.

"Felice, let's stop and take a look at the cartograph," he said.

Felice extracted herself from the corridor and, he thought, made a show of waiting for him to make his way out.

Sharp stones grasped at his arms as he wound his way from the darkness to a torchlit chamber.

"Don't you hear the screams, 'Ratio?" Felice said, running toward the end of the hall.

Horatio growled, trying to keep the sound of disgust in his throat. She was making things up now, he was sure of it. Yet he followed her still.

They huffed around the corner, and Felice stopped as though getting close to her prey, planting her heel down and then her toes.

"Let's have a look," Horatio said.

"Shh." Felice placed a finger to her lips.

"Do not shush me." Horatio grasped her sleeve at the shoulder and shoved her into the wall. He quickly let go, backing up to the other side of the passage. Counting to ten.

"I think you're getting frustrated," Felice said. "Ares said that the labyrinth has driven people mad in the past."

Horatio pressed his fingers to the bridge of his nose, exhaling loudly. His arm brushed the wall behind him and he felt a steady vibration in it. Was it electricity? He turned to it, placing his palm along it.

"What is it?" Felice asked, coming to him. She placed her hands on the wall beside his.

Horatio looked down to the ground. There, a small puddle began to form from a crack in the stone. He traced the wall with his flashlight, seeing a larger pool of water forming just outside a stone door. There, beneath a few hanging roots, was a labrys. He traced the fossilized ax with his fingertips and gasped. The writings of Hexalodorous were right about their depiction of the deadly innovator's door. His whole body surged, wondering if these plants fossilized here were the ones from the history. The ones used as part of the Icarus Folio.

"It's Daedalus' workshop," he breathed, tracing his fingers along the stone. "And it has been disrupted."

33

The girls climbed the staircase. It began unclut-
tered, but as they ascended, it became busier
until they reached the top and stared into a long,
rock-strewn corridor. Tremors gripped the walls
again and again, and Lil squinted into the distance as she heard
a loud crack and rumble. There were torches in this passageway
and they were dim, but bright enough for Lil to see a stone come
crashing down fifteen yards ahead. It burst against the opposite
wall, shattering and contributing more broken rock to the heavily littered path.

They hadn't walked far before Charlie leaned against the
wall. She set her foot down, then gasped, lifting it back up.

"We should stop and take a look," Lil said, feeling Charlie's
trembling arm across her shoulder.

"We can't stop here. We're out in the open," Charlie pro-
tested, her voice breaking.

"Yeah, we're probably much safer if we find another death
chamber," Sydney said, turning toward them. Lil looked up at
her, trying to detect her expression in the shadows. But her face
was nearly invisible.

"We have few options—"

"We *had* options," Sydney growled. "Before we stepped foot
in here. I haven't seen a single option since then."

Lil felt her throat tighten. Was Sydney saying this was all her fault? Hadn't she told them she would go it alone? "I said—"

"Let's have a look," Kat said, her calm voice smoothing the air. "We can discuss this later. When we're out."

"Yeah, if we get out," Sydney whispered.

Lil lowered Charlie onto a boulder, trying to stay focused. Kat was right: it wasn't worth arguing about. The only thing that mattered was getting Charlie and the rest of them out alive. Charlie groaned as she adjusted herself on the rock. Her breath quickened, and her chest rose up and down in jolts.

Lil knelt in front of Charlie, lifting the heavy fabric of her pant leg. It was cold on Lil's fingers, and she stifled a gasp as she held the torch down to see. Not only was Charlie's leg twisted at an awkward angle, but the skin was broken and bleeding, the clear bump showing that the bone was attempting to cut through midway up the shin.

Lil looked up at Charlie's face. Her brown hair was drenched and hugging the sides of her forehead. It was sweat, not water, Lil realized. Her eyes were closed. Lil's voice strangled, an overwhelming sense of guilt rising in her. "Charlie," she whispered, "listen to me. It's going to be okay." But she wasn't so sure as she watched a bubble of blood rise from Charlie's skin and slide down her leg in a red river.

Charlie's arm went out to the wall, and she leaned her forehead into her torn shirtsleeve.

"Don't touch it," Charlie said. "Please. It hurts."

"We have to stop the bleeding," Lil said.

The sound of fabric tearing echoed nearby, and Lil looked over to see Kat pulling three bands of fabric from the bottom of her cardi-wrap.

"Good thinking," Lil said, taking the bands. "Can you hold the torch?"

Kat nodded, accepting it. She stepped close.

Lil took the first band, letting the others drop into her lap, and squeezed the water from it. "Charlie, listen to me," she said. "This is going to hurt, but it has to be bandaged to stop the bleeding and give your bone support."

Charlie's chest rose and she breathed more rapidly, but she nodded.

The fabric was damp in Lil's hand and she squeezed it again, trying to get all the water out.

"She's going to need antiseptic," Sydney whispered from behind them. "There is no way that water is clean. This is not good."

Charlie's brow furrowed and she glared at both of them. "Just hurry up and do it if you are going to do it," she said through clenched teeth.

"We'll do this," Lil said, "and then we're going to get out of here and get you some antiseptic. Get you to the doctor." Lil folded the fabric into a square and aimed for the center of the shinbone. As soon as the fabric made contact, Charlie stifled a cry, balling her hands into fists. She jerked against the wall. Tears sprang out of her eyes and slid down her cheeks, but she didn't pull away as Lil used the second band of fabric, winding it from the top of the patch toward the bottom. Then she took the third and went from the bottom of the patch toward the top.

Charlie trembled, her eyes blinking rapidly, and Lil lowered her pant leg, hoping that it would at least be slightly more comfortable. Charlie's eyes fixed over Lil's shoulder, and she froze.

"You're all right," Lil said, watching her. "Listen, I know this isn't going to be easy."

Charlie reached out, pressing her hand hard over Lil's mouth. Her eyes fell to Kat, who was staring in the same direction.

"We have to move," Sydney whispered from the shadows, her voice barely audible.

Lil turned and looked over her shoulder, back toward the Daedalus chamber. Back the way they'd just come. Please, let it be water, Lil thought, but she saw the faint glimmer of a stark light, rapidly expanding.

34

L il positioned herself back under Charlie's arm. "Move, move, move," she said as she turned to Kat. "You and Sydney run up ahead."

Kat shook her head as Lil teetered onto a rock, grounding her feet, wiggling her toes in the ends of her sneakers.

"Just go. Leave me behind," Charlie said, veering off to the side, but Lil held her close.

"We're not leaving anyone here." She clamped her arm around Charlie's waist.

"Let's go," Sydney said to Kat. "We'll find the next chamber."

"We'll meet you there," Kat said, looking back at Lil and Charlie.

They turned toward the passageway, and Lil watched as they picked their way over the stones. The mountain rumbled around them, and another cracking sound met her ears.

"Be careful of the rocks!" Lil hissed as one cascaded downward.

Kat and Sydney linked arms, and Lil watched as they made headway, the torch dwindling to a small ball in the distance. Lil tried to relax her muscles. Just like running the ropes course, she told herself. Muscle over mind. Instinct over thought. A rock shifted underfoot as she moved forward, helping Charlie hop onto the next boulder.

"Okay, we'll keep quiet and move as quickly as you can," Lil said, concentrating on landing her feet. Charlie gasped as her foot dragged across the top of a rock. Just aim for the light, Lil thought, eyeing the next torch. Lil turned back toward the doorway. For a moment it was dark, and then the white light appeared again. Blinking and bouncing. A flash, matching the beat of her heart.

"When they appear," Charlie grunted, "you leave me behind. Run for it."

"You know what I think?" Lil said, jumping off a boulder and swinging Charlie down next to her. "I think you've read too many books with noble heroes."

She felt Charlie laugh as they moved forward.

"We've got to go faster," Lil hissed. Her foot caught on a root as they met the shadows. Her arm ached from Charlie's weight. Her legs grew wobbly as she tried to balance on each stepping-stone.

"Stay close to the wall," Lil said. "Stick to the shadows." She moved to the right, pushing Charlie to the stone. Charlie rested a hand on it and hopped as fast as she could over the rough terrain. They passed under a torch, and Lil held her breath until they reached the dark stretch between the last torch and the next one. She slowed, unable to see the ground in front of her as they exited the pool of light, but soon the edges of the rocks were visible, and Lil aimed for their flat tops. Just like the balance beam, only more options, she told herself. Less of a need to land one foot directly in front of the other. Just keep moving. Keep moving. Keep alive. Keep moving. Keep alive.

"It's easy," Lil said, more to herself than to anyone else. Charlie swooped against her arm—up and down with each breath, with each hop. Rhythm.

Lil aimed for the next patch of torchlight. But suddenly it

melted into a stark white puddle, pushing their shadows long and dark in front of them. Lil blinked hard as her eyes tried to adjust to the difference.

A voice echoed from behind them.

"There! Fe, look."

"We're dead," Charlie said as they dove under another torch.

"Shh," Lil whispered as she picked up the pace.

She didn't need to look. They were coming. The beam of light flicked toward them. How far ahead were Kat and Sydney now?

"Just—" Charlie started.

"Just keep looking forward," Lil grunted, feeling the sweat drip down her sides. The light of the flashlight had consumed them now. This is good, Lil thought. She could use the extra light to their advantage. She trained her eyes. Saw each footfall. Each toehold. The nooks of each stone, clear to her like a blessed path leading them on. Jump, step, hop, climb. Breathe, breathe, breathe. Her muscles moved without her. She liked that feeling. That feeling past total exertion, where you become light as air. Her sneakers barely kissed the stones as she carried over them. Charlie held fast on her shoulder, her weight becoming nothing, as if they were as buoyant as water.

"Give up," the woman said, her voice just behind them.

Lil's stomach twisted as she heard metal click, the crisp sound of a firearm being cocked.

"We are dead. We are dead," Charlie said, hopping faster.

"Don't shoot, Fe," a voice huffed. "You'll loose an avalanche on us."

Lil's lungs expanded as if filled with new life. The man was right. They could all be crushed if she discharged the weapon. The rocks were precarious enough already. Now, if only she and Charlie could outstrip them. She pictured herself at ten years old, running up Snake's Vein behind her mother. Momentum. Ignore everything else. She reached up, cleared sweat from her eyes. As they hit the corner, she looked over her shoulder. All she could see was the flashlight beam just a few yards away. It sent a series of mini explosions into her vision, and she immediately regretted it as her feet caught between two rocks. She began to tumble forward.

Charlie gasped, her fist tightening on Lil's shirt. They were falling.

The deafening sound of a crashing wave met her ears. But there was no ocean, not here. Lil's body shot forward as a shadow appeared from above. She felt a hand on her shoulder. Not Charlie's—a second one. It yanked her back as the crashing sound got louder. Rocks rained down, but something bigger was coming, shaking the ground beneath their feet. Lil's hand slipped from Charlie's waist. She fought to keep upright. Charlie was slipping away. A rock exploded just past her shoulder blade, sending huge chunks of stone shrapnel into her side and back.

The second hand released Lil. She toppled over Charlie, rocks grinding into rock. Lil clutched the disk to her side as she tumbled forward.

A gasp met her ears and then a voice, coming from the other side of the pile of rocks that was now right behind her.

"Fe!" the voice said.

Lil fought the knot that appeared in her stomach. Forced her lungs to breathe. She stumbled to her feet. A rock slid from her shoulders and crashed to the floor at the base of the pile. She yanked Charlie to standing. The rock slide had saved them.

"Mon dieu!" Charlie gasped, her voice high and tight.

"We're not stopping here," Lil said through gritted teeth.

They surged ahead again. Lil aimed for the shadows, knowing it wouldn't do much to protect them, but she had to try. A door creaked. A hand grasped her neck. She pulled against it. It twisted her shirt, tightening it fast against her windpipe. Another hand grabbed her arm. She struggled, but her efforts were futile. She tumbled toward the grasping hands, blindly falling toward the wall.

35

Fe?" Horatio said, fumbling back the way he had come.

He stumbled on a rock and careened to the side. He reached his arm out to catch himself, and he heard the crunch of his flashlight as it wedged between his side and the wall, blinking momentarily before it went out.

Horatio righted himself, searching the shadows, trying to get his eyes to readjust. "FeFe?" he said, tossing the broken flashlight to the side and rushing to his sister. He carefully placed his feet as he crouched down. He let out an involuntary gasp as he saw his sister crumbled in a pile of shattered rocks.

Heat built in his chest, and he tried to breathe clearly as he lifted a shaking hand to check her pulse. A small life force tapped against his fingers, and blood seemed to thunder into his throat, his head.

"Eefcharisto, patera dia," he whispered under his breath. He closed his eyes, drew the necklace from his shirt and kissed it. Then he opened his eyes. "You're fine, sister," he shouted, swatting at her cheek. "Wake up. Wake up."

His face scrunched as his hand batted at her once more. "Now is not the time for sleeping games," he said, thinking that might make her laugh. Thinking of how she had always tried to get out of their morning chores and Sunday meeting by pretending to be in a deep sleep.

Her eyes blinked open. She gasped, "I'm hurt."

"You are being overdramatic," Horatio said, even though he knew that he had always been the one to overdramatize things. He pushed himself in beside her and lifted her arm over his shoulder.

"Ah!" She jerked away, her breath growing fast.

"Where does it hurt?" Horatio asked, watching her shaking hand clutch her stomach. Watching her chest rise and fall swiftly.

"Everywhere," she said.

"It is probably just a broken rib," he said, smiling, though he knew she'd had a broken rib before.

She looked up at him. "You were always Mom's optimist," she whispered, pulling up to standing.

Horatio tucked his machete into his belt as he leaned her against his shoulder.

"And you were always Mom's comedian," he said, his throat twisting like tree roots.

"Perhaps I can manage to go a little bit farther." She laughed and sucked in a breath.

"A little farther is all we have to go. I'll show you. Then you'll see the nebulous chamber. We'll get the Icarus Folio, Fe. And when you have that, you'll feel better."

He stared into her eyes. "You'll never have to suffer again."

But her eyes fell from his as she slumped against the wall. "Give me a moment, 'Ratio. Then I'll go. I promise."

36

Lil's shoulder smarted. She blinked her eyes open, trying to steady the room as it dipped and twirled around her. It went dark. Then Sydney's face appeared. Darkness. Kat's face. Darkness. Charlie's face. Sydney's lips were moving, but Lil couldn't hear what they were saying. She couldn't hear anything, but she did see the room upend itself as a wall came into focus on her right.

She blinked again. She could feel the cold stone against her cheek. Then the hand holding her arm. Then something rubbing her neck lightly. She panicked as the sound of rushing water filled her ears, but a moment later it was followed by the distinct presence of her own heartbeat, and then, finally, voices erupted around her.

"Can you hear me?" Sydney asked. "Lil, are you there?"

Lil pushed herself up on her arm.

"Easy with the shoulder!" Sydney said as pain sliced through Lil's collarbone and into the top of her spine. She grasped at it with the opposite arm and supported it as she rose to her knees. Her eyes fell on Charlie. She was leaning up against the wall, her head rolled back. Kat was by her ankle, putting more fabric across her shin, wrapping it like a bandage.

"Is she okay?" Lil asked, pushing herself to an upright position.

"We have to get her out of here," Kat said, wiping at her face with her forearm.

Charlie's eyes blinked open as Kat's fingers worked quickly to tie a knot. She winced and let her head fall back again.

Lil turned toward the center of the room, searching for a door. Her blood seemed to freeze in her veins as she saw everything in front of her. Ropes twisted between statues, connecting them from waist to waist, from one side of the large room to the other. And each figure held something very familiar. The labrys. Not small like the one stamped into the disk around her neck, but real. Taller than the statues. Thick-handled and sharp-bladed. A weapon in every fist.

"The labrys was on the door," Kat said. "Impossible to miss. An actual metal one, buried in the stone."

Lil pushed herself up to standing. Her joints ached as she stumbled to the first statue. This one was a woman, holding a swaddled baby in the crook of one arm. The next a small child, maybe age three or four, tied by the waist to an adult, her small fist holding the labrys, which towered above her. The rope extended like an arm and circled the next statue. This one was a little bit older, her feet set apart, hair around her head in masses, unkempt and wild as if she had been turned to stone in a windstorm. She held the labrys in both hands as though wielding it against something. From her waist a rope extended to another sculpture, this time a teenager, in a running stance, the labrys in her left hand as if she were hunting with it. Lil stepped down the line, placing her hand on the ancient rope, feeling it bristle against her fingers. She stopped at the center of the room. There were two figures. A man and a woman. They leaned against each other. Lil stared at the creases and folds that created them. They looked as if they were made from the same piece of stone, only separated at the waist, where once again, the rope circled and hugged the woman. But, Lil thought, it couldn't be a symbol of captivity. In her hand was the largest weapon of them all. What did it mean?

Lil looked down the line once again, examining them more closely. Each statue also had a pitcher. Each statue was connected by rope. Each statue held a double-headed battle-ax. She squinted at their necks. Each statue had the disk emblem, hanging by a string. Lil lifted the disk from her own neck. She held it up. She spun it between her palms, looking for a place in the room where it might fit.

They were in the Ariadne chamber. Lil's heart pulsed in her neck. The Ariadne symbols were the ones that Mom wore. The ones that Bente wore. But what did it mean? She glanced around the room, looking for answers, searching for the meaning. But it evaded her.

"You didn't happen to see the riddle, did you?" Lil said, turning toward the others.

"We saw it," Kat said, swabbing Charlie's forehead with her shirtsleeve. "We couldn't write it down."

"Can you remember it at all?" Lil asked, making her way to the center of the room. She stood in front of the statue of the couple.

Kat took a deep breath. "I only remember part of it—"

"What do you remember?" Lil said. "Any details would help."

"I don't know if I got the words exactly." The yarn emerged from her pocket, and Lil watched as it flipped between her fingers like the tail of a snake. As if the yarn had soothed her, Kat spoke: "'To all gods, honey. To the labyrinth mistress, honey. To the most holy, honey.'"

She fell silent, scowling down at the yarn and lacing faster.

"Was there anything more?" Lil asked.

"There were a few lines," Sydney said from her place by the wall. "It was about Theseus and the guiding thread."

Lil glanced toward the door, wanting to step back out into the passageway. Even for just a moment. Had the rocks been successful in taking out their predators? Or were they on the other side of the door, waiting? Lil grasped the disk at her waist and pulled it up, staring at the labrys. The front of it reflected the torches as though it, too, was made of fire.

"Traditionally, Ariadne is the mistress of the labyrinth," Charlie said softly, her eyes barely opening. "Mistress of the labyrinth."

Lil stared at the statues. "But which one is Ariadne?" She stepped closer to the couple, most prominent in the center. "They all have the same items."

She ran her finger along the rough stone, stepping back again. As she did, a hint of sweetness tickled her nose. She looked down to see a capped urn at their feet. There was a small crack in the lid. A sliver was missing from the clay. She grasped the handle and lifted the lid off, immediately regretting her decision. Her hand froze in midair. She waited for the room to tip. Nothing happened.

"Honey," Kat said, next to her now. She deposited the yarn into her pocket.

"They're each holding a pitcher," Sydney said. "That must be significant."

A ladle hung idly from the side of the urn, and Lil lifted it gently from its spot.

"Ah," Kat snapped. "'To the most holy, honey.' We're supposed to give a gift. An offering of honey. A *libação*."

"A libation," Lil said.

"Right," Kat said.

Lil spun back toward the statues. Which was the most holy? Were any of them gods? She looked back and forth for religious emblems. Something sacred. Maybe the disk itself was sacred, a symbol of spirituality? But they were each wearing one. She walked back down the line from the eldest to the youngest. Why would Mom have had it if it was a religious item? She had never seemed to believe in much of a god. The only reason her mom's funeral had been in the church was to honor Lil's grandparents' memory. Lil came to the end of the line and stared at the swaddled baby. Her mind spun back to the day of her mother's funeral.

She and Dad went out to the airfield. There was one special rock on the edge of the woods that they had always sat on to watch Mom take off and land. She had found herself there after the funeral, looking out over the hangars toward the distant sunset. Feet tucked in. Chin to knees. She searched the horizon.

"You ran right off," Dad said, coming over to the rock and taking a seat on it, too. Lil tucked her head in harder, trying to keep her eyes clear, but when she looked at Dad, his eyes were red-rimmed and full. He held out half a sandwich.

"You have to eat something," he said.

Lil shook her head. "I'm not hungry."

"You know your mother doesn't accept that excuse," he said.

Lil extended her hand and took the sandwich. She bit into it, but the bread seemed to expand in her throat as her gaze met the horizon once more.

She worked to swallow, trying to form words. "Do you think there's a heaven and that Mom went to it?"

Dad's hand came down to rest on his knee, clutching his half of the sandwich. "I wouldn't claim to know."

"But if there is one, she's not getting in, right? Not for . . ." Lil's throat tightened on the word, strangling her voice to a whisper. "Not for suicide."

"Who told you that?" Dad asked, ruffling the paper over the sandwich.

"Some kid in my class," Lil said, her head starting to ache from trying not to cry.

"Which one— You know?" He took a bite. "It doesn't matter. You want to see religion?" He set the sandwich down on the rock next to him and pulled a picture from his wallet. Lil gazed through tear-filled eyes. "You want to see faith? You want to see miracles?"

He pointed at the picture. It was of her in Mom's arms on the day she was born. "Love," Dad said. Mom looked so happy. Her eyes tired, and full of light. Like there was something special behind them. "Pure love. Have faith in that," Dad said.

He pressed a hand on Lil's back as she dropped the sandwich and took the picture to her heart, because it didn't matter. Either way, heaven or no, Mom wasn't here anymore.

"She's gone," Lil said, her throat strangling her voice. She pressed her cheek into Dad's soft flannel shirt, and he stroked her hair while she tried to catch her breath.

"Not gone." A breeze blew toward them across the field. "Not really. Blood is older than breath, Lil. And outlives it. You're always going to have a piece of her." He kissed the top of her head. And Lil closed her eyes, feeling the cool breeze lick away the tears, sending them off into the air. "You are a piece of her."

Lil found herself staring at the first statue in the room. The mom and baby. The woman's hair was long, curling around her shoulders and down her back. It was decorated with a web of shells so tiny, one might mistake them for little pearls. "Most holy," Lil said. "Most pure. It's this one. It has to be."

"Based on what?" Sydney said. "I mean, how did you come to that conclusion?"

Lil's back bristled.

"The infant child is always the most holy, historically," Kat said.

Lil nodded appreciatively, trying to find her voice.

"Just making sure you're not making connections that don't exist," Sydney said, staring at Lil's hand. Lil looked down to see her thumb marking a line around the spiral in the disk. "If this is ancient lore come to life," Sydney said, "it had nothing to do with your mom."

"Well, what do you think it is, then?" Lil snapped.

"I'm just making sure. I wasn't saying I had a conclusion."

"Fine," Lil said, walking briskly back to the center statue. She plunged the ladle into the urn. She pushed it down and pressed as it broke the surface. It submerged in slow motion. Then she pulled it back from the bottom. She carried it to the first statue. Took just one breath. Aimed for the pitcher and poured. The honey ran from the ladle in a long, thick golden ribbon, curling over the sides with lazy elbows, and then streamed steadily inside. As it emptied, the pitcher sank. *Click.* The ladle emptied more. *Click.* It emptied completely, with only the thinnest stream visible. *Click.* It stopped.

Lil's gaze hurried from wall to wall. Nothing happened. She examined the statue, unchanged before her eyes. She examined the back wall, spun to locate a new door. It had to work. Something had to change. Her eyes fell briefly on Charlie, who looked paler by the second despite the warm glow of the firelight.

Sydney stepped toward her. "Maybe it needs more hon—"

Lil's chest twisted. "Oh, stop," she said through gritted teeth. She dropped the ladle to the ground. Maybe she was crazy to believe any of this. Maybe Sydney was right. Maybe no connection even existed. Maybe this was all a bad dream. And she had brought them here. And she had leaped in—completely and stupidly forward. And now she had made this mistake. The cord of the disk itched her neck, and she yanked it up and over her head.

"What are you doing?" Kat said. "Please stay calm."

"Wait," Sydney said.

Lil grasped the disk in her hands, her knuckles going white.

"No, seriously," Sydney said. "Wait. Listen."

A sound met her ears. The sound of something slowly rolling. Almost as though it hadn't been freed in ages and had taken a moment to begin. It seemed to pick up speed. Lil turned, tensing. Her muscles contracted, sending a shooting pain into her collarbone. But it didn't bother her, not much, because as she watched, a thin door opened at the base of the pedestal, and out rolled a small disk. A replica of the one that she held. That her mother had worn around her neck. It was the same size as Mom's necklace, only older and made of stone instead of metal. It stopped on its side like a coin in a slot machine. She looped the larger disk back around her unhurt shoulder, and clasped the smaller version in her hand. Just like the others they had collected throughout the labyrinth, this charm had a leather thong wrapped through a hole at the top, and Lil lifted it.

As soon as the charm was freed from its pedestal, the chamber began to shake. Lil scrambled backward. Doors on each side sprang open like hungry mouths. Rocks skittered down from above, and Lil shielded the disk Bente had given them with one arm and her head with another. The statue of the nearest child creaked and spilled forward, an arm shattering against the floor. The labrys spinning free, its blade biting into stone.

And as everything came to a standstill once again, ten passageways extended out of the room. Lil searched for the small brick in the wall, the one that had opened like a drawer at the exit of each chamber, assuring them that their path was true. But the walls surrounding the doors remained intact, their surfaces completely smooth. There was no way of knowing which way to go.

37

Lil clutched the disk in her hand and stared open-mouthed at the doors around her. She looked back at the statue of the woman holding the child. Somehow she'd chosen wrong. She must have. Otherwise, they would have been pushed one way or another, just like in all the other rooms. Her hands shook, and she bit back tears.

"I'm sorry," she said, her hands landing in her pockets. It didn't lead anywhere. It took all her will to upturn her eyes and look to the others.

"It doesn't add up," Sydney said.

"What doesn't add up?" Lil asked, slipping the stone charm over her head.

"Well, we got the artifact, but it doesn't go anywhere." Sydney rubbed her arms with her hands. "It goes everywhere."

A slight rustle and crack of wood echoed around the chamber, and Kat was right in front of her, gesturing toward the door and mouthing something. Lil's heart jumped into her throat as she looked up to see the edge of a machete wedged between the wood and the door frame.

"They're coming through," Kat said quietly.

"Everyone up," Lil whispered.

"Please," Charlie said, pushing Lil's arm away. Her head lolled against the stone.

"Help me," Lil said, grasping Kat's arm. They pulled Charlie to her feet. "We need to hide," Lil hissed as she looked around the room.

The wood on the door creaked and moaned, and a few slivers of timber cracked off and fell to the floor.

Lil scanned the room, her eyes glancing from door to door. There was no way of knowing what was beyond them. Some looked less intimidating than others, lit at the corners by soft interior light.

A pain pierced Lil's neck and blurred her vision momentarily as Charlie squeezed her shoulder. The wood moaned and cracked behind her like teeth gnashing, and Lil lurched forward.

"Kat," she whispered. "Leave the torch."

Kat handed the torch off to Sydney, and Sydney hurried to the nearest statue, the couple in the center, and placed it into the man's hand. Then, all together, they hurried into the darkest doorway.

Shadows surrounded them as Lil pressed her back against hard roots. She leaned into them, trying to become a part of the wall. She couldn't detect anyone else, except for Charlie, whose arm rested limply over her shoulder. Sydney and Kat were lost in the darkness. Lil took a deep breath and released it as quietly as possible. She felt Charlie shake as the door in the chamber gave a final jolt and crashed into the room, sending out a loud thud that echoed against the stone. Lil watched as the large, barrel-chested man entered the room. He looked around, and then disappeared back out the door. As he entered again, a woman was hanging on his arm. Lil flicked her eyes away. Ashamed that there was a flutter of hope in her chest. A sense of pleasure that one of them was hurt—badly, it seemed—and the other bruised.

"Over here," the woman said, pulling her arm across her

face. Then she gestured toward the first statue. The man walked over to it, and they leaned down, peering in at where the charm had been.

Lil squeezed the artifact in the palm of her hand. "They have the virtue?" the man whispered.

"Yes," the woman answered.

"Then they've collected them all," the man said.

But what, Lil wondered, did he mean by virtue? And how did these people know about the disks?

"They've proven themselves extraordinarily useful," the man said as he made his way over to the torch. He came to the fallen statue and paused, examining its shattered arm. Then he stepped on the only intact piece, three fingers, which crunched and crumbled under his boot.

The pair disappeared momentarily behind the monument of the couple. Lil could just see his hand take the torch from the statue.

"They've gone forward without light," he said.

Lil pushed herself back even farther. She could feel her heart begin to race. Her fingertips throbbed with blood.

"Then they're headed to the nebulous chamber," the woman gasped, clutching her side. "But by which purification path?"

They stepped forward, toward the tunnels, and Lil held her breath. They circled first to the left and disappeared from Lil's view. Time seemed to slow down as she waited for their faces to appear again. Each second went by with the *thump thump,* then pause of footsteps as they traced their way from one side of the chamber toward them. Lil reassured herself that the light didn't reach into this passageway. That they were well hidden.

Please choose one of the first doors, Lil thought, squinting her eyes closed and then open. But a moment later, a shadow stretched out in front of the passage the girls were hiding in, and Lil couldn't stop the tremors that convulsed her body.

The shadows morphed into a giant swaying monster until an arm appeared and a foot, and there they were, right in front of her. A few yards away. She should have led everyone farther in, Lil thought. They should have run forward ceaselessly. The torchlight tickled the door, and Lil felt her back grinding into the hard roots behind her. If she could become part of the wall, she would. If she could stop the shaking. Surely, she thought, the rustling was too loud. They must have heard it. She watched as the man's eyes went wide. His nostrils flared, and the woman covered her mouth with her hand. Lil followed her gaze to the ground. The torchlight crept over a pile of bones littered at the entrance. She had assumed she had tripped over sticks, roots. But instead she saw an upturned rib cage, a tangle of arms and legs. She pressed her lips together and wondered what it was at her back that dug into her so hard.

"Perhaps this way?" the woman asked.

The man pulled a handkerchief from his pocket and dabbed at his forehead. "Doubtful," he said, smiling.

The woman smiled as well, but Lil could see it was strained.

A rumble shook the mountain, and the man took a deep breath as his gaze went skyward. "Follow the father's roar."

Lil shivered.

The man clasped at something just under his shirt. Lil wondered what it was as they stepped out of sight. The light slipped from between the bones and scurried out the door after them.

Lil didn't realize she had been holding her breath until Charlie breathed in next to her, her arm beginning to tremble once more. She weighed more heavily on Lil's shoulder, and Lil blinked to clear her sight as the pain shot to her collarbone. She lowered Charlie down the wall, and they sat in darkness for a few moments more, until the chamber no longer echoed with footsteps.

Once it was quiet, the girls slid toward the mouth of the passageway. There was no going farther without light. Lil stepped cautiously over the bones and reached a hand out the doorway, feeling for the torch that was stationed on the wall of the chamber. Her hand found the wooden stem quickly, and she lifted it from its casing. Just as she did, a crack echoed above her. A door sailed down like a guillotine in front of the passageway, slashing at her knuckles as she lurched and fell back, pulling the torch in as the stone grazed her knuckles. The door slammed to a halt, and sparks erupted from the bottom as flint met flint. A river of flame flowed on either side of her, and when Lil turned, she could see everything.

38

The flames ran down the walls, catching on loose debris, which floated toward the center of the passageway like miniature burning kites. The tangle of bones in the doorway weren't the only bones there. Rags of varying colors hung loosely from the skeletons. Flags of surrender, waved too late. One rag close to the fire lit and curled back, sending a horde of maggots skittering to the shadows of the walls. And scattered among the bones were those same pendants Lil had seen on the corpses in the arrow chamber. Little circles, with jagged lines cutting across them, glittered in the firelight.

"Oh God. I can't," Sydney said, curling over and throwing up.

Lil swallowed hard as she tried not to do the same. "It's okay," she said. "Don't panic."

Kat covered her mouth, her eyes filled with tears.

"It's okay, Kat," Lil said. "We're going to get out of this."

"You think so?" Sydney said, wiping her mouth. "'Cause as far as I can see, no one has *ever* made it out of this."

Lil shook her head. "You know that isn't how this works."

"Do I?" Sydney growled.

"Yes," Lil said, trying to believe. "Each one's a test. We just have to think of it as a test."

Kat shook her head. "A test where the wrong answer means death."

"Yes," Lil said, moving closer to the bodies. "We just have to figure out what's going on here."

"Ha!" Sydney closed her eyes and shook her head. "You're losing your mind. We should never have followed you." Her voice was bitter. "We should have moved that pile of rocks and gone out of the side of the mountain to get help, but instead you led us into a torture chamber."

"Stop, please," Charlie said weakly from her position on the ground.

"How can you say that?" Sydney said. "You're the worst off."

"Enough, please," Kat said. "We all came. We all made a decision."

Sydney's face scrunched into angry lines. "You two are defending her? We sent you into a watery grave because we have no idea what we're up against here." She turned to Charlie. "Your shin is shattered. We're being stalked. We have no idea what this is." Then she looked back at Lil. "You think you're going to find your mother here?" She flicked her hand to the river of bones. "Do you see her here, Lil? We're following an ancient symbol from one room to the next to the next, but never getting anywhere. Do you see any answers?" Her chin jutted to the disk that hung around Lil's neck. "You're completely delusional. And so are the rest of us for running along after you."

Lil lurched at her before she could stop herself, slamming Sydney up against the root-scrabbled wall.

"What the hell's the matter with you," she growled, her eyes blurring.

"You can't tell?" Sydney's face twisted.

Lil felt a pull on her arm.

"Stop, please, stop," Kat said. "We have to work together. That's the only way this works."

"What part of this whole night has *worked*?" Sydney shouted, kicking out.

Lil's shin smarted, and she gasped as Sydney's knee landed hard in her stomach. She dropped her hands, and Sydney fell sideways into Kat. Kat teetered, dipped to the side, her arms waving for a moment. Lil reached for her, but she seemed to tip in slow motion. Flailing like a windmill, then falling backward. Hip first, then side, then arm. Almost before Lil could comprehend what had happened, an arrow was there, *whump*, quivering to a standstill in the thick of Kat's left biceps.

"Ahhhhh!" Kat screamed, clutching at her arm. Lil was on one side of her and Sydney on the other a second later, pulling her from among the bodies. The blood trickled through Lil's hands as she examined the wound. Her head spun.

"Kat!" Lil gasped.

"Oh God," Sydney said, clutching her stomach and dropping to her knees.

Lil shook her head, tearing a chunk out of the bottom of Kat's cardi-wrap. "It's okay," she said, fighting to catch her breath. She wiped her eyes. "It's going to be okay."

Kat's nostrils flared in and out as Lil grabbed the arrow.

"Leave it in," Sydney hissed, hitting her hand away. "It'll help clot the blood. Just wrap around it."

Lil grabbed the arrow and snapped the end off, so that only a small part of it stuck out. Her hands shook as she dropped the shaft of the arrow onto the ground.

Kat's eyes remained closed as Lil wrapped the fabric around the wound, pressing to stop it from bleeding.

"It's going to be okay, Kat," she stuttered. "We're going to get you out of here." Lil reached over to Sydney. "It's going to be—"

Sydney thrashed out as she got to her knees. "Don't touch

me," she said, helping Kat up. Sydney leaned her against the far wall next to Charlie. "You've done enough already."

Charlie reached out her hand, closing her fingers over Kat's.

Lil swallowed hard. Her body ached as she looked from one of her friends to the other. What had she done? She cleared her eyes and turned to the center of the passageway, filled with bones, trying to steady her vision. Her heart beat in her head. Unwanted noise when she had to think. It pulsed in her throat. In every corner of her bruised body. She stood at the edge of the gauntlet. Sydney was right. She'd gotten them in here. And now, it seemed impossible to get out. And her mother was everywhere. And she was nowhere. And Lil's chest was on fire as she stared at the littered bones and the arrows that had struck them.

Sydney's voice echoed in her ears and doubt blurred her mind. Had she chosen wrong and sent them into a dead end? Was this like the arrow chamber, where every answer would mean death unless you could figure out a way around the mechanisms?

"But, but," she stammered, trying to convince herself, "we have this charm. It's the same size as the others, on a leather thong just like the others." She indicated the charms that decorated the girls' necks. Surely, it meant something.

"Ariadne," Charlie muttered, barely blinking her eyes open.

Lil had to get everyone out. Both Charlie and Kat were fading quickly.

"Ariadne," Charlie said again.

"She's going incoherent," Sydney said.

"Mistress of the labyrinth," Charlie whispered.

Kat squeezed her fingers. "It's okay, Charlie, we're here."

"No," she blinked in frustration. "Mistress of the labyrinth . . . would know every path."

Tears sprang to Lil's eyes. "Of course," she said. "Of course her chamber would lead everywhere." She squeezed the charm. "Ariadne would be able to navigate any one of them. Maybe I did choose right"—she clutched the stone necklace and turned back to the passageway—"which means that this is a test. One we have to solve."

Sydney looked unsure, but Lil watched her gaze dart back and forth as though her mind were constructing a diagram. Lil scanned the passage. Perhaps together they could still get everyone out alive.

The arrows were scattered among the bodies. Poking out of the piles. Two were closest to her, and she noticed they had landed in the same place. A solid slice through the ankle. She rose to her feet and scanned the other bodies. Her gaze jumped from arrow to arrow. Each embedded in the back of the ankle, bound there loosely by a tendon, for eternity.

"They bled to death," she whispered.

"You think?" Sydney said, but she turned, holding the back of her hand to her nose. "Look, each arrow has gone through the back of the ankle. Which means . . ."

Lil lifted the torch, scanning the sides of the wall, searching the shadows.

"Which means . . . " Sydney knelt down. "See?"

Lil leaned over next to her, following her gaze to a nozzle just a few feet away.

"Yeah," Lil said.

"They only shoot from ankle level." Sydney sniffed and pressed her lips together. "Probably a weighted system. When there is a change in weight on the center of the path, they're triggered. Kat fell in. Weight landed. Arrow released."

"Could we figure out how to go between them? I could run

really quickly." Lil stood up. "Hop between them." She thought of running through the tires on the ropes course. It was all about an even gait. Muscle memory.

Sydney got up and shook her head. "I wouldn't—"

"I know *you*—"

"Let me finish, please," Sydney said, glaring at her.

Lil conceded.

"What I am trying to tell you is"—she pointed toward the arrow shafts—"see how some come from one side and some from the other?"

"Yeah," Lil said, looking at the tails of the arrows. Pointing in different directions, indicating which side they flew from. "They alternate."

"Right," Sydney said.

"So I can't jump between, because if I jump between the ones on the right, I'll be hit by those on the left. If I jump between the ones on the left—"

"You'll be hit by the ones on the right," Sydney said, wiping her hands along the side of her jeans.

"So how do we get across?"

Sydney shrugged. "I don't know," she said, squinting down to the other end. "You're not meant to. That lever"—she pointed to a big wooden lever sticking out of the wall on the opposite side. Lil could see a skeletal hand reaching for it. One of them had almost made it—"is not meant to be reached, but I bet if it was, it would shut off the mechanism."

"Maybe," Lil said. "Maybe I could climb along the wall?"

"No," Kat said from the floor.

Lil turned to them.

"You swing." Kat pointed up above her head. Lil turned,

peering into the shadows. A thick rope hung about five feet above them, and five feet from the entrance to the arrow canal. Just out of sight and just out of reach. It wasn't like the ropes on the course, not manicured and colorful and held in place by fasteners. It was old and knotted. And it swung in the shadows— back and forth—an empty loop at its end, waiting for the weight of a human body.

39

Horatio hesitated at the edge of the tunnel. It was darker than the others and somehow louder. On the other side, he could see a flickering of light. He looked up toward the ceiling.

"Put me down here, 'Ratio. You'll have to go without me."

"No, Fe, we'll finish this together. Do you see the lightning?" He turned slightly so Felice could peer down the darkened hallway. It flickered, like a wink from heaven. "That's the end. We're near the chamber. We're near the truth. We're near destiny."

"That's what I am afraid of," Felice whispered, her weight becoming heavier on his arm.

"We'll be fine. Just a few more chambers. This one doesn't even look so bad. Then we'll be out and we'll be heroes."

Felice removed her arm from his shoulder and sank toward the ground. "The plan is not as simple as Ares made it out to be."

"Ares wouldn't lie to us."

"You believe in his word more than I do."

Horatio shook his head and crouched in front of his little sister. "Listen, sister, your doubt has been poisoning you. You're just tired." He reached into his satchel and pulled out a kerchief, wiping her brow with it. "Let me see what's ahead of us, and then I'll carry you through. We'll go out the other side together."

Felice's eyes shuddered closed and then open. She heaved a sigh. Sweat dripped from her brow, and she trembled from head to foot. Horatio turned his eyes away. What was it? he wondered. Internal bleeding? He would have to move quickly to get them out. Then back down the mountain. Would he be able to do it in time? His stomach clenched, and he turned toward the passage, thrusting the torch forward. A rat jolted to his hind legs, as if studying Horatio, before he skittered toward the shadows.

Horatio turned to an oil well on his right-hand side. Like all the torches, he thought, it was run by Greek fire, an ancient concoction used in battle—and for practical purposes—that was similar to lighter fluid. He placed the flame against the liquid. Spires of fire rose toward the ceiling and revealed that they weren't in a corridor, but in a tall, narrow room. About halfway up the chamber were six stone doors in the walls. Horatio spun, looking at each of them. They were unmarked.

Just as the fire reached the belly of the mountain far above them, the ground shook, and Horatio hurried to Felice. Rock and soil flew from the ceiling and they began to rise toward it, turning as though they had landed on a spinning pedestal. He crouched over her as rocks tumbled toward them. One lurched into his shoulder as they rose ever higher.

Horatio reminded himself that each passage past the Ariadne chamber was a challenge, for purification, letting only those most honorable toward the interior chamber. How many times had Ares told the story of their ancient brethren fighting their way through the purity challenges? How many times had Horatio tested his own strengths in preparation for them? He had to focus on keeping his head clear and getting them through one of the doors above. He looked up as they approached, picking up speed.

The spire of flame reached the ceiling, revealing javelins and sharp arrowheads, glinting like rows of teeth.

Another rock careened down, and he covered his head, crouching over Felice to protect her. The rock smarted as it hit his shoulder. He winced, and when he opened his eyes once more, he could see Felice, her eyes closed, her breath ragged.

"Get ready to jump into the next door," Horatio said, noticing that the platform was turning fast now. His vision blurred as he tried to keep his eyes steady on the approaching door. He knelt to stand. "Put your arm over my shoulder."

Felice smiled and raised her hand to his face. She shook her head, weakly. Reached toward the strap of her bag and pulled it from her shoulder. Her hand seemed to quake uncontrollably as she set the pistol down on the platform and laid the satchel next to it. What was she doing?

"FeFe, please, now's not the time. You must listen."

She leaned up, gasping. "I'll tell Byron . . . and Mom you made . . . it," she said. Her eyes perked to life with tears. "You fulfilled your destiny."

Then, before Horatio could move to grasp her, she rolled to the edge of the platform.

"Felice, no!" He scrambled toward her, invisible hands squeezing his throat as he watched her tip over the edge and plunge from sight.

"Noooooooooooo!" Horatio scrambled back, covering his eyes with his arm. He wiped away the tears, tried to clear his vision. The doors. He was nearing the doors. He gulped past the lump in his throat.

"Felice," he said, clutching the pendant at his neck. He stumbled to his feet. Grasped the bags and the pistol. He clutched them in his shaking hand and dove into the nearest archway, crumpling into the shadows.

40

Lil's mouth was as dry as clay as she watched the rope swing. Her mind flashed to the kitchen as she crept to pick up the garlic skins and to turn off the burner under the pot of blackening soup. Her eyes had followed the slant of light spilling from Mom's office. And Lil could see the bottoms of her feet where they were not supposed to be. Back and forth. Back and forth. Swinging just like the rope in front of her.

Lil blinked her eyes clear of tears. It wasn't the same, she told herself, even though death surrounded her. It was just like running through the trees. She rubbed her hands together. She knelt down with one foot in front of her and adjusted the tongue of her sneaker, flipped feet and readjusted her other one. She stood and took the disk that Bente had given her and tucked it into the waist of her pants.

"Listen, this is crazy," Sydney said, wringing her hands. "If you land in there . . ."

"I'll be dead," Lil said. "I'll be riddled with arrows."

Sydney swallowed.

"We don't have a choice," Lil said. "Anyway, you're right. It's my fault we're down here. And you're right. I have no answers."

"No—" Sydney said. "Just listen. We can find some armor or something. A shield."

Lil looked around. "There's nothing to make it out of. This is the only way. I want to get us out of here alive. And if I don't go, this is where we'll end up." She looked around at the bones. The cavernous eye sockets, the shattered ankles of older eras.

"You can't just jump and get that," Sydney said. "Let's be serious."

"Well, not like this," Lil agreed. "We need to clear a path. Make a short runway. Then I'll jump off this wall." She nodded. "And I'll twist and catch it."

They made their way back to the door, pushing the bones to the side. Moving them with their feet until a black path led to the head of the arrow canal.

Lil examined the trail. Run straight, curve to wall, step on fire well with left foot, leap off wall with right, angle, catch rope. She ran through it again in her mind, then went over to the fire well and did a mini step on it with her left foot. "Turn and catch rope," she said quietly.

"What if the rope isn't secured?" Kat said weakly. "What if it breaks and falls?"

Lil looked at the rope, swaying in the breeze. She closed her eyes and shook her head. "It won't. I'm sure it will hold steady."

Lil felt the charm from the Ariadne chamber sitting on her chest. Just like the way its metallic twin had sat on Mom's. She closed her eyes and pictured Mom holding the necklace, rubbing it as though it would grant her a magical answer. She clutched it and pictured her mother on the opposite side of the counter, her eyes clearing as her thumb twisted around the spiral. Lil tucked it safely under her shirt, then lowered herself into a runner's stance. She pictured the woods out behind the airfield. The ropes course, the challenges, the logs to jump over, the walls to push off, the trapeze to fly to. The balance beam, the vertical ropes, the rock wall. She'd done them all. Over and over she'd done them all. Unharnessed. This was the same. This was basically the same. Just run hard, jump high, aim.

"*Min zeis aplos. Zeis tolmira,*" she whispered, hearing her mom's voice in her ears.

Lil flexed her back heel. Licked her lips. Tensed her muscles. Charged forward. Everything seemed to move in slow motion. Her feet hit the ground. Her muscles expanded and contracted as if they breathed on their own. Her eyes landed on the fire well. Her foot met its mark, her hamstrings tightened, her left foot hit the wall hard. She sprang. The charm weighed against her chest as she turned. The cord twisted across her neck.

She aimed.

Reached.

Abs squeezing.

Fingers extending.

Lungs expanding.

The walls around her spun.

She grabbed the rope.

Knuckles clenching fast.

Weight dropping.

Swung.

Her shoulder screamed in pain and her eyes blurred with tears. She stared at the bones below, wondering how many had attempted this before falling to their deaths.

The rope extended to the end of the canal, and Lil's feet sailed over the last of the bodies. She released the rope and landed, stumbling forward until she could steady herself. She knew she had made it past the lever, but she still waited for an arrow to zip free and sever her ankle. When nothing happened, she turned. Grabbed the handle of the lever and pulled. She watched as the shafts in the wall retracted. Disappearing into the stone. She stared down the passageway and saw Sydney helping Charlie up.

"Wait!" Lil said. She searched the ground until she found a heavy rock, grabbed it and tossed it into the center of the passage. It landed with a *thunk*. Nothing happened.

Lil saw Kat push against the wall and stand. She stepped toward them, but they stopped in their tracks, faces frozen, staring at her. She stopped, too, wondering if she had been hit and hadn't sensed it. She scanned her body. No arrows. Nothing. Then she felt a hand come down hard on her shoulder. The room wobbled as a knife-sharp pain cut into her neck and the cold end of a barrel pressed against her temple.

"You three. Come here," a gruff voice said. Lil looked out the corner of her eye. She could see his hairy knuckles wrapped around the gun's grip. Something like the smell of stale bread and wine met her nose. She watched as Sydney helped Charlie over the valley of bones. Kat leaned against the wall with her good arm and pushed herself forward, looking as if she might pass out. Lil moved to help, but a meaty hand gripped her. He pushed the barrel into Lil's head, turning her face to the wall. "Take that torch." She grasped the torch and pulled it off. "Give it to the short one."

Lil turned, catching Sydney's eyes. She took the torch with a shaking hand as Charlie bowed against her. Eyes closing and opening slowly.

"You'll lead the way," he said to Sydney. "And the others will follow nicely. And if they can't, they will remain here and die. That is the way of the labyrinth."

"I'll help you," Kat said, settling her good arm under Charlie's shoulder. Charlie opened her mouth to speak, but no words came out. It had to be the cut, Lil thought. Blood poisoning? They were losing her.

"Move," Horatio said, grasping the back of the necklace draped around Lil's neck. It rose sharply against her windpipe. "This way."

41

L il choked as they plunged down a long passageway, following Sydney through the darkness. She could hear Kat breathing heavily behind her, the slight rustle of her loose pants keeping up with them, somehow, but she didn't dare turn to see how she or Charlie were managing. She couldn't have if she had wanted to, the way the leather cut into her, making her dizzy.

"Please," Lil gasped, attempting to swallow.

Sydney came to an abrupt stop, and the torch revealed a large wooden door. The top rounded into the ceiling. Carved into it was a picture of a man with a Mohawk and a ring through his nose. A bolt of lightning ran across his chest. Just as she had seen on the necklaces on so many of the corpses. A boot hit the back of her knee, sending her buckling to the ground. Suddenly, the leather loosened from her neck and Lil sucked in a greedy breath.

The man pulled the necklace from her neck and tossed the charm in front of her. He whirled to the others. "Virtues down." There was the word again. Why did he keep calling them virtues? What did it mean? Sydney pulled the one from the Daedalus chamber from her neck and threw it into the pile. Kat appeared next to her, leaning against the wall, and took a moment to get the one from the Minotaur chamber from her neck. Then she helped Charlie remove the charm from the Europa chamber.

They plunked to the ground. "Thank you for collecting the four virtues," he said, shoving Lil toward them.

"What do you mean?" Lil said. "The four virtues?"

The man squatted down to her height. This was her first time seeing his face, which she thought looked surprisingly sad. Her eyes flicked to a golden chain around his neck. As he tilted his head, a pendant he was wearing slipped to the center of his chest, and Lil could see that it matched the door. One lightning bolt cut across it diagonally. One side of his lips curled up in a smile.

"But you jumped in so readily. Surely you know."

"No," Sydney said, turning from the door. "We don't know anything, and we don't want to. We'll do whatever you ask. Just let us go."

The man shook his head, wiping his hand across his mouth, and stared up at her. "A bit late for that, I'm afraid."

"Then tell us," Lil said. "What are the four virtues?"

Sydney shook her head in the torchlight. Her jaw twitched as she glared at Lil.

"You heard him," Lil said. "He's going to kill us anyway."

"You're observant," he said, standing up and waving the barrel of the gun toward the door. He looked down at the virtues. His eyes darkening. He sniffed and wiped at his face. "They're the symbols of an evil group. Murderers all. Isn't it obvious?" He gestured around him.

"I don't believe you," Lil said, her voice coming out in a low growl.

"No?" He pointed his gun at her. "Look around you. Smell the death in the air."

He pointed to Charlie and to Kat. "Not even you have escaped its clutches."

Lil's eyes landed on the ground once more. It couldn't possibly be true. Why would Mom have— She banished the thought.

"Pick up the virtues and stand," Horatio whispered.

Lil collected the charms and rose to her feet. She took a moment to peer over her shoulder. She could see Kat leaning up against the wall, crumpling under Charlie's weight. Sweat ran down her face and soaked through her clothes. Blood soaked her right arm, but she still stood. She gazed back into the depths of the labyrinth behind them. They couldn't run, of course, even if they had been able-bodied. There was nowhere to go.

"Place them in the wheel." The man grasped Sydney's hand roughly and pulled the torch to the side of the door. There under the sconce was a wooden wheel. It had four indentations in it. A place for each of the virtues. Lil's hands shook as she matched the pendants with their keyholes and pressed them in. *Kikpop. Kikpop. Kikpop. Kikpop.* Each one clicked into place. The man gestured to a crank at the center. "Turn it to the right. Four times," he said. He placed the barrel of the gun against Sydney's temple and stared at Lil. "Do not mess it up. Turn it a full rotation four times. If you fail, your friend will die."

Lil grasped the spokes and pushed it to the right. She let it wind once around until the virtues made their way around. She spun it again, listening as something within the door seemed to move, unhitch, creak. She spun it a fourth time, making sure to stop it at just the right moment. It landed with a click, and the door opened.

Lil stared into the dark. Deep within the shadows, the yawn of old wood echoed, like a ship whose masts are bent on breaking.

"Step inside," Horatio said, pushing the barrel of the gun

against Sydney's head. She placed a hand on the door frame, steadying herself only slightly, and stepped forward.

"Find the light," Horatio said. Did Lil detect a quiver in his voice? Did he know where they were? Sydney turned toward the wall and Lil saw the oil well protruding from the stone. She watched as Sydney set the flame to it. With a click and a pop, torches perked to life around a large cavernous room. Stalagmites and stalactites took shape from the floor and ceiling. A great hall. In the center sat a large wheel. Rising out of it was what looked like a very old potbellied stove. A clay chimney soared toward the ceiling. Several bronze rods hung from hooks around it. A door sat at its center, handle dark with ash. It had multiple spouts winding from it, giving it the look of a long-necked spider with floppy legs.

The man gasped, looking around the room. "It's even grander than I had imagined." His hand rose to his necklace, and he stroked the gold. "Get in. All of you," he barked.

Lil fell into step beside Sydney. "The symbols aren't of murderers," she whispered. "Please don't believe him, Sydney." Lil tried to meet Sydney's gaze as it circled the room, but despite her best efforts, Sydney would not turn her way. Lil pushed her hand into her pocket, feeling the damp picture of her mother, trying to reassure herself.

"Everyone to the center." Horatio pushed them to a stalagmite. Kat tipped to the side, and Lil grabbed her arm.

"We're losing her," Kat whispered. Charlie's head rolled sideways and Kat slowly slid to the floor, lowering her to lean against the stalagmite, her own breathing heavy.

Lil pushed her fingers to Charlie's neck, trying to find her pulse. A small beat rapped against her skin, and Lil breathed a steady sigh of relief. At least she was alive.

"I think she's just passed out," Lil said. As she lowered her hand, Charlie's eyes fluttered, straining to open. Sydney joined them in the huddle, saying nothing. Kat struggled to get comfortable against the stalagmite. Lil surveyed them, looking from one to the other. Never on the ride up the mountain had she imagined that this was what she would find. That she would race for hours into an ancient labyrinth after—she pulled the water-damaged picture from her pocket—riddles and ghosts. The only people willing to help her, sacrificing everything to do so.

Lil had brought them in. She had to get them out. But as her eyes spun around the room, she saw no door. There was no obvious way out. There was no telling what lay beyond this place, but she had to try.

Lil turned to the man keeping them captive. "You seem to have found what you wanted. Now, why don't you let us go?"

He pulled a decorative satchel open. "Not before we fetch the Icarus Folio. Stand." He leveled the gun at her.

The Icarus Folio? Lil wondered at the name. Icarus was the one who had flown too close to the sun. "What is it?" she asked as she stepped toward him.

He placed the gun at the back of her neck and pushed her toward the strangely shaped stove in the center of the room. With his other hand he pulled a large leather scroll from his satchel and unrolled it. Lil spotted it out of the corner of her eye. Lines were carved in the hide. It looked like some sort of map.

They stopped in front of the stove, and Lil noticed several small urns around its base. She looked down into one. It looked to be filled with ash, just like they had seen in the Minotaur chamber.

The man muttered to himself, then placed a foot on the urn nearest him and pressed it down. For a moment, nothing happened, but a second later, it sank into the floor. Lil risked a look at her captor. His eyes filled with greed as he stared at the floor. Lil turned just as three stones at her feet twisted away from one another. The barrel slammed against her head, and she was forced to her knees.

"Reach in and get it," he said.

Lil gulped, staring into the dark. She couldn't see anything in the shadows.

She heard the hammer of the gun click. "Reach in and get it," he said once more.

Lil lifted shaking hands and reached into the darkness. Something, probably cobwebs, she told herself, tickled her fingers. Her knuckles hit stone. She moved her hands sideways and grabbed. Her hands hit stone once more.

She turned, and the man's eyes widened.

"There's nothing there," she whispered.

He pushed her to the side, but the gun remained pointed at Lil as he scooped a meaty hand into the hole. He grasped at nothing.

"No," he said. He lurched up, grabbing Lil by the arm. He looked around the room. "The cartograph says it is there." He looked at the leather map as though it had betrayed him.

His eyes darted up and down. Lil peered around, too, looking at the room from a new angle. There, just opposite her, was a labrys. She gulped. It was in a circle, the exact same size as the one at the entrance. She stifled a gasp, feeling the disk still heavy in the waist of her pants. Where would it lead?

"Ah. Well, look there, now. It's the tome of the order. It will have . . . everything we desire to know. It will show us the location. I am sure of it." The man's hand tightened like a cinch around her biceps. He gestured toward a ledge above the door. "You. You seem fit enough to climb." He yanked her toward the wall, gesturing to what looked like an old book, high up on a wooden pedestal. "Fetch it."

The order? Lil stumbled toward the wall, her eyes flicking from the door with the labrys, then to the book high above it.

"I'll take the key," he said, gesturing to where the cord had looped and was visible below the hem of her shirt. Lil reluctantly pulled the disk from her waist. The key. They had used it to enter a similar door. Lil licked her lips. Could they use it here, perhaps to exit? Before Lil could stop him, he yanked it from her grasp, the disk spinning away. He replaced it with a plain satchel, the one that had the map inside. "Climb!"

Lil raised her eyes to the old book on the ledge above them. Pieces of broken wood poked out of the rock, as if at one time or another, stairs might have existed there. At the top, the stone leveled off on a tiny platform, and there, the book lay open on the pedestal.

He pushed Lil toward the wall and she slid along the slick ground, hitting it hard. She clamped her hand around the first piece of wood sticking out of the wall. Perhaps if she could climb, she could use the book to distract him, or use it as a bargaining chip. Or . . . something. Get the key. Maybe get them out of here once and for all.

She pushed herself up, her collarbone immediately erupting with pain. She reached with her other hand. Her weight would have to rest on her weak arm.

"Climb, brave one. Do it for your friends," came the man's voice behind her. She looked over her shoulder and saw Sydney held fast in his grasp.

"She's not my friend," Sydney growled.

Lil shook her head. If she could get them out, she could make amends.

"Nevertheless," he said.

Lil planted a foot, her body fighting her as she reached once more. She closed her eyes, her mind swirling to the first times she had climbed with her mother. She could see her, for a moment, there. The trees in the woods moving with the breeze. Lil had clung helplessly to the side of a rock, wanting to jump down instead of go up, into even more of a snare.

"When you take a moment to embrace your surroundings," she heard her mother's voice say in her head, "the correct path will reveal itself. Embrace your surroundings."

Lil opened her eyes. She climbed, feet scrambling for footholds along the stones. Her arm ached and her back smarted. Something in her rib cage burned. But she swung and dipped and rose higher and higher. All muscle groups worked together. And against one another. Like her joints had become coarse rock. But she climbed. "And if you do not see an opening," her mother's voice came again through memory, "you make one. *Zeis tolmira.*"

Lil's feet found crevices, and her hands found broken pieces of wood. And her lungs, somehow, found air.

She pulled herself up onto the tiny platform. It was slick with water, or mildew, and she jammed her toe into a crack to keep from sliding. The pain in her shoulder seemed to fill her head with ringing, and she leaned into the wall once more, trying to catch her breath.

"Place the book in the bag," Horatio said.

Lil leaned into the wall as she reached down and lifted the cover of the satchel. She held the edges of the book, the pages wavering before her eyes. They were split into four columns, and

Lil drew her arm across her eyes, trying to clear them. The first one was filled with symbols, just like the ones they had seen on the plaques throughout the labyrinth. The second was a similar type, but made up of more lines. In the third column, she recognized a few Greek letters. And in the far right column there was English. Lil's throat tightened, and she gasped for breath. The air seemed as thick as soup. Her fingers met the bottom of the page, leaving a dirt smudge under the final line. Under the last name listed in the last column.

Helene (Panagakos) Bennette. Extinguished 2012.

"Mom," she gasped.

"Let's go!" the man shouted from below.

Lil jerked, the book in her hand sliding free of its pedestal. Her fingers buzzed as shooting pains stabbed down from her shoulder, and she reached for a better grip. She lurched too far, her foot slipping free from the ledge. She scrambled for a handhold, but could not find one. The book slipped away from her fingers and plummeted.

Lil followed.

42

Lil could feel water on her face. Soft and cool, it tapped into her forehead and drizzled down her nose. She felt a rumble in her shoulder blades and heard a crash of thunder. She winced, trying to pull her eyes open. Everything hurt. Her lungs. Her arms. Her legs. Her shoulder pulsed with pain, and her foot echoed it. She pried her eyes open and stared up into the rib cage of the mountain. The ceiling, high above, seemed to blink. Several heavenly eyes, snapping open and shut. She tilted her head, trying to understand what she was seeing. She squinted past a stalagmite. A drop of water sailed down onto her forehead as more little eyes blinked open. Lil felt the water land on her lips. Her hand leaped involuntarily to her face. She felt the soft water against her skin and smelled the earthy aroma. Rain? She stared back up to the ceiling. It was lightning winking through holes in the mountaintop. Outside. Freedom.

Lil swallowed hard, trying to find strength to stand.

Then she heard the man's voice. "Help me move her."

Sydney's dirt-smudged face appeared above Lil. And she suddenly became aware of her breathing. It was ragged, and it hurt to take in a breath. How many broken ribs did she have? she wondered. Lil could see the distance she had fallen from. She must have rolled back down the rocks. The lightning flashed, illuminating the empty pedestal. *Extinguished.* The word danced in front of her face once more. She yelped as her back spasmed. She was moving, being pulled across the cave floor.

"Never mind, sweet," the man said softly. "It'll all be over soon."

The wall switched with the ceiling as she was propped up against something cold and hard. Something soft moved beside her, and she turned to see Kat, pressed up in the same way. And Charlie on the opposite side of her. Lil tilted her head, looking up. They sat against the potbellied stove at the center of the mountain, the wheel, stationary, just above their heads. "What are you doing?" Lil growled.

Horatio knelt down and Sydney landed beside him. He tucked the book under his arm.

"Why don't you take the book," Lil said, struggling for breath. "Take the book and just leave us here."

Her captor clutched the ancient book to his chest. "Because, you see, Father Zeus needs a sacrifice from the messenger in order to reveal the location of the folio." He looked up at the ceiling. "I understand now. A sacrifice, and I will know where to look." He knocked on the cover of the book as if trying to summon the answer to the top with his fist.

Lil's stomach twisted as he made the lightning bolt sign over his heart and then tapped his chest twice. She had never seen a prayer like this. He had to be in some sort of a cult. He clasped his hands together.

"Father, I thank you for your guidance. I thank you for the privilege of fulfilling my destiny. I thank you for your strength through spirit. And most of all I thank you for accepting my kin, Byron and Felice, into your arms this day."

He paused and Lil watched his face tense. He swallowed. "For all of this, I pay you homage with life, that you may reveal to me the location of the Icarus Folio and all of its secrets to immortality."

Lil's head spun as his words echoed in her ears. She glanced at Sydney, but she would not meet Lil's eyes.

The man reached above Lil's head, and a moment later his hand appeared holding one of the bronze rods that had been secured to the machine.

"Our father Zeus loves a sacrifice," he said, appearing at eye level once more. He pulled a rope from a satchel, the very satchel that Lil had been wearing moments before she fell. This was it, then: they were going to die. Lil felt the blood rush to her face, and she lashed out. He deflected the strike easily with a wave of his forearm. She looked to her right. Sydney stood leaning into the huge turbine. Why wasn't she being secured like the rest of them?

"Sydney—" Lil gasped, trying to get up, but gaining no ground.

"The short one will come with me. The only able-bodied one left. I think she prefers me over you, anyway." His face glowed like a jack-o'-lantern in the torchlight. "But you shall serve a greater purpose."

The man took Lil's hand and pressed her knuckles closed around the metal rod. "When I open that door"—he gestured to the labrys on the far wall—"and go on my way, the center oculus will open up and let in the lightning." He wrapped the rope around her fingers, pressing the rod into her hand, so that she couldn't loosen it from her grasp. Her fingers bent around it despite her best efforts. "It will find its mark and your pain will be over."

Lil's body filled with rage as he turned to Sydney. As lightning flashed, Lil could see Sydney's hair trembling in the night.

How could she just stand there? "I may have led you in," Lil said through gritted teeth, "but you stand idly by, leaving the rest of us to die."

Lil saw Sydney glance at her, and tried to read her expression in the dark. There was something in the way she propped herself against the machine. The way she was leaning heavily to one side. The lightning flashed from the portals in the ceiling, and light flickered into the chamber. She could see Sydney's gaze move skyward.

Horatio aimed his gun at her. "Let's move."

Sydney looked at Lil. Then at the bronze shaft she held in her hand, and then at Lil again. Lil watched as Sydney shifted, removing her arm from the machine. Lil felt a vibration against her back. It started as a dull thrum and picked up strength and speed. Before she could process what she was doing, Lil swung the bronze as hard as she could. The strike landed neatly across the man's neck. He tumbled sideways, the gun falling from his grasp. Lil scrambled toward it, the rod clattering along the stone, an unruly extension of her arm. Sydney jumped out of the way.

"Sydney, help!" Lil shouted, struggling to free the rod from her grasp, to shake loose the rope that secured it there.

But Sydney crawled out of sight around the machine.

"Sydney, please," Lil gasped as she raced across the floor after the gun. It sped to the wall, stopped and spun in place. She crawled toward it, but the man dove on top of her, crushing her beneath him. Lil's body screamed in pain, her broken ribs crunching. Her fingers extended, but were short of the barrel. His calloused hands twisted around her neck like raw ropes.

Lil struck out once more, trying to free the rod from her hand, or at least to get it to an angle where she could use it as an effective weapon. The man's weight shifted just enough for her to flip, and she grasped the rope, unwrapping it from her palm. She searched for Sydney. Lil jabbed him with her elbow, feeling the satisfying thud of a lip against teeth.

The hold on her windpipe weakened, and Lil crawled toward the wall. But the man redoubled in strength, lunging over her. His hand reached the gun first. She bit at his biceps, and he cried out, pulling his arm back. He struck Lil with the back of the barrel, and a crack resounded through her head as her vision swam.

"It's less glorious, but we can do it this way, too," he said hoarsely, cocking the gun. She slowly raised her hands as he leveled the barrel against her temple. She looked up to the ceiling, her gaze landing on the blinking portholes far above. Then she closed her eyes. Shutting out the nightmare around her.

She heard a crack of thunder. A flash cascaded just beyond her eyelids. The rain cooled her brow. Then a wave of heat met her face, blowing back her hair. Was this what it felt like to die? Lil wondered, waiting for the pain. Sparks flashed against the backs of her eyelids like fireworks. Had Mom felt like this when she died?

A scream met her ears and Lil grabbed at her chest. Had she made the sound? She peeled her eyes open. Lightning was firing through the chamber, arcing from a spout leading off the stove to the back of the man's neck. For a moment he was frozen in midflight, the electricity holding him with a tight arm. The gold pendant around his neck was stiff and shaking as if alive. Then he dropped toward the ground. Flat on his stomach. The arm of lightning dissipated immediately, and Sydney appeared behind him, holding one of the machine's nozzles in her hand. She dropped it and ran around to the opposite side. Lil hurried to her, seeing a wooden crank spin. Sydney pressed a wedge of wood, trying to lock it into place, and Lil held the handle with her, rotating it up. Sydney jammed the wedge in, and the crank slammed to a halt, the winding slowed and then it stopped.

Sydney's face was covered in dirt and tears, and she blinked quickly, stuttering as she rose to a shaking stand. "It's the—it's the—" She shook her head. "Charged ash—" She gestured toward the soot-covered door on the potbellied stove. "And pressure." She gulped. "Makes lightning." She ran a shaking arm across her face. The curls in her hair sprang as she rested her hands on her knees and closed her eyes. "Zeus?"

Lil stood up, trying to comprehend. She looked from the turbine, to Sydney, to the spout that fell from her hands, to the man who lay unmoving on the ground, to this ancient machine that had somehow produced a bolt of lightning.

"You're a genius," Lil said, her voice shaking. "You're a goddamn genius."

"Thanks," Sydney said. "Now let's get the hell out of here."

Lil hurried around the other side of the machine. She yanked the disk from the man's lifeless body. Then she grabbed the book from where it lay now, by his side. Kat attempted to rise onto one knee. Lil reached her, tucking her shoulder under Kat's arm. Sydney did the same with Charlie, slapping at her face.

"We've lost her," Sydney said. "I think we've really lost her."

"Hang on," Lil said. "We're there. We're nearly there." Though she wasn't sure. They could end up in another chamber. They could end up in endless chambers. She ran as quickly as she could to the door. Then lifted the disk, lining the labrys up just as she had done so long ago at the entrance to the labyrinth. She pressed the disk into place. The room wailed. The torches went out. Lightning split the chamber in jagged beams.

A door slid open.

43

Lil careened up a set of steep stairs, dragging Kat with her. The way was dark and a moment later she felt her head hit the ceiling. It smarted with pain and she crumpled into a crouch on what seemed to be the top step. She reached frantically in front of her, a small handle fitting into her palm. She said a silent prayer and twisted it to the side. A short door swung open. The air seemed different, fresher somehow, and she yanked Kat through. As Sydney pulled Charlie out, Lil ran blindly forward. She slammed into what felt like the edge of a table or a chair. She stumbled to her knees.

"Help!" she shouted, wondering if they had come out of the mountain or if they would end up at another test. "Help, someone!"

She spun in the darkness as Kat moaned next to her. Lil's heart pounded in her ears. She felt the wall and ran her hands along it, feeling for cool air. Feeling for an exit. But before she could, a door was opening in her hand. She was stepping back. A small light entered the chamber. A silhouette of a person in a cloak stood before her.

"Oh, thank heaven," a woman's voice said. Was it Athenia or was Lil dreaming?

She rubbed her eyes. A creak came from the other side of the antechamber and Lil jumped, moving back the other way.

She stopped halfway across the room as she saw two figures

enter from another door. It was Trudy—she could see her silhouetted hair in the moonlight—and by her side, Colleen. The counselors.

"A light," Athenia said from behind her. "Flip the light!"

Trudy lit a match and held it to a wick next to the door. The antechamber burst with candlelight. Lil shielded her stinging eyes.

She looked up at Athenia. "Help," she said, grabbing at her sleeve.

"Get Aestos and Atticus up here, now!" Athenia shouted.

Lil watched Colleen disappear into the dormitory.

Athenia slammed a hand under the table, and hinges yawned. Lil turned to see the door that they had just come through, a small square at the base of the wall, close. And as she looked just above it, she found herself staring into a set of familiar eyes. A picture of her mother's face. She shook her head and blinked, reaching to it.

"Lilith, I need you to stay calm," Athenia said, pushing her arm down by her side.

"Mom," Lil said, but she couldn't find her breath. Her heart was moving too fast. Her head spun. The picture faded. The room melted into darkness.

Lil slept like the dead and dreamed she was among them. Deep in the caverns of her mind she ran the labyrinth again. Arrows flew. Monsters of times past erupted from the walls. Assassins waited in the shadows. Flashes of lightning shattered the chamber. Dead eyes stared at her. Blood ran from the walls. She woke to light. Aestos' face. Then plunged into darkness. Woke again to light. Athenia sat by her side. Then she again plunged into darkness. Woke to Atticus' kind eyes. Then darkness.

The sheets twisted around her. Hugging her waist, shoulders. The neck of her shirt wound itself into a noose and squeezed her throat. She gasped for breath, clawing at it until her fingernails dripped with blood, sending rivers down her chest. The rivers bled together and became the corpse sea, and everyone was in it. She saw herself, her mom, Sydney, Charlie, Kat, Bente. The disk spun in front of her. A coin with a side made of fire and a side made of soot. The spiral sucked her in. The labrys chopped her to pieces. A rope circled her waist. And she ran through endless corridors, looking for her mother's face. That man's voice rang through her dreams. *A tribe of murderers.* She pushed her hands over her ears. But the farther she plunged into the depths, the louder it got. Soon the walls faded and she reached a pit, where she leaned against a wall and thought of nothing.

44

Below Melia Mountain, the day began as usual. Tour buses found their way on the winding mountain roads to the coast of the Libyan Sea. Sheep had already gone to pasture and shepherds roamed amid their flocks on the rocky mountainsides. Old women hawked honey on the roadsides, their jars catching the sunbeams as the chorus of *"agno meli"* explained that it was the purest in the land. The leaves rustled quietly as a light breeze carried out the memories of a few days of rain. The garden buzzed with bees, soaring back and forth from the flowers to the apiary.

And a small stone path led from the open kitchen, through the garden to the *mitato* behind the manor. It was not exactly like any other *mitato* on the island of Crete. It was not full of the traditional wheels of cheese, hides, kettles and other items a shepherd might need in his herding settlement. Instead, herbs were strung from every beam. Mortars and pestles of all different shapes and sizes were scattered across the center table. Herbal medicines specifically made for every ailment filled small cupboards. Supplements, tonics, powders and poisons hid under the large washbasin sink. Shelves against one rounded wall bowed under large volumes. Cookbooks sat by religious texts. Books on mysticism toppled over books on natural science. Western medicine texts leaned on natural medicine books, which rested on small notebooks on alchemy. The fire sizzled under a pot of water. Several beds, each with a nightstand, clung to the opposite curved wall.

In the bed closest to the door, Lil flipped over, her body aching from head to toe. It had been two days since they had exited the labyrinth. And she was just now stirring. She groaned as she forced her eyes open. She shielded them with her hand as the light pierced the open window and blinded her. She leaned back into the soft pillow and blinked several times.

"You're up?" Aestos said. "Atty, get the verbena tea and the menthol rub."

Lil shifted to look at the other side of the room. There in the bed next to her was Sydney, and just beyond her, Kat smiled. Lil pushed herself up. There just to the other side of Kat was Charlie. Charlie's eyes fluttered open, and she gave a weak wave and a smile. Lil's heart rose.

"We made it?" she asked, her voice coming out in a croak.

"We made it," Sydney whispered.

Atticus appeared in front of her, pushing a pair of glasses up his nose. He set a long-stemmed pot and a teacup on her bed stand.

"Thank you," Lil said. She reached up, rubbing her sore throat.

"The menthol rub," Atticus said, pulling a small, dented tin from his pocket. He unscrewed the cap and showed it to her. She looked at the goopy salve, splintered with leaves. The strong smell of mint stung her nose.

"You put it on to soothe the muscles," he said. He handed it to her. "Aches and pains." She remembered him from the dining hall. He had looked so unsure of himself there. Now he walked away from her to a mortar and pestle, and diligently began pouring things into its base. She peered out the window. Nothing was what it seemed here.

"Very good," Aestos said. "Atticus is very good at his job. You are lucky."

"Where are we?" Lil lifted the long-stemmed pot with shaking hands. She poured the tonic into her teacup and took a sip of it.

"You are in the house of healers," Atticus said, gesturing to the arms of herbs that reached down from the ceiling.

Lil felt the warm, lemony water make its way down her throat. It soothed her, clearing her head. The image of her mother's picture in the last room swirled in her mind's eye. Had she dreamed it? Was it a hallucination? She felt a surge of blood go to her face as she sputtered—

"Athenia, the chamber—"

Aestos moved to her bedside, pulling a chair over to it, and for a moment he reminded her of her father, sitting diligently by her side whenever she had been sick. "She will be down soon. She will come and talk to you now that they know you are awake."

"I don't understand. That man who tried to sacrifice us. The Icarus Folio. The labrys. My mother's portrait. What happened?"

Aestos smiled and nodded, waving a hand. "Yes. Helene. You are just like her. If you are lucky, you will heal as quickly."

"You knew my mother?" Lil said, setting the teacup down on the bedside table.

"I knew your mother," Aestos said, nodding. He looked down at his clasped hands. "Atticus knew your mother. We all knew your mother."

Lil's throat tightened. "You know why she died?"

Aestos looked up, his eyes lined with tears. His lips worked into a tight line, and he swallowed hard. Nodded. "But you must hear it from the beginning. You can't know it without hearing it from the beginning. And that job is not mine."

A knock came at the *mitato* door, and Athenia appeared in the sunlit doorway. "Are they all awake?" she asked, peering in.

Lil picked up her teacup again and pushed herself to a full sitting position.

"The room is yours," Aestos said, getting up. "We have much to do for the leadership lunch. I'll leave the full health report on your desk, but they are all doing quite well." His eyes surveyed the room, all the way to Charlie. "Considering."

"Thank you," Athenia said, stepping inside.

"There's extra tea on the stove!" Atticus said, picking up a basket and going to the door.

Lil watched as Athenia took some time to pour tea and settle into a chair. She held the cup between her hands and stared into it for what seemed like an eternity. Lil was about to say something when Athenia finally looked up.

"You have all been through a great ordeal." She spoke haltingly. "You have many questions. We have many answers and much to discuss."

Lil felt the breeze blow in the open window and tickle her hair, and she sucked in a breath, creasing the picture of her mother in her hand—the face of the picture split from the water in the Daedalus chamber—waiting for the answers that she had spent years trying to piece together. She adjusted herself on her pillow, hoping that now, finally, she would hear the truth. Kat, Charlie and Sydney pushed themselves up, too, fully alert. Sydney reached for her glasses on the bedside table and put them on.

Athenia placed her cup on the center table. Lil noticed that she wore a long flowing wrap that looked soft and breezy, and from a large sleeve, she pulled the virtues that they had collected through their night in the labyrinth. Lil's breath caught as she saw the gold pendant the man had worn tied in with the others.

Her mind raced with thoughts as she relived the journey and her dream. They had visited ancient chambers, gone into a surreal passage. They had seen the wings of Daedalus, a lightning machine with the symbol of Zeus. Charlie had thought many of the artifacts looked real. The dead bodies, Lil knew, were definitely real. The terrors of the challenges were etched in her memory, and yet there was so much fact and fiction melding together in her head that it was impossible to separate the two. It was almost as though she had lived a nightmare and, even now, couldn't wake from it. She leaned forward, her questions bubbling to the surface.

As if Athenia knew she was about to begin, she raised her hands. "Still your questions for now. There is much I have to say."

Lil watched as, like her, Sydney, Kat and Charlie tightened their hands and lips and waited, impatiently, for Athenia to begin.

"You have been through a great trial," Athenia said. "One I had hoped you wouldn't have to experience." She paused, setting the pendants down in her lap and pulling a loaf of bread from the center of the table. "But I'm afraid what's done is done." She tore a piece of bread from the loaf and handed it to Lil. "You have been into the labyrinth. You secured the virtues and made your way to the nebulous chamber." She stared down at the charms as if they were old friends. "You saw artifacts from Minotaur, Europa, Daedalus and Ariadne." She gazed out at the bright sun. "You likely saw their shadows and spirits in the chambers. They're never too far from here, after all."

Lil gulped, following her gaze out the window. "But—"

Athenia raised her hand once more, slicing her words out of the air. "When you entered the labyrinth, you saw the inscription."

The others nodded.

"'Everything you think you know abandons you within,'" she said, picking up a bowl of olives and handing it to Lil. Lil accepted the bowl, taking a few and jamming them into the bread, then set it in her lap and extended the bowl to Sydney. Her mind was far too busy to sit and eat.

"It was real, then?" Charlie said quietly from three beds down. "It was all real."

Athenia closed and opened her eyes, and she took a breath as though to summon the courage for what she had to say next. "The history of Crete dates back much further than the classical Greeks, much further than our written histories. Well, our known written histories. During this time, the Minoans populated the island. They were a people who started society in the Western world. They were creators, innovators. They built their own community dwellings."

"Like the palace of Knossos," Charlie piped in.

Athenia continued, almost as if Charlie hadn't said anything. "They made olive oil and wine, and they harvested from the fields and they even had their own alphabet."

Athenia plucked the Ariadne virtue from her lap and flipped it over, revealing the spiral side with the many pictographs. "As you also know, from your lesson with Colleen, the Greeks wrote down the stories of their ancestors. These have come to us as modern-day mythology, but what we often forget is that the Greeks thought of the mythology as their history.

"There was a time long, long ago, before 1600 BCE, when Zeus, not a god"—she raised her index finger—"but a man, roamed this hillside."

Lil pictured the Mohawked man drawn on the door of what the man had referred to as the nebulous chamber.

"He was a serious warlord with a thirst for blood and power. Though kings didn't technically exist, you could say Crete was his kingdom. Because he was the most powerful, at least the most feared, he was also the most revered." She dropped the Ariadne virtue and picked up the golden Zeus pendant: the circular design crossed by the lightning bolt. "He wished to become immortal, and he had a plan for it."

"Through story," Charlie said.

"Through science," Sydney added.

Athenia nodded.

"He needed a team of innovators to build him into more than he was. To give him the resources he needed to conquer the Aegean." She flipped the bundle of pendants and selected the tablet that they had pulled from the Europa chamber.

"He had taken Europa from her home in Phoenicia, knowing full well that her family were skilled historians. Her brother Cadmus is given credit for bringing the Greek alphabet to the Western world. That script was Linear A, the roots of the Greek language. Europa was also a writer and historian, and she was forced to write stories of Zeus' conquests. These stories became staples in the oral histories of the island, spreading and expanding throughout the Aegean.

"Next"—she flipped the bundle and pulled the horns of the Minotaur to the surface—"Minotaur. The artist," Athenia said, "Minotaur was the bastard son of Minos, and Zeus' grandson. He was banished to the labyrinth because it was foretold to Zeus by an oracle that he would overtake him, be twice the king that he could be. Contrary to the modern-day myth of Minotaur as monster, he was a sensitive artist, nay, a visionary, who would have brought peace and prosperity to Crete. Zeus' medium was power and fear, so he locked him away and turned him into a monster, so that all people who came to Crete might fear the island even more than they already did."

Athenia flipped the pile again as Lil's head buzzed. She held up the winged hands from the Daedalus chamber.

"Daedalus, the ancient world's greatest innovator, was brought to Crete and forced to create a labyrinth, his own prison. He was promised tools and resources, but ultimately those tools and resources would be used to gain more land and power for Zeus."

Lil stared at the final virtue once again, the sign that her mom had worn.

"And Ariadne, popularly and rightfully known as the mistress of the labyrinth. As a young one she was bound to her grandmother in the darkness of the passageways by a rope, spinning her way in and out of the shadows. Then she was able to navigate the unraveling twists and turns on her own." Lil pictured the statues bound to one another by the ropes.

Athenia flipped the pendant, revealing the labrys. "She was a bold warrior, and it was her job to protect the labyrinth and those sacred secrets inside it. Her weapon was a double-headed ax." She flipped the pendant over again, showing the spiral with the pictographs. "And on this side, a map, written in Linear A. A complex tool to navigate every path to the nebulous chamber . . . and beyond. Only decipherable to a rare few."

A weapon and a map, Lil thought, but why would her mother need it? It didn't make sense. She pushed herself farther upright, her ribs screaming in pain.

"But what does this, what do these things, these people, have to do with the leadership conference, and Bente . . . and my mom?"

"And if this is an archaeological site that would reveal ancient history—all those tablets could redefine what we know about our past—" Charlie said, "why hide it?"

"And why," Sydney said, "is the labyrinth set up in a series of riddles?"

"Deadly riddles," Kat added.

Athenia dropped the pendants into her lap once more and pulled her teacup up to her mouth, taking a sip. Lil gritted her teeth, trying not to be annoyed by her casual unraveling of the story.

"Valid questions, all," Athenia said, swallowing. "Ultimately, the secret—the importance of keeping the secret—far outweighs the necessity of it being public knowledge.

"You see, as Zeus saw the skills of his captives, his desire for more power became insatiable. Looking to nature as the unrivaled phenomenon in the world, he wanted to be its equal. And so he observed it. He decided he wanted to harness lightning, so Daedalus created the *cheir thanatou*: hand of death."

"The pressurized oven . . . the volcanic ash," Sydney said.

Athenia nodded, gulping more tea.

"He created multiple weapons for Zeus. The charged ash was the most powerful and unique of the arsenal. It could wipe out more people than a battle-ax and from a greater distance. As time passed in the labyrinth, Daedalus, Europa, Minotaur and Ariadne saw that his power was growing, and even to them, he was becoming greater than human. With his new demands, the group tried to destroy him. Zeus had longed to fly like the birds for a long time, and"—she looked down at the Daedalus pendant—"Daedalus had it in his mind that he might make a set of wings that were triggered to fail. They would fly Zeus far out to sea so that he wouldn't be able to make it back. However, Zeus had caught on to their game, and he forced Daedalus' son Icarus to take the flight instead."

Lil looked down at her hands, thinking of Daedalus watching his son fly out to his death. She remembered the line in the riddle at the door of the chamber, "creation to destruction bends."

"Needless to say, he didn't make it," Athenia said. "And Daedalus retrieved his body from the shore a few days later. Devastated, defeated and half mad. The Minotaur longed to give him a proper departure, cast a beautiful urn for the child, but Daedalus coveted the body almost as if he thought the boy would breathe again."

"That's terrible," Kat said quietly.

Athenia placed the mug on the table. "Wracked with despair, Daedalus began a project beyond any he had attempted before. He would spend the following months decoding the secrets to life and death—creation and destruction—designing the blueprints to resurrection."

"But that's impossible," Sydney said. "I mean, beyond cryogenics—"

"He didn't have the means, but in his fervor, he had unlocked the key to immortality."

"That's also impossible," Lil said.

"Mostly," Sydney interjected. "Some scientists would say that death is merely a flaw in human cell reproduction. There are many living organisms that far surpass human life." Sydney's eyes popped wide open. "Oh, those fossils in his chamber? Were those part of his experiments?"

Athenia's eyes glimmered. "Extremely observant, Sydney," she said. "He did hundreds of experiments on natural species that were known for living forever, or at least for surviving an exceedingly long time. Daedalus longed to create something that wouldn't ultimately lead to destruction."

Lil pictured opening the floor, reaching her hand into the empty chamber. "The folio, what the man was looking for, it wasn't there."

Athenia's hand curled around the Zeus pendant once more. "Yes, the Icarus Folio, the secrets to eternal life. Zeus had found out about the blueprints, and Daedalus and the rest of them could see that once again, something created for good would be turned to evil by his hand. They met and made a plan, hoping that they might, at long last, truly free themselves from the cycle. They could still kill the man while he was, well, mortal.

"So, Europa, able to win Zeus' eyes, knew him best. She knew the son of Kronos had almost been destroyed by his father, eaten in a cannibalistic ritual like the rest of his siblings. But Zeus had been saved by his mother, Rhea, and told by all those who met him how special he was to have escaped his warmongering father's clutches. Europa played on his pride. She told him that a man, a god, of his height did not need a mere inventor to harness nature for him. He could harness nature himself. And if he did so, he would go down in the books greater than their forebears, greater than Gaia, the earth, greater than Uranus, the sky. The greatest that history would remember.

"And so Zeus, filled with delusion and wine, on a night long, long ago, met Europa. Together they made their way to the nebulous chamber. There, lightning began to shake the sky, pulse and electrify the air. And Europa had received a simple bronze rod from Daedalus. She was to give it to Zeus, tell him that this was the path to immortality. To become one with lightning, the greatest power known to the natural world, would make him immortal at last. They created an oculus in the ceiling. And Europa pushed it open so that the lightning would find him. But in the last seconds, as the lightning bore down and shattered the sky with its fury, Zeus implored Europa to become immortal with him."

Athenia lowered her eyes to the floor. "She bore the ultimate sacrifice. Knowing he must die, she clasped her hand around his as he raised the bronze to the sky. Lightning found its mark. And nature did not spare her vengeance."

Lil felt needles climb up her back as she listened.

"That night they disbanded. Daedalus, heartbroken by another loved one's death by his invention, could no longer stay in the labyrinth. Minotaur would see him on a pilgrimage across the sea, and Ariadne would stay to govern what was left. To protect the Icarus Folio and the secrets of the labyrinth from those who would seek its power. The same month Daedalus left, Ariadne walked the labyrinth. The ash had grown stronger over the nearby island of Thera—you know it today as Santorini—and she could see it billowing in the air at the top of the mountain. When it erupted, it sent waves fleeing, and a giant tsunami engulfed Crete, wiping out nearly an entire civilization like ants.

"Those who knew that Zeus had reigned on Crete longed for what he had, longed to become him. So it's no surprise that as the tsunami's effects dissipated, others arrived on the island. The people that the historians call Mycenaeans would come to rule the land, taking the remaining men to be unwilling soldiers of the sea, and the women, unwilling bearers of a new generation. Ariadne hid from her fate high in the mountains. And over time, a few others would stumble upon the cave entrance at the top, looking for a sanctuary from their destinies. Ariadne accepted those worthy into the fold, and a secret society was born—always made up of only four and those four taking the roles of the originals." She held up the pendants once more so they swung in the sunlight that pooled in from the window. "Historian, Inventor, Artist and Protector."

All of a sudden Lil's mind began to click, the puzzle pieces finding one another and snapping into place. If Mom had worn the symbol of Ariadne, then . . . Her heart thundered as Athenia continued.

"Ariadne had vowed to protect the archives from the outside world," Athenia said, "and her mission in this way would not change. Everyone who joined swore a solemn oath. The labyrinth became an initiation chamber. The center became a study, a laboratory, a place of exploration, creation and innovation. From the death of Ariadne and the Minoan civilization to today. Those who had heard rumors of the mountain, who sought designs and weaponry, who were sick with power and seeking immortality would be put asunder time after time by the so-called Daughters of Ariadne, the Keepers of the Labyrinth," Athenia said.

The image of Lil's mother danced on the antechamber wall and filled her head. The Protector, Athenia had said. "My mom was the Protector?" she whispered.

Athenia finished her cup of tea in one swallow and placed it on the table beside her. "Yes. An initiation happens every twenty-five years. Helene was the most recent Protector." She lowered her eyes to the floor. "When your mother passed away, Bente returned in her place. She had preceded her and would fill her shoes until a new recruitment could take place."

Lil's nose tingled, and she took a moment to peer out the corner of her eye at the others. They seemed to be as stunned and tongue-tied as she was.

"When she passed away?" The words on the page filled her mind. "When she was . . . extinguished?"

Athenia lifted her head and looked Lil in the eyes. "Helene would never take her own life."

Lil's body twitched into motion, but her sore muscles stilled her. "Then who took it?" she growled. "It was that man? The one in the labyrinth?"

Athenia licked her lips. "Ariadne has kin, and Zeus brethren. They call themselves the Zephylites. They seek the Icarus Folio. They believe that when Zeus died that day on the mountaintop, he in fact did become immortal. The story is that he rose and dashed out the Minoan civilization with the volcanic eruption. And he did it out of vengeance. The Zephylites would use their power for evil, to take control of the world and of mortality, that they might also become Zeus. They are his keepers, but their ways are greedy."

"They have a god complex," Sydney said.

"A small order," Athenia said, "just like ours, but extremely powerful in the workings of the world. Now imagine power unchecked by time."

Lil's eyes stung with tears, and she could feel the heat rising in her body. "So he . . ."

Athenia shook her head. "The one sent to retrieve the folio? He was a mere henchman. Don't dwell on him."

A knock came at the door, and without pause Colleen stuck her head in.

"Your workshop is about to begin," she said to Athenia.

Athenia rose from her chair. "Is it that time already?"

"Wait," Lil said, shifting to get out of bed. She needed more answers. The story was only half finished. Why had her mother died, and by whose hand? Lil clutched at the bedsheets, trying to rise.

"There will be time for more discussion later," Athenia said.

Lil stilled herself, her mind working to keep the information. She needed to go home with answers for Dad. With something more tangible than a story about a near-invisible secret society longing for immortality. Her father would never believe it.

As if reading her mind, Athenia leveled them each with a grave expression.

"As you likely know, everything I have said here is absolutely confidential."

Colleen placed a basket on the chair that Athenia had just occupied. "We had not intended for you to go into the labyrinth," she said. "We had a series of other, less threatening tests that would require you to display your skills aboveground. However, Bente—" She choked on the name. "Bente ended up with you. And by some catastrophe, you were pushed through the door. You have made it through the labyrinth. You have proven yourselves to be bright, bold, thoughtful and creative. You do possess all the virtues of the order, and now you know its secrets.

"In this basket," she said, lifting the top, "there are two rocks for each of you." Colleen reached in with both hands and extracted a red rock and a black one. They were egg shaped and no bigger than her hands.

"Tonight you must make your choice," Athenia said. "If you choose to stay, you will place the red rock outside the door of your dormitory. If you choose to leave, you will place the black rock outside the door."

Lil gulped, wondering what would happen if she chose not to stay.

Athenia continued. "If you choose to depart, you have nothing to fear. You will receive an amnesiac from Aestos and all of this will fade away into dream. If you choose to stay, then more will become clear as time passes." She turned to the door. "Besides the dangers of the labyrinth and protecting it from the Zephylites, I assure you there are many benefits in joining us. You will have state-of-the-art resources at your fingertips. Your connections will be worldwide. You will have special missions that will fit your key roles, and you will become leaders in our world. Just as the original four influenced humanity, so must we as future Keepers."

Lil pictured the airfield with the empty spot where the Longhorn had sat. Had her mother been doing special ops for the government, or had she been doing something special for the Daughters of Ariadne? Every time she had left, where had she gone and what had she been up to?

Colleen placed the rocks back into the basket and closed the lid. And with a nod, she and Athenia left. Lil, Sydney, Kat and Charlie stared at one another. Lil didn't know what to say. Her mother had been here. Had done this. Had believed it. Had died for it. Had even deemed it worth dying for. Perhaps, Lil thought, she would do the same.

45

That night, Atticus handed Lil a basket as she readied to leave the *mitato*. He lifted the lid. Inside she saw a Turkish coffee pot, the tin of menthol salve and a small terry-cloth wrap that seemed to emit a heady herbal aroma.

"The fresh essences will sharpen your senses and calm your mind enough for you to sleep," Atticus said, pulling the wrap from the interior of the basket. "The stones"—he lifted a cloth to reveal the two stones that Colleen had shown them—"are here as well. You must decide tonight."

"Thank you," Lil said, accepting the basket from Atticus' hand.

"So you know everything?" she said, looking up at his tanned face.

He nodded. "My family have been healers for the Daughters of Ariadne for nearly as long as the history of the order itself."

"But you're not doctors?" Lil said.

"We're better than doctors," Atticus said.

Lil turned to see Aestos at the potbellied stove in the opposite corner. He poured a liquid into a small vial and placed it into a basket next to him. Then he brought it over to Charlie. "This will be good for the wound, numb away the pain when it gets bad. Rub it on gently."

"*Merci,*" Charlie said, leaning on a pair of crutches that looked like they had been freshly whittled that morning.

Sydney lifted her basket from the bed, and Kat joined her.

"Oh, I retrieved all of your dormitory keys from the chaos," Atticus said, pulling two of the large cast-iron keys from each pocket. He held them out.

"We'll see you in the morning," Aestos said. "At breakfast. It goes without saying—you must not mention a word of this to anyone." He went over to the freestanding sink, lathered his hands with a bar of soap and ran them under the water.

"But what do we tell the other girls if they ask?" Kat said.

Atticus wiped his hands. "Do not fret. I have made up a story for each of you. Sydney, keep calm. Nerves are the worst you have to battle. Lil, you're bruised up. You fell down the stairs on Tuesday night when you left your room without your candle." He turned to Charlie, who held the crutches securely under her arms. "Wednesday, each group went on a field trip to Samaria Gorge. Charlie, if you can manage, say you fell on the first part of the trail. It's the steepest and most dangerous. You had to ride the rest of the way on the back of a mule."

"I would have liked a more adventurous story, but it will have to do, I suppose," Charlie said.

"And, Kat, you attempted to catch her as she was falling, yanking your arm from its socket. You'll keep it covered, but this will help explain away the sling. Understood?"

They all nodded.

"All right, follow me." Atticus turned toward the door and opened it.

Lil looked outside to a moon-soaked garden, then jumped as the shrubbery next to them shifted. Sydney grasped her arm, but out into the moonlight shot a small goat, who fell into stride beside Atticus.

"It's only Baskin," Atticus said, reaching down to scratch the goat's head. "Not to worry now."

All together, they walked a stone path through the garden and back into the kitchen. Atticus lit four candles, handing them off one by one. Lil took hers and Charlie's, so that Charlie wouldn't have to manage the stairs with the basket, candle and crutches.

"I think you know the way from here," Atticus said, sliding the kitchen door open to the stone stairwell to Hall D.

"Thank you," they said as they made their way slowly up the stairs and into the quiet of the hallway. No one said a word. Lil helped Charlie with her door and candle.

"I'll see you in the morning?" Lil said. "At breakfast?"

"Definitely," Charlie said, leaning the crutch against the wall.

Lil set the candle down on the dresser and turned to the door. She stopped and looked back before leaving.

"Charlie, do you think you'll stay?" Lil asked.

Charlie pulled two fountain pens from her pocket and laid them side by side on the dresser. They were both badly cracked, and ink stained her fingers. She wiped them off on her pants. "There's a lot to consider, isn't there?" she said.

"I suppose for some," Lil said. But she'd chased after her mother, chased after answers, for what seemed like ages. She longed to wipe the sleepless nights out from beneath her eyes. From beneath her dad's eyes. She longed for truth. She pictured her mom kissing her dad good-bye. Off on another mission. She had been coming here. Lil was sure of it. She could continue her work. She could follow in her footsteps. Catch up to them.

She stepped into the hallway, wondering if she could talk to the others before they closed themselves inside, but Sydney and Kat slipped into their rooms, doors closing softly behind them.

Lil went to her door and pressed her key into the lock. The stained-glass window had been repaired with an exact replica and cast a soft moonlit glow down on her arms as she turned the key. The door itself had been put back together, and when Lil opened the door, all stood as it had when she first arrived. She went over to the window seat, sat down and placed the basket in front of her. Lifting the lid, she pulled the wrap out and placed it on her collarbone. The ache around the break quickly subsided, the warmth of the wrap sucking it away. Then she pulled out the two rocks and placed them in front of her: the red one on the right and the black one on the left. She picked up the red one and clutched it in her hand as she extracted the picture of her mom and Bente from her pocket. It was so badly damaged it looked like it was under a cracked frame. The glossy front split. Colors in the right-hand corner ran. But her mother's smile remained unchanged.

She could learn more about Mom. Lil's fingers tightened, but more important, she thought, she could extract some answers. She would never take an amnesiac. Lil clutched the red rock and went to her door, sliding it open and peering into the dark hall-way. She glanced quickly from one rush mat to another at the base of each door. No rocks were set out yet.

The door in front of her swung just slightly in the breeze, and she noticed that Sydney had left the top half open just a crack. Lil stepped across the hallway and pushed the door open gently. There was Sydney, holding up a frame with a picture in it. By the light of the candle, Lil could see two girls. One was definitely Sydney, and the other one was nearly identical to her. Younger, but had her features.

"Is that your sister?" she asked.

Sydney turned, placing the picture on the table. "So much for that scholarship."

Lil rolled the clay rock in her hand and deposited it into her pocket.

"Still thinking about that, huh?" Lil said, wondering how she could possibly be considering that after all they had been through.

"It's why I'm here," she said, crossing to her bed where she had laid out the shirt and pants she had worn into the labyrinth. The shirt seemed to have taken on a new, darker color, and the pants were dirt-covered and torn.

"So you won't be staying? Even after everything Athenia has told us?"

Lil looked her over as Sydney sat down on the bed and began to scrub a patch of dirt off her shirt. Sydney looked up and leveled her with a stare.

"Do you think they're really trustworthy? Blueprints of immortality. It's a bit far-fetched, don't you think? Even our greatest scientists haven't figured it out. How could some ancient man have the resources to understand it?"

"But there are people who seek it—" Lil started.

"The Zephylites?" Sydney stopped scrubbing, her eyes going wide. "You realize they are utterly psychotic, right?"

"So you've made up your mind, then?" Lil asked.

Sydney guffawed, as though it were all a joke. "I would say so."

Lil felt the weight of the rock in her pocket.

She went back into the hallway. Stopped and turned. She wrapped her elbows over the bottom half of the stall-like door.

"Hey, Sydney?"

"Yeah?" she said, switching her shirt for her pants. She held them, surveying the damage. "Might as well just throw these away," she muttered.

"You know we wouldn't have been able to survive without you, right?"

"Nah." Sydney shrugged, as if trying to throw off a hand on her shoulder. "You would have found another way. That's all. I slowed you down."

"You saved my life. You saved all of our lives," Lil said. "You see how things work. How they're put together. We would have died in trap after trap without you."

"Okay," Sydney said, dropping the pants into her lap. "Thank you for the awkward pep talk."

"If you stayed, it would be a great asset to . . . to whoever else stays."

Sydney looked toward her. Lil watched as she glanced at the picture of her sister and then back at her bag.

"Think of it," Lil said. "If not for us . . ." She remembered the words Athenia had said. "Unlimited resources. Perhaps to help find a cure—"

"I'll take it all into consideration," Sydney snapped, turning back to her pants and shaking her head in dismay.

Lil turned toward her door, stood for a moment in front of her mat. She pulled the rock from her pocket and placed it in the corner. She stepped back into her room, glancing at her watch. The front of the watch was scraped and scarred, but she could see it said 11:00. She pulled her pajamas on, got into bed, set her sneakers securely at the foot of her night table, placed the picture of her mother on her nightstand and stared at it until her eyelids grew heavy.

Then she fell asleep until morning.

46

The sun began its climb over the eastern side of the island. It swam the length of the tides and speckled the sea foam with pink tips before it reached shore and swept from beach to mountain. It dipped through the gorges, sneaking and peeking into caves and running fire-dappled feet up riverbeds. Finally, soaring ever higher, it tore toward the manor and soaked the walls with golden morning rays. It climbed in the window and stretched the length of the hallway that Lil walked, curled the edges of urns that hugged the corners and twinkled through the stained glass that topped the doors.

The dining hall was alive with a happy hum as Lil made her way inside.

Charlie, Kat and Sydney had already taken their seats at the center of the table. The same place they had sat on the first night, but completely different, Lil thought as she took a seat beside them. Sydney was bent over her homemade GPS, a small screwdriver in her hand. She turned it and dropped a screw into her palm.

"Morning," Lil said.

"Morning," Sydney muttered, looking over the top of her glasses as she pried the back off the device.

"It's broken," Kat said. "She's been obsessing over it for the last fifteen minutes."

"Can't imagine how it might have broken," Charlie said, grabbing a roll from a basket at the center of the table. She turned a fountain pen between the fingers of her other hand.

"What are you writing?" Lil asked.

"Just putting down a few observations about the conference." Her hair was back to its original style, swooping down to her forehead and framing her bright eyes. She winked at Lil.

A moment later, Atticus and Aestos appeared in the doorway. And Lil's mouth started to water as she surveyed the yogurt, honey, breads, boiled eggs, oats and olives that occupied their trays. Atticus appeared over Lil's shoulder, extending the tray down to the tabletop.

"You're all looking well rested today," he said quietly. "It must be those ergonomic mattresses they have in the dormitories."

Lil smiled, and each accepted a plate except for Sydney, who continued to stare down at her device. Atticus placed a plate in front of her. "You must eat a hearty breakfast," he said. Then he was gone, working his way down the table.

Lil lifted her spoon and raised it to her mouth, but a moment later, a large head shoved its way under her arm, upending the yogurt onto the table.

"Disgusting," Sydney said, looking up for just a moment as it landed in the center.

Crumbsy panted and lapped her tongue toward the table as Lil attempted to push her giant head away.

"Hey, big girl, hello," Kat said, giving her a scratch behind the ears. The dog panted happily, and Kat pulled a piece of bread from her tray, pressed an olive against it and held it out to the greedy dog's mouth. Crumbsy slurped and swallowed, covering Kat's hand with saliva.

"Sydney's right. That is disgusting," Charlie said.

"Told you," Sydney said, looking up from her device long enough to snatch an olive and throw it into her mouth.

Lil picked up a small pitcher of honey from the side of her plate and poured it over the rest of her yogurt. She watched it swirl, and smelled the sweet aroma.

A familiar laugh met Lil's ears, and she looked over Charlie's and Sydney's shoulders to see Vivi Lancaster striding by. She was dressed in hot-pink shorts and a tiny tank top. A sweatband pressed her hair flat to her head. She paused as she landed between Sydney and Charlie.

"Oh, so it's true! We were hoping to show you up on the trail run yesterday, but heard you wouldn't be participating due to half your team taking a tumble in the gorge." She looked from Kat's sling to Charlie's leg. "I heard you barely made it past the entrance." She clapped Charlie on the shoulder and Lil could see a new story starting to stitch together in Charlie's mind.

Lil stared at her and chewed, imploring her to stay silent.

"We had a rough time with it," Charlie gulped, moving her gaze back down to her paper. Vivi peered over Sydney's shoulder. "Oh, honey, did your cell phone break? Would you like to borrow some money so you can buy a new one?"

Sydney set her device down, and Lil froze with the spoon halfway to her mouth.

"I'm sure you have more important people to bother than us," Sydney said, setting her arm on Charlie's crutch, which rested against the table.

Vivi glared at her for a minute and then started to make her way down the aisle once more. Only midstep, she jerked awkwardly and spilled onto the ground, the crutch slamming into the table as she tripped over it.

"Whoops," Sydney said, letting go of the crutch and picking

her device back up. As if oblivious to the scene unraveling behind her, she pulled out a wire and scrutinized it. "It's completely fried. Too much water damage."

Kat, Lil and Charlie tried to keep their chuckling to a minimum as Vivi dusted herself off and huffed to the far end of the table.

After breakfast, they made their way back to Hall D. Everyone fell quiet, and Lil was afraid to ask what their decisions had been. They weren't supposed to talk about it. What if the others said they weren't going to stay? What if they had already taken the amnesiac? Lil wondered if any of them had eaten yogurt that would make them forget. Atticus had selected the bowl for Sydney. Had she opted to return home?

Lil pushed her door open and set the key on the bureau. There was something different about her room, and it took her a moment to detect it, her eyes finally landing on a red puddle of cloth on the bed. She slid the door closed and crossed to it. It was a robe. She lifted it from the mattress, soft fabric falling loosely between her fingers. The clasps were a threaded gold, the emblem on the sleeve twisted like a band of honey, marking the initials of the order: *DOA*. As the end whisked off the mattress, a small cream note card fluttered to the floor. Lil crumpled the robe in her hand as she bent to pick it up. It was a piece of paper just bigger than her hand and as thick as card stock.

Please join us for the initiation ceremony
10:00 p.m.
Antechamber in the west wing
Min zeis aplos. Zeis tolmira.

A breeze fluttered in the window, and the words wavered in front of Lil's eyes. *Do not just live. Live boldly.* The words reassured her. She placed the note card in her back pocket, took the robe and set it aside.

She sat through three workshops and had a free study period, because Bente, the teachers explained at lunch to the entire group, was still ill and regrettably would be unable to teach her course that afternoon. Or for the duration of the conference. How easily the others accepted the lie, Lil thought.

Aestos served a dinner of stewed lamb with thyme and white wine sauce. Fresh mixed greens seemed to melt on Lil's tongue. It was all washed down with a homemade mulberry lemon soda and followed by a dessert of loquats and honey cakes.

The evening wore on, and Lil made her way to her balcony, watching the night come in. The day darkened, and the mountain around her became an inky black. She kept an eye on the balcony next door to see if Charlie would emerge, but instead, a pair of trousers just flapped in the breeze, adding a *thwap, thwap* to the punctuated beat of shutters hitting stone. Girls gathered in the common rooms below, and their giggles reached Lil's ears. She wondered at the pain and the laughter that this mountain had seen. And in a way, she felt a part of it. Like that had also been her path, and that perhaps it was natural that her path would lead her here.

Lil watched as candlelight spilled, soft-edged, from the windows of Melios Manor. Everything within began to settle. She could feel the night moving, the wind carrying a piece of history, untranslatable to the human ear as it brushed through the bay leaves and lifted the smell of lavender into the air. A heady feeling surrounded her as she got up and made her way from her balcony back to her room. She fumbled in the darkness to light her own candle, placed her robe around her shoulders and proceeded down the hall. She checked her watch. It was 9:55. She listened for a rustle in the other rooms, but only heard the ceaseless beat of shutters tapping against stone.

She secured her robe, lifted the light and made her way to the end of the hall.

47

The instructions on the back of the invitation included a map to Athenia's chamber that led immediately into the west wing and avoided the other dormitories. She traipsed through halls she hadn't been in before, walking slowly and steadily past large ornate doors, wondering what they held behind them. She was alone as she reached the counselors' chambers. She checked in front of her and held up the candle to see behind her as she stopped outside Athenia's door. She was sure Charlie would come. And wanting her to appear, Lil paused at the door. Took a few extra beats waiting to hear the sound of footfall or crutch upon stone. But nothing met her ears. Only silence. Lil raised her hand and knocked twice. On the second knock the door gave way on its own and swung open. She entered the dark room, looked up toward the stained-glass window, grasped the sconce and pulled it down. The picture flipped in its frame and stuck upside down in the top of the door. Pendants on the far wall shimmered in the moonlight, and a small door swung open. A sliver of golden light drew a knifelike line on the floor.

Lil stepped toward it and stopped. She stood in the moonlit darkness, surrounded by skeins of yarn and piles of fabric. Could she really go in alone? Who else would be there if Charlie and Sydney and Kat weren't? Who else had proven themselves over the week? What had they missed while they were deep in the labyrinth and in the healers' house?

Lil stepped forward again and hesitated again, crinkling the note card in one hand. Her candle wavered in the light, and she shivered despite the warmth of the room. Whispers tickled the air beyond the door, and Lil was drawn to the golden ray. She had no choice. A test of faith, Athenia had said, and then more would be revealed. She could go home with an answer. With a part of Mom. Lil pushed the note card into her pocket and reached for the edge of the door. Her fingers rested on the stonework.

Just then a creak echoed behind her. Lil spun to the dormitory door, peering past her candle flame and into the darkness.

"Nous sommes désolées," Charlie said. "We tried to get here earlier, but I'm not used to the time it takes to get around on these crutches. Then we took a wrong turn. Adding the robe didn't help, either."

Lil's heart catapulted into her throat as Kat's face also appeared, just beyond Charlie's shoulder. Her hair popped from beneath the crimson hood, framing her face in layered curls.

"You came," Lil said as they made their way across the room to her. Lil stared past them to the darkened hallway. It was empty beyond Kat.

"No Sydney, though," she whispered.

"We didn't see her," Kat said.

"Well," Lil said. "I guess we go on without her from here."

"I guess so," Kat said.

"They're probably waiting for us," Charlie added, jutting her chin toward the door.

"Yeah," Lil said.

She turned to it once more, grasped the edge and pulled it

open. Athenia stood a few feet from the door, where she lit a candle atop a podium.

"Enter, please, and take a seat," she said, gesturing toward a table. Colleen and Trudy sat across from each other, closest to them. Next to Trudy was an empty seat with a single candle. And next to Colleen was another hooded figure. A fourth new initiate. She turned, and Lil's heart rose as she saw Sydney's features peering out of the shadow cast by her hood.

"Late as usual," she said, grimacing.

"Well, no one was there to remind me," Lil said.

Sydney rolled her eyes as Lil made her way around the table and took the seat next to her. Athenia stood, clasping her hands, and waited for everyone to quiet down. "Let's begin, shall we?"

Lil had not seen the antechamber clearly before this moment, and she took the time to look around. Alcoves ran down each wall, each one lit by a flickering candle. At the center alcove stood a sculpture and Lil saw that the figure, with the disk under her arm, was Ariadne. From there, more statues decorated the space. Then it turned to paintings, and from paintings to black-and-white photographs, and from black-and-white photographs to colored ones. It was like an alumni wall, only dating back much farther than any she had ever seen. Her eyes stopped at the picture of her mother. She smiled confidently out of the frame, her eyes on Lil. And Lil wondered if she had sat right here, in this very chair, at one time or another.

"Trudy, please retrieve the virtue boxes," Athenia said.

Trudy got up from her seat and went over to a small cabinet near the antechamber door. She pulled out four olive-wood boxes, stacked them one on top of the other and brought them to Athenia. She placed them on the small stand beside the podium, and Athenia nodded at her.

"Before we honor the new members," Athenia said, lifting a tall candle from the edge of the podium, "we honor those of the past. Those who have gone before us, fought, suffered and died, most recently—" Athenia paused, holding a flame sideways over a round candle with eight wicks. "Bente Formo." She lowered the flame to the candle and it caught, casting a warm orange glow on her face. "You will always be with us, friend."

She placed the single candle back on the edge of the podium and lifted a large book—the large book from the nebulous chamber—in front of her. As she pulled the book open to a marked page, Lil wondered what brave soul had gone in and retrieved it. She watched Athenia run her fingers along the page. Then she began to read, first in Greek, then in English.

"*Fotia Akloniti. Deste ekeinoi pour yposchontai edo se mia moira san athanato oso elia.* Fire unwavering, bind those who promise here to a spirit as enduring as the olive tree.

"When your name is called, you will rise and come to the table with your candle," Athenia continued. "You will receive the four virtues. If you choose to accept them, you will use your candle to light the immortal flame and then return to your seat. Counselors will renew the bind first."

Athenia lit a wick next to the one that had already been lit for Bente. Then Colleen and Trudy rose from their seats and each lit a wick themselves. Once the mentors had taken their seats, Athenia looked down the table.

"Lilith Bennette," Athenia said, "please come forward."

Lil shook as she rose from her seat. She gathered the robe as she stood, so as not to trip over it, and made her way to the front.

"Lilith Bennette, please kneel."

Lil dropped to her knees as Athenia pulled a chain from where it nested in its box. She held up the metallic disk, and it twisted in the firelight. A modern depiction of the ancient charm that they had found in the labyrinth.

"The face of the Melios Disk on one side with the labrys on the opposite, the symbol of Ariadne. It is a thread, moreover, a clue. A key. It is the virtue of the Protector. Your sign and your seal." Lil watched it spin like a coin, winking in the candlelight as it turned. "Let it be a reminder that your virtue is your honor and boldness. But let you be reminded, Lilith Bennette, that boldness also has an antithesis. Weakness. Weakness will lead you astray, from a path of protection to one of retribution. May you always stay to the path of the bold and never fall to retribution." Athenia leveled her with a stare, and Lil felt her gaze slip from Athenia's and find the wall just over her shoulder.

She raised the necklace up and Lil bowed her head. Lil felt its weight as it was lowered across the back of her neck.

"Weighted with your virtue, you may accept the bind by joining the unwavering flame."

Lil took her candle and placed the flame to the farthest unburnt wick. It lit and Lil pulled her candle away.

Athenia stared into her eyes. "This bind serves as a promise. That anything within these walls stays within the walls of your soul. And cannot be shaken—not by trickery, not by greed and not by pain. Do you make this promise?"

"I do," Lil said.

"You may be seated."

Lil made her way back to her seat as Sydney was called forward and the symbol of Daedalus, winged hands, which stood for both creation and destruction, was placed around her neck.

Lil held her disk. She could see the full portrait of her mother now, and stared into her mom's eyes as Athenia's voice continued in the distance.

Charlie was given the symbol of Europa, a tablet, which stood for knowledge and its antithesis, ignorance.

Lil thought about the virtues and their antitheses. They always seemed so closely tied. Wasn't the point of the Daedalus chamber that creation always led to destruction or that destruction led to creation?

Finally Kat stood and was given the symbol of Minotaur, the artist, whose crossed horns stood for empathy. "Empathy, like the horns of a bull," Athenia said, "must be fierce and never surrender to its antithesis: apathy."

Lil stared into her mother's eyes: she had been here and done this. Died for it. Bente, too, had given the ultimate sacrifice.

"You have taken the vows," Athenia said.

Lil turned to see her holding up the round candle, now lit with eight flames. She made her way around the podium to the table and set the candle down before them.

"You are now initiated into the oldest sisterhood in human history. I invite the experienced Historian to close the ceremony."

Colleen stepped to the podium, flipped to a page near the end of the book and lifted a pen. She looked up and locked eyes with Lil. "Lilith Bennette, Protector." The pen moved as she wrote in the book and then looked to Sydney. "Sydney Bennington, Inventor." Sydney nodded and Colleen, once again, made notations in her book. "Charlotte Babineaux, Historian." Charlie held the tablet close and smiled. "And Katrina Andrande, Artist." She finished inking the page and set the pen down.

"The vow you have taken here will go with you through life, and to the grave. Your blood is now bound with the blood of those who have gone before you. A blood of virtue. A blood of justice. A blood of depth and knowledge. From now until you gasp your last breath, you are the Keepers of the Labyrinth."

48

The moon dipped into the windows of Melios Manor and lit the white patches between stones with little blue rivers. It was long past midnight as Lil, Sydney, Charlie and Kat made their way back to their own dormitories.

"I wonder if we'll wake up in the morning and it will all have been a dream," Kat said as they reached Hall D and made their way to their doors.

"I hope not," Lil said, clutching the pendant at her neck.

"But if not, what do you suppose is next?" Charlie said.

"I don't know," Lil said, "but whatever it is, we'll do it together."

Lil slid her key into the lock.

"You guys want to meet for breakfast?" Sydney said as she pushed her door open.

Charlie and Kat nodded.

"Yeah," Lil said. "What time?"

"Seven," Sydney said. And then, "Let's meet at six forty-five just to be safe."

"Six forty-five," Lil agreed.

"*Boa noite*," Kat said.

"*Bonne nuit*," Charlie and Sydney said together.

"Night," Lil said, stepping into her dark room. She placed her candle down on the bureau. It wasn't until she reached down to pull her sneakers from her feet that she saw something had been slipped under her door. She crouched to it and lowered her candle. Her breath caught in her throat. She picked up the folder. *Helene Bennette,* the tab said. Lil clutched the file in her hand and looked out the door and down the hallway. It was empty. Everyone had filtered into their rooms. Who had dropped it off, she wondered, if all the counselors were in the antechamber?

Lil slid her door closed and took the file and her candle to her bed. She placed the candle on the bedside table and flipped the folder open. Her robe splayed out around her as she sat on the soft mattress. There she stared down at the torn-out pages of her mother's journal. She traced the rough edge as her eyes raced over the words.

Ariadne 399,

The Zephylites have a new leader, and he seems to be more informed than any before him. His name is Herbert Peskins, but he has been ordained among the Zephylites as Ares. He is an information analyst at Rockview Military Systems and teaches weekend classes at NYTI. Because of a lack of time, I am enclosing his full file.

He is here, believing he goes undetected in my shadow. But do not fear. He will not extract information on the Icarus Folio. I have already provided for its security and moved it from the nebulous chamber. It rests in location 3546, just as Daedalus would have wanted.

*Along with this note, I send you my virtue, in case
what I fear may happen tonight does indeed occur. If
I am found and tortured, you will have this symbol
to pass on to my successor. My P.E.T. is en route as
well.*

As always, min zeis aplos. Zeis tolmira.

Ariadne 400

Lil's mind raced and her eyes welled with tears. The Icarus Folio had existed. Mom had moved it. Lil reread the letter again and again. These were her mother's final words. Written in a shaking hand. How close had they been when she wrote it? Lil clutched at the virtue around her neck. Athenia's words filled her ears. "May you always stay to the path of the bold and never fall to retribution."

She read the name over. *Ares.*

"Never fall to retribution," Lil said, but her thumb circled the back of the disk, feeling the shape of the spiral under her thumb. Around and around and around it went.

She wondered if protection would sometimes be the same as retribution. The Cretan wind dipped in the open window, huffed at the candle flame, bending it back against the wick. Lil reached for it, but despite her best efforts, the flame sizzled and drowned in the wax. Plunging the room into darkness.

ACKNOWLEDGMENTS

There are so many people to thank for helping, encouraging, inspiring and supporting the writing of this novel.

Thank you to the professors who so willingly answered my random, and often confusing, e-mails. Professor Curtis Runnels at Boston University, thanks for the resource list that laid the groundwork for this story. You have no idea how the e-mails back and forth and the additional reading sparked my imagination and fueled this journey. Thanks to Professor Martin Uman for the note on lightning. It greatly helped me envision the trick of volcanic ash. Thanks to Dr. Sarah Ekdawi for your help with the Greek and Ancient Greek translations. And, of course, for the key phrase: *Do not just live. Live boldly.* May it be so. Thank you to Stahl, who handed me the right poem at the right time. "There is a thread that you follow . . ."

Crete is an absolutely beautiful place. The setting of Melios Manor is inspired by Milia Mountain Retreat. Thank you to Giorgos Makrakis and Iakovos Tsourounakis for building it, and thank you to Tasos Gourgouras for hosting us, feeding us delicious food and sending me the information on the Nikos Psilakis cookbooks so that I could have a little taste of Crete when I returned home. Thank you also to Costas Dritsas, who hosted us when we visited the eastern side of the island, and for teaching us about the olives and olive oil.

Thank you to my Unreliable Narrators for all your support

through the weeks, months and years of our lives. Especially, Trinity Peacock Broyles, Katie Mather, Tamara Ellis Smith, Kelly Bennett, Jennifer Wolf Kam, Sarah Wones Tomp, Sharry Phelan Wright, Kerry Castano and Cindy Faughnan. You are the best writing sisters a girl could ask for.

Thank you to my amazing literary agent, Joan Paquette. I'm lucky to have you in my corner. And thanks also to the Gangos near and far. And to the wonderful Vermont College of Fine Arts community, from where so much of my inspiration springs.

Thank you to Ginger Johnson and Jessica Dainty Johns for writing days. You are two of the most gifted and dedicated writers I have known.

Thank you to my friends at the Derry Public Library who put up with me while writing this novel and hashed things out with me, especially Susan Brown, Sherry Bailey, Eric Stern, Meryle Zusman, Jessica Drouin and Evan Bush. Also, thanks to my DPL teen writers group, who listened to and gave input on the opening pages. You are all brilliant.

Thanks so much to my super editor, Jill Santopolo. Your patience, support, patience, guiding questions and patience are beyond compare. I hope, although doubt, you had as much fun with this as I did! Thank you also to the amazing team at Philomel, who made the whole package come together. Especially Talia Benamy for the input along the way and the finishing touches.

A special thanks to my longtime friends Kim, Tris and Sam for brainstorming this manuscript on girls' weekend—and for encouraging me.

Thanks so much to my family. To Casey, Moie and Ambs for your brains, brawn and beauty. I catch glimpses of you in all my stories. Thanks to Mom for leading the way. I think the motto of the story may be yours more than the rest of ours. And to Pa for checking in and finding useful historical tidbits that inspired the manuscript on several fronts. Especially for the indomitable LILITH.

Thank you to my sweet baby boy, Tucker, who listened to the whole darn thing over and over again. I only assume that is why you wouldn't flip over. You can't hear as well the other way around.

And thank you, most of all, to my husband, Jason—my love, my high school prom date, my forever best friend—for supporting me along the way. You're the best.